PRAISE FOR *ATLANTIS: THE ACCIDENTAL INVASION*

"A fascinating twist on the Atlantis legend.
Filled with action, adventure, and a great deal of heart."
—Stuart Gibbs, *New York Times* bestselling author of
the Spy School series

"Features expeditious pacing, ample secrets,
and imaginative science and tech creations
that are zippy indeed."
—*Kirkus Reviews*

"This steampunkish sci-fi/fantasy adventure
is quickly paced, an inventive, if far-fetched,
engagement of plastics pollution and climate change
—as well as a diverting vision of Atlantis's
underwater technology. Lewis's middle-grade
wackiness is quietly funny and realistic."
—*Horn Book Magazine*

"Full of action and adventure."
—*GeekMom*

ATLANTIS

THE ACCIDENTAL INVASION

by Gregory Mone

AMULET BOOKS • NEW YORK

Cataloging-in-Publication Data has been applied for and may be obtained from the Library of Congress.

ISBN 978-1-4197-3854-8

Text © 2021 Gregory Mone
Cover and map illustrations © 2021 Vivienne To
Book design by Brenda E. Angelilli

Published in paperback in 2022 by Amulet Books, an imprint of ABRAMS. Originally published in hardcover by Amulet Books in 2021.

Printed and bound in U.S.A.
10 9 8 7 6 5 4 3 2 1

Amulet Books are available at special discounts when purchased in quantity for premiums and promotions as well as fundraising or educational use. Special editions can also be created to specification. For details, contact specialsales@abramsbooks.com or the address below.

Amulet Books® is a registered trademark of Harry N. Abrams, Inc.

ABRAMS The Art of Books
195 Broadway, New York, NY 10007
abramsbooks.com

TO MY DAD,

WHO LED ME UNDERWATER
EARLY AND OFTEN

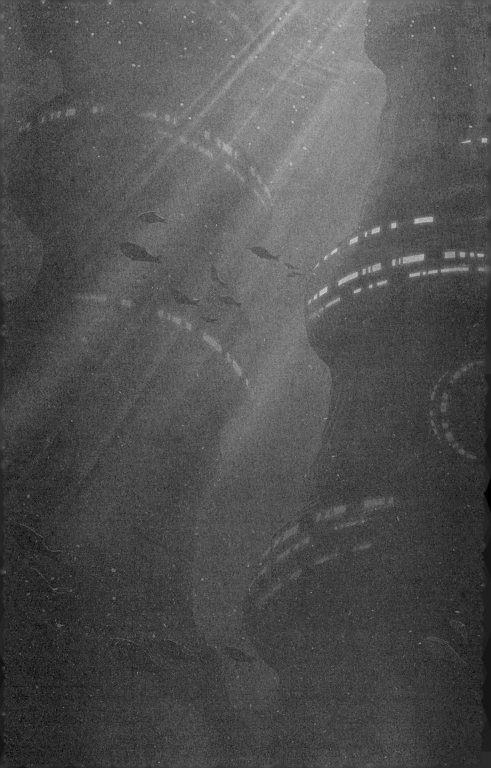

CONTENTS

1
THE STORYTELLER

KAYA quietly opened the large, multicolored glass window and stepped out onto her balcony. The streets below were crowded with people. Her vest, ankle straps, and gloves were powered up. She could run to the show, listen, and drift back before anyone discovered she was gone. Easy. Right?

Her dad was in the living room, listening to some kind of debate about the future of farming. Something about how the city was going to feed its growing population. Important? Sure. Boring? Absolutely. Her dad didn't sound too fascinated, either—his breathing was heavy and slow. Soon he'd start snoring.

Kaya looked left and right, up and down. A dozen families lived in their wall. Any one of them might tell her dad they'd spotted her sneaking out again.

Still, this was her chance.

She leaped.

Falling was the easy part.

She dropped like a rock past the windows of the homes below.

On the street, people were packed like fish in a food tank. Kaya couldn't even find a spot to land. She switched on her suit's gravity drive and hovered in the air a few arm's lengths above the crowd. A woman with thick gray hair suddenly soared up and over the swarms, toward a balcony across from Kaya's wall. The space she'd left was already closing. Quickly, Kaya dropped, knifing down into the gap. Then she crouched, blending into the crowd, pushing her way forward like everyone else.

"Spoiled floater," a man behind her growled.

She hurried away, snaking through the people, and pulled a thin cloak out of her bag. Then she wrapped it around her shoulders to cover her gravity gear. That guy didn't need to growl at her. Sure, she had a suit, but her life wasn't perfect or anything.

Her neighborhood, though, was undeniably beautiful, even down here on the ground. The polished stone walls were lined with crystals, not the jagged rough rocks you'd find in other areas. The windows of the homes were framed with sparkling blue and green glass. And it didn't smell, either. On the way home from school, she had to pass through a neighborhood that stank of rotting fish. The air here was clean and fresh.

The city was warmer than usual. Kaya was starting to sweat, so she tapped her belt. Her clothes loosened, which was more comfortable in the heat.

Up ahead, across a plaza, Rian was waiting as planned. The area around the vent was empty. No surprise there. No one wanted to be close to the hot, steaming air.

Rian shook his head when he saw her gear underneath the cloak. "Did you seriously jump again?"

"I can't exactly sneak out through the front door."

"Someone's going to rip that stuff right off you one of these days."

"I used your earpiece trick," she said, changing the subject. Rian had a way of making his parents think he was in his bedroom when he was out in the neighborhood. He spread some putty on his door, stuck an old earpiece and a miniature speaker to it, then synced them with his own earpiece. If someone knocked or spoke through the door, he'd hear them and respond. As long as he wasn't too far away from his apartment, his voice played clearly through the speaker. To his mom or dad, it sounded like he was home. He always bragged about it. Kaya had never actually tried it, though.

Hopefully it worked.

In a rush, she unbuckled her gravity gear—ankle straps, gloves, and chest plate—and folded them into her backpack along with the cloak.

"Ready?" Rian asked. "Let's go."

Her friend knew the side streets and tunnels of Ridge City better than anyone. Most people shuffled along with the crowd or rode the boats and ferries along the painfully slow waterways. Rian? He had mastered all the shortcuts, and now he led Kaya through narrow, curving alleys, down dark stairways to passageways below. You had to be careful when you hurried along these routes. Pick the wrong time of day, and a flood might rush through and carry you out with the trash.

"Hurry up," he called back.

The air smelled of metal, and the stone ground was wet and coated with grime. Rian was running. This was risky. One wrong step, and you'd slip and smash an elbow or knee. "Slow down," she called to him.

"Not a chance."

They cut left and right, and when they arrived at the old theater, Kaya was dripping with sweat. Loosening her clothes had only helped so much. Rian was studying the building with his hands on his hips. The sign over the entrance was crooked. A few letters were missing, too. Green mold grew along the sides of the rough rock wall. There were two large windows above the entrance, high above the ground, but neither one looked like it had been opened in years. "This is it?" she asked.

Rian thought for a moment before responding. "I think so."

Kaya clicked her belt again, then shook her arms and legs. Her sweat-soaked clothes dried instantly. She had expected crowds outside, or at least a few people. After all, this was an Elida show. The woman used to tell her stories to audiences of thousands. Then the government began shutting down her concerts, claiming that her tales were too revolutionary. Too dangerous. Of course, Elida insisted that they were just stories. But were they?

Years ago, people bought tickets months in advance to see one of her performances. Now her shows were free and held in secret, announced only hours before they began and sometimes canceled even faster if the government found out. Rian had alerted Kaya earlier that a performance was happening at this theater. Now she wondered if it had been called off already. "Are you sure this is the right place?" she asked again.

He was quiet for a second. Doubtful. Then his expression lightened. He motioned to a group of a dozen or so people hurrying out of a dark alley behind her. The group hustled past the two kids. The last of them turned back toward Rian and Kaya before stepping inside. "Won't be many seats left," the woman said. "What are you waiting for?"

The theater was a wide cave with high ceilings and long rows of polished stone benches. At least a hundred people crowded the main seating area. A few dozen more packed onto the balcony above.

"Two seats down there," Rian said, pointing to the third row.

The lights on the stage glowed brighter as they sat.

The rest of the auditorium grew dark.

The crowd began to applaud as Elida walked slowly into the middle of the metal stage and sat on a small stool. Her hair was long and curled and white. A kind of energy shone around her, and there was no introduction. She didn't need one. Kaya's grandmother had told her that when Kaya was little, her mom used to tell her Elida's stories at night. Supposedly the idea was to help her sleep. But instead, her grandmother said, they had infused her with wonder, excitement, and a burning desire for adventure. She was always bouncing on her bed at the end, and question upon question streamed out of her. Apparently her mother was only too happy to answer them, and in the end, it was her father who came in and tried to calm her excited brain so she could sleep.

Sometimes Kaya wondered if the stories weren't meant to help her rest.

Maybe they were supposed to spark her dreams.

That was years ago, though. She barely remembered those days.

She almost couldn't recall what her mother looked like anymore.

An emptiness grew inside her. She breathed it out.

"What is it?" Rian asked.

Luckily she didn't have to explain. Elida was already launching into her tales of adventure, tragedy, and comedy. The stage, the theater, the crowd of listeners soon disappeared. Kaya was transported to the worlds of the stories, to faraway places and wondrous realms. After more than an hour, Elida finally got to Kaya's favorite, an old tale about a boy who traveled far beyond the borders of their world, all the way up to the surface of the sea. Her mother had told Kaya this story when she was young. This was the one that had really set Kaya's imagination on fire. There were different versions, different tellings, but they all had the same basic details. Her heart always beat a little faster when the hero first broke through the ocean's surface. The air above was supposed to be poisoned. The surface was supposed to be lifeless and bleak. But in what should have been dangerous air, the boy gazed at strange flying creatures and glittering, floating palaces of glass, crowded with bright green plants and trees. And people, too—Elida called them People of the Sun. The storyteller made the world above sound so real. And yet so magical.

The story was almost perfect, really. Except that the boy should have been a girl.

When Elida finished this final tale about the People of the Sun, the crowd applauded wildly. The storyteller rose carefully to her feet, bowed, and said, "At my age, there are no encores. Thank you all, and remember—"

A man dashed up onto the stage and whispered an urgent warning. The storyteller breathed deeply and shook her head.

He pleaded with her. She held up her hand and sat back down on the small stool. Then she made an announcement.

"My associate has informed me that we will soon be visited by unwelcome guests," Elida said. "I encourage you all to leave in a calm and orderly fashion."

The audience panicked. People started rushing up the aisles, swarming the exits. A man literally stepped on Kaya's leg to climb over her. Rian stood and yanked at Kaya's sleeve. "Let's go!"

But she couldn't leave. Not yet. The old storyteller was so calm. So peaceful. She had ordered that man and the rest of her staff to flee. Now she sat alone. Her eyes found Kaya as Rian coaxed her to run. "Why don't they want you to tell your stories?" Kaya called up to her.

The old woman held a hand to her ear. "What was that, young lady?"

Rian let go of her sleeve.

Elida was talking to her. She was almost too nervous to call out again. Almost. "What's so dangerous about your stories?"

Now Elida smiled. "There is truth in them, dear. And truth can be dangerous." She pointed to the doors. "Very soon, government agents will rush this theater and arrest everyone they find. Some will be released. But these lucky few will never speak of what they experienced while in the care of those agents. Nor will they speak of my stories."

"And the ones who aren't released?"

"They will never be seen again."

"Let's go, please," Rian begged her.

Only Kaya, Rian, and the storyteller remained in the theater.

Again, Elida looked at Kaya. Right at her.

"I will not run," she said, "but you two will."

Outside, sirens whirred and whined.

"They're already here," Rian said. "We're too late."

The front doors were no longer an option. They'd run right into the agents. And then what? Elida pointed high above them—the balcony. If they could get to the balcony, there might be another way out. Hurriedly, Kaya pulled her suit out of her bag.

"What are you doing?" Rian asked.

"Getting us out of here."

Now there were shouts outside the building.

There wasn't enough time to strap into all the gear. She buckled on her chest plate. "Hold on to my back."

"What?" Rian replied. "Why don't I put on the gear, and you hold on to my back?"

"Don't be weird," she snapped. "Do you have a gravity suit?"

"No."

She grabbed his right hand and whistled to turn on the drive. "Then hold on," she said, and leaped off the ground.

The drive struggled against the weight of the two of them. Rian was practically yanking her arm out of the socket. They barely rose above shoulder height.

"Drop me!" Rian said. "Drop me and go!"

Nice of him. Sure. But a little dramatic, too. Kaya whistled again, holding the last note to turn the suit up to full power, and they floated high above the seats. She tilted her head back. The ceiling was approaching fast. Rian swung his legs, then let go of her, slamming into a balcony bench overlooking the stage. "Ouch," he muttered.

Without him, Kaya drifted faster, straight for the ceiling. She threw her hands up and pushed off the jagged rock overhead. Her wrists stung. She whistled again, dialing down the drive, and somehow landed on her feet in a crouch a few steps from Rian.

"Luck."

"Skill," she replied.

He paused. Then he pointed to the end of the aisle. "Huh. Stairs."

Right. That would have been easier. Faster, too.

She heard the heavy footsteps of the agents rushing into the auditorium below.

Kaya and Rian stayed low to the floor, then crept closer to the balcony railing. They raised their heads, slowly, just enough so they could see over the edge. The first agents were already charging up onto the stage. The sound carried easily in the now-empty theater.

Rian pulled Kaya down. "Careful," he whispered. "The plan is to not get caught."

She nodded. He was right. He pointed to his ears. They could still listen.

Down below, a woman with a scratchy voice was addressing Elida. "You're under arrest."

"For what?" Elida asked.

"You know very well."

"Was it the story about the boy who drifts to the surface and finds not poisoned air and barren landscapes, but a world bustling with life and advanced technology? Should I not have spoken of the People of the Sun?"

"Quiet. That's enough."

"It's just a story, dear," Elida continued. "Unless it's not?" Her tone had changed. Now she sounded as if she were mocking the agents. "Could that be it? Could the story be true? I suppose that would be one reason for you Erasers to silence me."

Kaya and Rian stared wide-eyed at each other. Erasers? Pretty much every kid had heard about the Erasers. They weren't police, exactly. Supposedly they worked in secret. They grabbed criminals and revolutionaries and made them disappear. Some said they tossed people out into the deep sea. Others said they threw them in a secret jail. Kaya and Rian used to argue about whether the Erasers actually existed or if they were a legend.

At that moment, they were frighteningly real.

"Get up, Elida, or I'll—"

"Yes, that's it! The story is true. You're silencing me for telling the truth, aren't you?"

The words hung in the air. She'd pronounced them in a powerful, defiant tone.

As if she wanted to be sure that Rian and Kaya heard her clearly.

Kaya heard a click.

Then a deep, powerful buzz.

The thump of someone hitting the floor.

Rian practically wrestled her down to keep her from looking over the edge.

"Pick her up carefully, and get her out to the cruiser," the woman ordered. "I'd prefer to get her out of sight before she wakes."

Kaya couldn't just sit there.

She tried to jump to her feet.

Rian pulled her down.

"What was that?" the woman shouted.

"Someone's here," one of the other agents declared.

"Did you check the balcony?" she asked.

"Well, we didn't—"

Kaya's heart was racing. This wasn't good. Not at all.

"Did you not see the giant balcony behind us?"

"Well, we—"

"Get up there before I erase you, too!" the woman shouted.

Seconds later, the agents' heavy footsteps were thudding up the stairs.

Kaya and Rian raced to the two large windows at the back of the theater. One was rusted shut. Kaya kicked the other hard. The window swung open. She whistled to dial up her drive. "You're not going to argue this time, are you?" she asked Rian.

"Nope."

He climbed on her back as the agents stomped into the aisles behind them.

The two kids jumped off the window ledge and drifted into the distance, higher and higher above the street below. In front of the theater, a few concertgoers were being shoved into a black, windowless transport. Kaya whistled again, turning her drive up to full power, and they crossed two neighborhoods in silence. Then she lowered them down to the ground.

For a moment, they stayed quiet, each of them catching their breath.

"Do you think those were really the Erasers?" Kaya asked.

"Definitely," Rian replied.

"You heard Elida. That stuff about the surface . . . the People of the Sun. What if they're not just stories? What if there is a whole world up there?"

"Kaya—"

"I'm going."

"Me too. My parents will be wondering—"

"No," she said. She pointed up. "I'm going to the surface."

"Great. While you do that, I'll head down to the planet's core."

"I'm serious, Rian," Kaya insisted. "I don't care what everyone says. There has to be life on the surface. Maybe even people. We're being lied to. All of us. There has to be more to the world than Atlantis, and I'm going to discover the truth."

MYSTERIOUS EXPLOSION OFF NEW YORK CITY

Navy calls blast in Long Island Sound a standard military training exercise

—*The New York Times*

GEOPHYSICISTS SEEK ANSWERS AS TSUNAMIS PUMMEL COAST

Experts stumped; leading scientists fail to find explanation for destructive waves

—*Popular Science*

WORLD ECONOMY IN PERIL AS SHIPPING LANES CLOSE

Unpredictable tsunamis render ocean travel too dangerous for container ships

—Xinhua News Agency

SENATE APPROVES PLAN TO MOVE U.S. CAPITAL

Rising seas, dangerous waves prompt vote to shift government inland

—*The Washington Post*

SCHOOL PLAY A SMASH

Local production of *Romeo and Juliet* deemed hilarious due to dancing costar

—*Plainville Gazette*

2

A PERFECTLY GOOD PLAN

THE HOVERCAR had a few dents. Some rust. One of the headlights flickered, and the motor had kind of sputtered when his dad had piloted the vehicle over their backyard and down onto the grass. But the thing had character, too. If the hovercar were a person, he'd have a bulging belly and more hair in his ears than on his head. He'd tell hilarious stories, and his name would be Carl.

No, Chet.

A beam of moonlight broke through the thick clouds.

The moon was like a spotlight shining only on Chet.

Lewis had to go. How could he not? The moon even liked the idea.

He wasn't just excited now. He was excitement. If he were a superhero in a comic book, exclamation points would shoot out of his fingertips. Or even his . . . toes.

Slipping quietly out of his first-floor window, he dropped into the garden below. He stopped to listen. The backyard was empty. To his right, he could hear his parents arguing in the kitchen.

Nobody called out to him.

His bedroom stayed dark.

All that day it had rained, and as he tiptoed through the soaked garden, his left foot slipped out of his untied sneaker and sank into the muck. The cold muddy water seeped through his sock, between his toes. But he would not be stopped. No. Forget the shoe. Who needed two shoes, anyway? He didn't even like the left one. A spot of pizza grease stained the canvas near his big toe. Plus his dad would probably buy him a new pair of hiking boots when they got to the mountains.

Creeping forward, he already felt like an adventurer, or even a secret agent. An undercover spy with one shoe. His code name could be Lefty. Other spies would wonder how he earned the name. Did he have a deadly left foot? Or a particularly odorous one? Did he use it to coax confessions out of his enemies? Tell me everything, you villainous traitor, or you will breathe these foot fumes for the rest of your life!

Behind him, his brother yawned. "What are you doing?" Michael asked.

He was leaning out the window. Michael was eight years old, four years younger than Lewis. Alien slime hung from his left nostril. "Wipe your nose," Lewis whispered.

"Why are you wearing one shoe?"

"It's the new trend. Everyone's doing it."

"Why are you in the garden?"

"I'm checking the kale."

"I think you killed it."

Lewis looked down. His sneakered foot was crushing a clump of greens. The kale was definitely dead. "It's a science experiment. I want to see if it recovers."

"You look like you're sneaking out."

"I'm not."

"Then why do you have your backpack?"

The backpack was undeniable. Overstuffed, too. But it's not like he could travel without a soccer ball.

Lewis backtracked to the window. He was almost at eye level with his brother. He sniffed the air. "Did I ever tell you that you smell like cheese?"

"Do not."

Oh, but he did. Cheddar, in particular. A cloud of cheesiness hovered around Michael wherever he went. If a lactose-intolerant supervillain ever tried to take over the world, Michael could be his archenemy, the Batman to his Joker.

"I'm telling Mom."

"Telling her what?"

"That you're going to hide out in your dad's hovercar."

"I'm not—"

"Yes, you are."

"What if I give you twenty dollars when I get back?"

Michael wiped his nose before responding. "Then I never saw you."

In the moonlight, Lewis noticed that his little brother was wearing one of his favorite T-shirts. Michael pulled up the collar and sneezed into the cotton. "You can have the shirt, too," Lewis said.

Michael wiped his nose again. "Really?"

"Really. But you never saw me. We're not even speaking now."

"Except about the twenty bucks. You promise you'll actually give it to me?"

"Promise."

Michael yawned again. "Okay. Good night, Lewis."

"Good night, buddy."

"Don't stay away too long."

"Okay, buddy."

The window closed behind him. Did spies bribe their little brothers? He didn't know and didn't care. Chet was waiting. Lewis snuck through the garden, across the damp grass of the backyard, and into the back of his dad's hovercar. He squeezed himself onto the floor behind the front seats. Something metal pressed into his ribs—a wrench. He tossed it up onto the back seat, then allowed himself one final glance at the house.

The solar panels were clean. The wind turbine spun gently. The pipes snaking down from the water collectors on the roof were shining and white. The place wasn't big, but it worked. His mom and stepdad, Roberts, slept at one end. Lewis and Michael—who was really his half brother, since Roberts was Michael's dad—squeezed into a room on the other side, through the kitchen. The only thing the house was missing? His own dad. Well, and maybe one of those robotic kitchens. A kid on Lewis's soccer team had one, and it made whatever you ordered, no questions asked. Thick milkshakes, grilled chicken, peanut butter and banana sandwiches. Lewis even demanded a fried rat burrito once, as a test, and the kitchen churned out a hot dog. Close enough.

Tonight, his dad was here at the house, but it wasn't a happy visit.

Roberts was probably in the basement, fixing something, or polishing his gleaming red hovercar out back. Lewis could see his parents arguing in the kitchen.

His mom was circling the table.

His dad sat with his arms crossed, grimacing.

Their conversation wasn't going well.

But their talks never really went well anymore.

This time, his mom was mad because his dad had tried to cancel their trip to the mountains and the Blackwater River. Again. She said it was the fourth time he'd canceled. Lewis thought it was only the second or third. His dad had apologized to him. And sure, Lewis was disappointed. Totally. The Blackwater overflowed at this time of year, so there were pools for swimming and diving, and water rushed through wide channels in the rocks. You could jump in and ride them like slides. Lewis had been so excited about the trip that he'd been packed for weeks. Then his dad messaged him to say he couldn't make it because of work.

Now he was here to apologize to his mom or something. But she didn't have to yell at him. His dad had super important stuff to do.

Plus, Lewis had figured out a solution.

One that would make everyone happy.

Suddenly his dad jumped up from the table.

Lewis slid back down into his hiding spot.

The kitchen door slammed against the side of the house, and he could hear his dad stomping across the lawn. Lewis was already smiling, almost laughing. His father was going to be so surprised! But he couldn't pop out now. No. Not yet. If he did that, his dad would probably tell his mom, and he'd have to go back inside. The whole plan would be ruined.

Patience, Lewis reminded himself. Patience.

"Battery power low," Chet announced. "Please recharge immediately."

The whole vehicle tilted to one side as his dad sank his huge body into the driver's seat.

He let out a long, slow seat rippler and sighed.

"Excuse you," the car replied.

Lewis tried not to laugh. Chet!

The four fans in the hovercar's short, stubby wings started spinning. "Never mind that," his dad replied. "And stop complaining about the battery. You're fine."

The fans spun faster. The motors hummed, and a whiff of the seat rippler coated the inside of Lewis's nose and mouth as the hovercar lifted off the lawn. He wanted to spit.

And yet his plan was working. Meriwether Lewis Gates was named after one of two famous explorers who had crossed North America centuries earlier. But Lewis wasn't much of an explorer himself. Not yet, anyway. He was only twelve years old. He did have plans, though. Enormous plans. And once his dad finished up his work at the lab, they were going on an adventure of their own, hundreds of miles from home, deep into the mountains.

When they arrived at the lab, he would jump up and shout . . . what would he shout, exactly?

Hi? No. That would be lame.

Surprise?

Too obvious.

Good evening?

A little formal.

Unless he bowed, and added an accent. Then it might be kind of funny.

Actually, though, what he said wasn't important. What mattered was that he'd finally get a few days with his father.

Chet roared forward, pushing Lewis back against the base of the seat, and the hovercar's computer continued to insist that his father recharge. Normally Lewis would've said something. Hovercars didn't just roll to a stop when they ran out of battery power—they literally fell from the sky. He'd seen one drop into a tree once on his way home from school. His friend Jet had laughed. The driver hadn't died or anything, but the crash looked like it had hurt.

Still, if his dad thought the vehicle had enough power, then it had enough power.

The hovercar tilted forward and dove.

The right kind of dive, though. Not a free fall into a tree.

Lewis squeezed his eyes shut. He didn't need to look around to know where they were and what they were doing. The edge of one of the thousand-foot-tall cliffs wasn't far from his house, and they were speeding down the slope to the flatlands below.

His stomach turned and tumbled as they soared down the side of the cliff. Then the vehicle's nose swung up, and the spinach from that night's dinner bubbled up into the back of his throat. A vile, wet burp erupted. Lewis clenched his teeth and breathed in through his nose. Normally, his talent for burping was unmatched. He could let out tiny little burps that popped as gently and quietly as soap bubbles, or he could call forth belches that poisoned the surrounding air with their power. His friend Kwan wanted to run an experiment on his burps. Kwan was convinced they could kill plant life. He wanted to test one on a tulip.

The hovercar steadied, cruising level to the ground.

Lewis grimaced and swallowed the spinach.

"Battery power critically low. Please land immediately."

That sounded important.

The warning kept repeating.

His dad kept ignoring it.

Finally, Chet slowed and landed with a gentle crash. Lewis's shoulder crunched into the seat and his ankle was uncomfortably twisted.

His dad patted the dashboard. "See? We made it back here after all. You had plenty of power."

Next, his father climbed out, and Lewis heard hurried footsteps.

Lewis waited a minute, then jumped to his feet. "Surprise!"

No response.

No Dad, either.

The air tasted salty. Lewis looked around. They'd landed on a building near the shore. The flat, empty roof was scattered with puddles reflecting the gray moonlight, and the dark ocean was only a short walk away. Far in the distance, Lewis could see the tall steel warning towers. They lined almost every coast, all over the world, and they blared out alarms whenever a giant wave was approaching.

The night was warm, but he shivered at the sight of the towers.

"Dad?" he called out. "Dad?"

He waited.

Nothing.

"Good evening?"

He tried it one more time, with a British accent.

Still nothing.

Lewis grabbed his backpack and hurried over to the edge of the roof. The building was bigger than he'd realized. Three stories tall, at least. Small waves were breaking on the sand below. The water was almost black, and the whole coast was empty. There were no other buildings around. No hovercars. No trees. And certainly no people. This part wasn't surprising. No one was crazy enough to build anything on the coast anymore. Not after years and years of huge waves, earth-shaking tsunamis that pummeled everything within a few miles of the shore. So what was his dad doing here? Was this his lab?

Near the front of the hovercar, Lewis found a square trapdoor in the roof. He yanked on it. The metal was cool to the touch. The hatch wouldn't budge. Knocking, he yelled, "Dad? Are you down there?"

His father didn't answer.

The warning towers did.

The towers were only supposed to sound their alarms when a giant wave was on its way. When Lewis was younger, the waves used to strike all the time. Sometimes the alarms would wake him up in the middle of the night. He would rush into his mom's bed and she'd sing him a song. Her voice calmed him every time.

If the alarms sounded when he was at school, they had to

climb under their desks, which seemed really pointless, since they were tucked away safely behind the giant cliffs. That was the whole reason the city had moved the school there in the first place. Nothing could make it over the cliffs. And if a wave did wash all the way in from the coast, up and over the towering cliffs, was hiding under your desk really going to help? The water would wash them all away. Plus Lewis always got gum in his hair when he crouched beneath his desk. He couldn't even get mad at anyone, though. He was the one who'd stuck the gum there.

So he'd heard the alarms before, but this time was different. This time he wasn't safely tucked behind the cliff, at school or at home. Now he was so close to the towers that the wailing made his whole body shake.

"Dad!" he yelled.

The wind stopped.

The horns blared another warning, and Lewis began to count. The time between alarms told you how close the wave was to the shore. They even made you calculate the distance on math tests in school. "One, two, three, four, five, six, seven, eight—"

Another chest-shaking blast cut him off.

Eight seconds?

Was that even possible? Maybe he'd miscounted.

The warning system was supposed to start when the waves were far away, so people would have plenty of time to move to safety. There should have been at least ten seconds between alarms; that would mean the wave was an hour from striking the shore.

He counted again.

Eight seconds. He'd been right the first time. His father had made him memorize the Everett Scale, which matched the number of seconds between warning blasts with the distance the wave still had to travel, and the number of minutes until it was expected to hit. The average tsunami rolled through the ocean at five hundred miles per hour. Ten seconds meant five hundred miles left to go, which gave people about an hour to flee. Nine seconds meant two hundred miles. Eight seconds? That translated to a hundred miles, or about twelve minutes until destruction.

Lewis rushed to the ocean side of the roof. For now, the water was still, but somewhere out in the darkness, a giant wave was speeding toward the coast. And when it roared forward and crashed onto the shore, it would obliterate the building.

The wave would crush everyone and everything in its path.

Including Lewis himself.

The horns blared again.

Lewis reached into the back of the hovercar and grabbed the wrench off the seat, then banged it against the metal trap-door. Pain shot through his forearm. "DAD!"

Chet was beeping behind him.

The lights on his control panel blinked red, then switched off.

Lewis tossed the wrench aside and leaned into the cabin. He could call Roberts. His stepfather was in the Coastal Patrol. He'd rescue Lewis.

When he tried to turn on the radio, though, nothing happened.

Chet wasn't lying when he had warned Lewis's dad.

The hovercar's battery was dead.

Suddenly the metal trapdoor in the roof swung open and his father popped out. He was a huge man, wide across the shoulders, with a thick chest, thick legs, and the fists of a brawler, but he moved quickly. Lewis was frozen. He felt like he was immersed in a game, watching everything through his virtual reality goggles, listening through his headset.

He wasn't really there. This couldn't really be happening to him.

"What are you doing here?" his father shouted. "How did you find my lab?"

Lewis stammered. "This . . . this is your lab? I thought—"

His dad pointed to the hovercar. "Can you fly one of these?"

"I . . ."

"Can you fly one?"

"No," Lewis said. "I'm twelve. And the battery's dead."

His father kicked the side of the hovercar, then cursed and stared out at the ocean. His jaw was crooked, and his hands were balled into fists. "Why now, Lewis?" his father asked. "The two of you! Why tonight, of all nights?"

The two of them? Who was he talking about? "I'm sorry, I—"

"Forget it. Never mind," his dad snapped. "I'm sorry." He rushed over and hugged him. Then he took him by the shoulders and stared into his eyes. "You have to come with us. It's the only way."

Who was *us*?

And where were they going?

The ocean roared, a low, deep growl. Nothing like a crashing wave.

Not yet, anyway.

The warning towers wailed. The blasts were getting closer and closer together. Was it down to six seconds now? Five? Lewis couldn't focus long enough to count.

But they couldn't have long. Eight or nine minutes at the most.

"Get inside," his father ordered.

A steel ladder reached down from the hatch into an enormous room. Lewis half slid, half climbed down. The light inside was blinding white. He squinted.

"Go, go, go," his dad urged.

He was moving as fast as he could. The straps of his backpack bounced against his shoulders. His father accidentally stepped on his fingers, but Lewis didn't make a sound, and his dad didn't notice. Jumping off the ladder onto a square metal platform, Lewis shook the pain out of his fingers and stared in wonder.

They were standing beside some kind of giant sphere, a metallic ball as wide as his house and two or three times as tall. Steel bands wrapped around the outside, each one riveted into place. There were windows, too, like the portholes of an old-fashioned ship, and some kind of fin was folded against the side. "What is this thing?" Lewis asked.

"I'll explain later. Get inside."

Lewis stepped through a small door in the side of the giant ball. His father closed and sealed the door behind them. A girl stood at the other end of a narrow hallway. A kid. High school, Lewis guessed. Ninth grade, maybe, or tenth. Only a few years older than him, but those were like dog years. She might as well have been twenty. She was tall and thin, with dark skin and a small nose. Her black hair was braided on top and shaved close on the sides. Even from a distance, he could see the wiry muscles in her jaw, her shoulders, her arms. Her clothes were torn in places. She kind of looked like a DJ. Was his dad managing a band now or something?

"This is Hanna," his dad muttered. "She's not supposed to be here, either. But if she hadn't heard you—"

"Not supposed to be here? I built this ship, Professor. I have every right to be here."

"You didn't build it. Robots built it."

The alarms went off again. The sound was muffled now, but clear enough.

"Yes, but they followed my design." She pointed to Lewis. "Why is he wearing only one shoe?"

Right. He'd forgotten about that. Lewis wriggled his wet toes.

"I don't know," his dad answered. "Why are you—"

The horns were almost constant now.

"That's only three seconds," his dad said.

"It's maybe fifteen to twenty miles away," Hanna replied. "Three minutes at most. I suggest we all strap in."

"Move," his dad yelled at him.

Lewis burped.

Hanna winced. "That was disgusting."

"He burps when he's scared," his father added.

"That's not true!" Lewis insisted. But it was definitely true.

They hurried forward.

"Two minutes," Hanna called back.

Lewis grabbed the back of his dad's shirt. "Dad? We're going to be okay, right?"

His father stopped, placed his heavy hands on his shoulders, and smiled. "We're safe in here. Trust me, son. Have I ever let you down?"

More times than Lewis could count. "Well . . ."

"Never mind. Wrong question. You can trust me."

"Or me, really," Hanna said. "It's my design."

Lewis wasn't sure he trusted either of them.

His dad turned his head slightly, listening. Hanna grabbed Lewis by one of the straps of his backpack and pulled him into the cockpit. Four cushioned chairs in two rows faced a large window. Hanna pushed him into one of the seats in the second row. "One minute," she said. "Get comfortable. Quickly."

He tossed his backpack on the floor as she and his dad started strapping themselves in. Lewis noticed that his dad wasn't even watching what he was doing. He was focused on the wooden wall out the window.

"You might want to tell your kid to buckle up."

His dad didn't even turn around. "You heard her, Lewis."

"Thirty seconds," Hanna called out.

The fact that each chair had seven different seat belts should have been a clue to what was going to happen next. Lewis buckled one belt across his lap and several others diagonally across his chest. His hands were shaking as he strapped in both legs, too. His heart was pounding. For a few seconds, everything was quiet, even the horns, and he hoped this whole thing was just a warning. A test, maybe. Or a false alarm.

Then the wall on the other side of the window exploded. An avalanche of water and splintered wood crashed against the reinforced glass, and Lewis flipped over backward as a powerful wave slammed into their giant metal craft.

3

THE ONLY WORLD

KAYA AND RIAN were still hurrying through the city. She was sure they were far enough from the Erasers by that point, but both of them kept glancing over their shoulders. And Rian was totally stuck on criticizing her plan. She had explained everything. She was going to travel out to Edgeland, near the border of Atlantis, then swim to the surface and back without getting caught. She had a deepwater dive suit—a good one, too. And she wasn't going to disappear for a week or anything. Her plan was totally doable.

But Rian wasn't supporting her. Not at all.

"Do you even know how dangerous that is?" he asked.

"I know."

"You could get into serious trouble!" Rian added. "People who get caught outside the ridge—they disappear." He lowered his voice to a whisper. "If the Erasers grabbed Elida just for telling stories . . ."

This was getting supremely annoying. Her friend should've been excited. He should've been offering to help her, not trying to scare her. "Look, I'm ready. I'm going. And the Erasers aren't going to harm a fourteen-year-old kid."

"What about your dad?"

"My dad won't even know!"

"How are you even going to get to Edgeland?"

"I've saved up enough money for a round-trip ticket on the vacuum train."

He stopped. "Really? That's a lot of money."

"Babysitting," she said. "The Murakis."

"The ones who are always yelling at each other?" Rian asked.

She nodded. "They pay really well. Anyway, if I take the vacuum train, I can get out to Ridge City, shoot to the surface, and return home the same day."

"Easy."

"Exactly!" For an instant she felt better. Then he sneered. Right. He was being sarcastic. "I want to see the surface. I need to see it, Rian."

"But—"

She held up her hand, signaling for him to be quiet.

"Are you shushing me?"

There was a voice in her earpiece. Her father's voice.

"Kaya," her dad asked, "are you still awake? Your door is locked."

Apparently the farm program hadn't been boring enough. She cupped her hands around her mouth to block out the background noise. "Just a minute, Dad."

"Okay," he continued. "I'll wait."

She muted her microphone.

"Go home," Rian said. "I'll talk to you later about the other thing. Okay? Just go. You won't get to the surface if your dad grounds you again."

31

She probably owed Rian a thank-you, but her dad was at her door, so Kaya scrambled into the rest of her gravity gear and sprang into the air. She was barely off the ground when Rian called up, "Are you sure I can't borrow that gear for a ride sometime?"

"Never!" she yelled back, smiling.

The walls to her left were lined with balconies overlooking the city square. She grabbed the railings as she passed, pulling herself along, building speed. She soared over the scattered people below, the ferry-packed waterways, the winding streams and steaming vents.

Her father was getting impatient. "Kaya? What are you doing in there?" he pressed.

The antigravity cruisers overhead were even faster than her suit. She spotted one turning in the direction of her neighborhood. Drifting closer to a balcony on one of the highest floors, she planted her feet on the railing and pushed off and up. She rose higher, grabbed one of the skids below the cruiser, and held on as the vehicle sped forward.

Her shoulder stung, but she didn't let go. In her earpiece, the knocking grew louder and louder. "Just a second, Dad."

Far ahead, she spied the sparkling, crystal-walled homes of her neighborhood.

She released her grip on the cruiser's skid and soared toward home.

Her wall was in front of her, but she was moving too fast.

A flag hung outside one of her neighbors' windows. She reached out and grabbed the folds, ripping it off its pole.

But her trick worked. She slowed, flipped, then dropped safely onto her balcony.

"Kaya," her father said. "I'm going to open this door in one minute."

She ripped off her gear and dropped it in a pile on the balcony. Then she crawled through the window, peeled the old earpiece and speaker off her door, threw the accidentally stolen flag onto her bed, and started doing push-ups.

The door slid open. Her dad stepped inside.

Kaya glanced up. "Privacy?"

"You're exercising?"

She stopped and sat up, resting her forearms on her knees. "What did you think I was doing?"

"Nothing, I—"

"Do you need something?"

He scanned the room. "No," he said. "In the morning, I'm heading away for a few days, for work, and I was just hoping to say good night." Her father noted the slightly open window to the balcony.

"I wanted some air," she explained.

"And that?" he asked, pointing to the flag on the bed.

"I was going to hang it on my wall."

He walked over and spread it out. "You hate the Narwhals."

The Narwhals? Of course she hated them. They were the absolute worst. Their music was torture. Why was he asking her—oh, right. The flag. The family on level seven loved their ridiculous tunes. Apparently they even flew the group's banner, which featured a narwhal banging on a drum with its tusk. "Yeah," she said. "I'm being ironic."

He crossed his arms. "Really?" She could see that he believed slightly less than none of her story. "Where were you? Tell me the truth."

Something about his tone, or the look in his eyes, broke her spirit. She couldn't lie to him—not when he looked at her like that. She sighed and stared down at her floor. "Rian and I went to see an Elida show. We were just listening to some stories."

He stiffened. "So you snuck out."

"Sort of."

"You could've asked."

"You would've said no."

"Because that woman tells lies for a living! Her shows are illegal for a reason."

"What reason is that?"

He paused. "We're not getting into that now, Kaya. Don't change the subject. You snuck out on a school night."

"I'm the best student in my class," she reminded him. "Plus, it's not like I was doing something dangerous. We were just listening to stories." In fact, what they'd done was ridiculously dangerous. They'd been chased by the Erasers. And they'd escaped! It didn't feel all that scary, though. Kaya was almost smiling—she hadn't had that much fun in so, so long. Still, her dad would lose his mind if she told him the truth. He was worked up enough already.

Pacing the room, he added, "You know how I feel about those fantasies, Kaya."

Fantasies? She hated that he used that word. "But I—"

He held up one hand and cupped the other around his right ear. A work call, she guessed. His expression quickly changed from annoyance to aggravation. "They what? Another one? I told them . . ." Her dad paused, listening. "We can discuss this more when I get there."

Finished with his call, he placed his hands on her shoulders. "You're not in trouble."

"I'm not?"

"No. I realize this is partially my fault. You're bored. I've been working too much. But once this project is done, I'll have more time. I promise."

"You always say that."

"I know," he said. "I know. But you have to trust me. And you have to get some rest, okay? Children need sleep."

"I'm not a child, Dad. I'm fourteen."

"You still need sleep. Promise?"

Kaya nodded. "I promise. And Dad?"

"What?"

"You really don't believe there's any life on the surface? Mom used to—"

He shook his head. "You are part of the only intelligent civilization on this planet, Kaya. I hate to disappoint you, but Atlantis is not just our world. It is the only world."

Michelle Moyer
Features Editor
Scientific American
700 Water Street, Suite 400
Denver, Colorado 80211

Dear Dr. Gates,

Thank you for submitting your article, "The Mid-Plate Anomaly and a New Theory of the Formation of Atlantis." Unfortunately, we will not be able to publish the piece, despite your impressive credentials. I imagine this will not discourage you and that you will continue to send us articles on your various theories of Atlantis, as you have for the last few years. But I can say with confidence that the Editorial Board will never publish any such theories without solid evidence. We work with facts, Dr. Gates, not fantasy.

Would you consider removing us from your submission list?

Regards,

Michelle Moyer

Richard—

Great to see you last week at AGU. I'd say you look well, but we've always been honest with each other. You are falling apart. This ridiculous Atlantis obsession is ruining you, Richard. You're one of the brightest geophysicists I've ever met, but this isn't science you're doing. You might as well be chasing Bigfoot.

Look, if you just drop the Atlantis thing, I might be able to help. I could probably get you on a project in a small role, but it would be something. You could get back to doing science again. Maybe get your life back together. What do you think? Send me a note if you're interested. But please, no more Atlantis papers.

—Hans

Gates! Good to hear from you, old friend. I can only imagine what you've endured. I'm sorry to say that I haven't had any success finding a home for your research yet, but please do keep sending your ideas my way. I'm always eager to hear what you're cooking up. Fascinating stuff. —R.B.

4
RIDING THE WAVE

"**DID YOU FORGET** the anchors?" Hanna shouted.

"Of course not."

"Then why are we moving?"

"Because I forgot the anchors," Lewis's dad confessed.

Lewis watched his thick fingers speed across the control panel's touch screen. The sphere lurched to a stop. Lewis was on his back now, staring at the ceiling, still strapped tightly into the chair. His backpack had tumbled behind him somewhere, and he kind of wished he'd taken off his one wet sock.

Water rushed past the windows as if they were trapped on the bottom of a giant river. "What's happening?" he asked. "This thing's a submarine?"

"It's not an airplane," Hanna answered.

"Yes, it's a submarine," his dad replied. "Just relax, son. I'll explain soon. This phase should last only a few minutes."

Lewis turned his wrist enough to check his watch, an old-fashioned timepiece that Roberts had given him. Normally, he removed it when he was with his dad; he didn't want him asking where he'd gotten it. But now he was glad he'd forgotten to take it off. He kept his eyes trained on the slowly moving second hand.

After a few minutes, the sphere stopped shaking. "Is that it?"

Hanna laughed. "We're just getting started."

The wave had rushed past them. Now the water was reversing direction. This, Lewis knew, was the most destructive phase of a tsunami. The first crash was brutal. But once the wave had reached as far inland as it could, all that water rushed back out to sea, carrying with it everything that wasn't anchored deep into the ground. Trees. Houses. Restaurants. Schools. Office buildings. Churches. Even bridges. The ocean was like a giant hand clawing at the land. That was why the coast was empty in the first place. Tsunamis had swept everything away.

His father's fingers flew over the screen again. Motors and cables started grinding below them, somewhere in the guts of the huge machine. "Releasing the anchors now," he said. The sub jerked slightly, then began to roll.

"Make sure you're still strapped in, son," his father warned.

Now the vessel pitched forward, and they started bumping along the seafloor as the wave carried them away from the shore. Hanna was whooping. The straps squeezed Lewis's stomach and chest, but at least he wasn't flipping over. He fought back another spinach burp as Hanna yelled above all the rattling and crashing. "The outer shell of the sphere is spinning like a ball," she said. "Yet our cockpit is stable. We're riding the wave!"

Before long, they slowed.

The sub shuddered as the anchors slammed into the seafloor.

The next wave tumbled past them. His father said nothing.

Hanna was quiet, too. Lewis studied his watch. A minute passed before the wave slowed to a stop, then flooded back out to sea. His dad released the anchors. Again the ship rolled forward.

"It's actually working," Hanna said quietly.

"You doubted us?" his dad asked.

"Well, I mean, maybe a little," she admitted. "I just didn't think it would work this well. The ride is more stable than I expected." She turned to Lewis. "What's your name again?"

How did she not know his name? "Lewis," he reminded her.

His dad corrected him. "Meriwether Lewis Gates."

"After the explorer?" Hanna asked. "Like Lewis and Clark?"

"That's right!" his dad answered.

"I'm going to call you Meri," Hanna decided.

"I like Lewis better."

"What do you think of the sub, Meri?"

"An airplane would be nicer, Susan."

"Really, though, what do you think?"

Everything was quieter, and they were moving slower now. He was alive. No, this wasn't the adventure he'd planned. They were supposed to go to the mountains. He was going to get new shoes. Hiking boots. The plan was to swim during the day and camp and cook soup over a fire at night. Delicious soup. Instead, he was inside a tsunami. And he was alive. Lewis had read stories about people who were found miles out to sea, clinging to boats or debris after a wave had struck. But he'd never heard of anyone riding out a wave on purpose. Most boating wasn't even legal anymore. Roberts talked about how you practically needed twenty different permits just to take out a kayak. They barely even let people fish anymore.

So this was good.

No, better than good.

This was amazing.

Hanna was still waiting for his answer. "Well?" she asked.

It turned out his dad's lab was a submarine.

A submarine built to ride a tsunami.

This was bigger, better, stranger than anything he could've imagined. He breathed out slowly and let himself smile. "It's awesome," he said at last. "Absolutely awesome."

"You're enjoying this?" his father asked.

"Sure." He breathed, swallowed, breathed again. The fear faded. His brain loosened up. Suddenly he had questions. "So where are we going? What's that grinding noise? And what's the point of all this? What are we actually doing?"

"That's a lot of questions," Hanna said.

"Also, is there a bathroom?"

"Yes," his dad said, "but you'll have to wait for that."

"Is this thing safe?"

"Probably," Hanna answered.

"Probably?"

"Since we're asking questions, why is it that you're wearing one shoe?" Hanna asked.

"It's a trend," Lewis answered. And maybe it would be, if he said it enough. Maybe celebrities and pop superstars would start going to parties wearing only one shoe. Sneaker companies wouldn't even bother making left shoes anymore. No one would want them. Everyone would go right.

"Whatever," Hanna replied. "As for the grinding, each time a wave rushes forward, we drop a few anchors, which aren't really exactly like anchors—"

"That's the noise," his dad added.

"—and we kind of tie ourselves to the seafloor as the wave rolls past. Then, when the water retreats from the coast, we release the anchors and—"

"We ride the water out to sea?"

"Exactly!" she said.

Lewis's grip on the armrests loosened. He could feel the blood rushing through his neck. How long was he going to have to wait to use the bathroom?

"You're okay?" his father asked. "No injuries?"

"I'm good," Lewis said. Mostly. He could last for another few minutes at least. "What's the point of it?"

"Of what?"

"Of all of it. This thing, the trip."

"The subsphere," Hanna said.

"What?"

"It's not a thing. It's a subsphere. Because it's a spherical, or ball-shaped, submarine."

"Okay, but what is it for?" Lewis thought of Roberts and the Coastal Patrol again. People actually got thrown in jail for illegal ocean travel. "You could get in a lot of trouble."

"Right," Hanna replied. "The subsphere allows us to sneak out into the deep ocean, past the Coastal Patrol radars, under the cover of the tsunami. We wouldn't get half a mile if we just drove."

That made sense. But she still hadn't really answered his question. "Right, but why? Are you studying tsunamis?"

His father coughed. "Sort of," he mumbled. The water slowed. The anchors slammed into the seafloor as the next wave rolled past. This one had only a fraction of the power of the first few. "Throughout the majority of recorded history, major tsunamis only happened once a century," his dad continued. "At most! But when you were younger, Lewis, there was an average of twenty a year, all around the world. All the oceans, all the coasts. That number has gone down a little, but even now, these waves are unnaturally frequent. Yet most of the scientific community insists that the waves happen because of natural processes."

"Your father here has a different theory about the source of the waves." Hanna motioned to Lewis's dad. "Do you want to explain it, Professor? Or should I?"

"Does she need to explain, Lewis?"

No. No, she did not. He knew. His dad believed that something else was creating the waves. A new kind of technology developed by a civilization hidden deep beneath the ocean. A lost world waging war against the people on dry land by sending giant tsunamis crashing into their coasts.

"Atlantis," Lewis said. "You're talking about Atlantis."

For a moment, they were silent.

His father sighed. "You're probably sick of Atlantis, like your mom. You probably don't believe me, either."

At first, Lewis didn't answer. He couldn't even say the word around his mom, let alone ask any questions. And she totally had her reasons. When his dad had begun working on his Atlantis idea, he was a professor, and Lewis's parents were happily married. As the waves pounded the coast, though, and his dad developed his theory, he became obsessed. He wrote articles and essays. He spoke with news reporters and politicians. A film company made a short documentary about his work. He was kind of famous—for a scientist, anyway. He even had some evidence, or what he thought was evidence. At one point, Lewis's dad had stores of strange, almost alien-looking tools and artifacts. Texts in ancient languages mentioning an advanced race of so-called sea people. Old newspaper articles about fishermen and others who claimed to have seen visitors from Atlantis. He had scientific data, too—something about links between gravity and the huge waves that Lewis had never quite understood.

Unfortunately, most of the physical evidence was lost in a fire at his old lab. But even when he had all that material, his ideas were rejected. People wanted real solutions to the wave problem, not strange theories about lost civilizations.

His dad lost his reputation first.

Then his job.

And, finally, his family.

But Lewis never gave up on him. No matter what his mother or Roberts or everyone at school said. This was his dad. His big, brilliant, strange father. If his dad said Atlantis was real, then it was real. "I still believe you, Dad."

"You do?" Hanna asked, her tone skeptical.

"Wait, you don't?" Lewis asked.

"No," Hanna answered. "Not entirely."

His dad slumped in his chair. This was not a surprise to him.

"Then what are you doing here?" Lewis asked.

She patted the control panel. "I liked the engineering challenge," she said. "Plus, your dad here doesn't need believers. He needs proof, and if he's right, I'll help him find it. See, I do think someone could be making these waves. I'm just not sure it's a bunch of fish people."

"You're not even supposed to be here," his father said. "Either of you!"

"I thought she was part of this—"

"I am," Hanna snapped. "I'm essential! But your father thought this trip was too risky, so he tried to go without me."

"It is very dangerous—"

"Which is why I designed an impenetrable submarine," Hanna replied.

"Your parents will sue me, I'm sure," his dad added.

"We'll be back before they even notice I'm gone," she insisted. "Mom's in China, and Dad's in London, and they programmed the house AI to babysit me."

Wait. She had a house AI? Those were ridiculously expensive. They could help you with your homework. They cleaned your room. If Hanna had one, she probably had a robotic kitchen, too. One smart enough to actually make a rat taco. Which wouldn't really be a good thing and would definitely be difficult, since the AI would have to find and catch a rodent, but still . . . Lewis really, really wanted one. The house AI with the robotic kitchen, that is. Not the taco.

"What if your parents try to message you?" his dad replied.

"I reprogrammed the AI and uploaded some videos of myself saying everything's fine in case they try to check in.

Don't worry, Professor, I'm good for at least a week. What about you, Lewis?"

He thought about his mom. She was probably panicking. Roberts, too. And Michael would be wondering about his twenty bucks. "We have to tell them we're okay," Lewis said.

"Your mother will be worried sick," his father replied, "but I can't send a message. There's a risk the Patrol could track us and prevent us from traveling any farther. They can't know what we're doing, or they'll bring us back and impound our ship. After all, this is slightly illegal."

"Slightly?" Lewis asked.

"Entirely," Hanna said.

"Then what are we going to do?" Lewis asked.

Hanna replied directly to his dad. "We could use the escape pod and send him to the surface for the Patrol to pick up. The water's still shallow enough."

"Too risky," his dad said. "I can't leave my son drifting out there on the open sea."

That was encouraging, at least. His dad did care about him. Besides, Lewis didn't want to get ejected from the subsphere like some unwanted human turd. "So, what are we going to do?" he asked.

His father stared out through the window and into the endless dark water. "We're going to Atlantis," he said, "and you're coming with us."

5

DARKWATER TRADING COMPANY

YES, she'd been forced to wait a few days, but now the timing was perfect. Kaya's father was away for work, thanks to the project that never ended, and her grandmother was staying with her. Kaya loved her grandmother. Totally. The lady was funny and smart. She told great stories, too, and always spiced them with little lessons. Oh, and she also slept a ton and let Kaya do whatever she wanted. Her grandmother didn't ask where Kaya went or what she did because, she said, her parents never bothered her when she was young. Be home for dinner. That was the only rule. Normally Kaya didn't abuse this freedom. She used the time to listen to stories at the library or dive and swim in the deepwater pools. Today? Well, today she was going to stretch the rules a little.

Okay, more than a little.

She chowed down on a plate of spicy kelp and stewed fish for breakfast. Stuffed her backpack with her gravity gear, spare batteries, food, her water bottle and tablet, and the last of her money. The deepwater dive suit was rolled up, jammed into her helmet, and crammed in there on top of everything else. She checked through her list in her head for the fiftieth time. Then she said goodbye to her grandmother and dropped a quick kiss on her forehead.

"Don't forget to be home by dinner," her grandmother said.

"I won't."

"You won't forget, or you won't be home?"

Interesting question. "I won't forget," Kaya said with a smile.

She had ten hours.

Ten hours to ride out to Edgeland.

Find her way to one of the darkwater pools.

Slip into her suit.

Speed to the surface.

See the glittering palaces of the People of the Sun.

Swim back down to Atlantis.

And hurry home in time for dinner.

Rian had said it was impossible. Edgeland was almost five hundred miles from Ridge City. A normal transport along the waterways would take a full day. Even an antigravity cruiser would take six or seven hours. But Kaya had thought it all through. On the vacuum train, the trip was thirty minutes at most. Sure, you had to pay for that speed, but she'd been saving her babysitting money. Thanks to the Murakis, she had the coins.

Once in Edgeland, she'd need an hour or so to find a pool. Then she'd get in the water and rise. Her suit was absurdly fast— she knew from testing it in the local pools. According to her calculations, she'd blast from the ridge to the surface in less than an hour. Spend a little time looking around, do a quick search for signs of life, for those floating palaces, and then race back to

Atlantis and the vacuum train home. Ten hours? Plenty of time.

She might even be able to do it in eight.

She grabbed all her things and rushed down to the street.

Rian was waiting for her. She should have expected that. Kaya hadn't actually told him her plan, but he had a way of unraveling her secrets. "Do I get your gravity gear if you don't return?" he asked.

"No, but there's a Narwhals flag in my bedroom. That's all yours."

Rian smiled. He hated them, too. "So, what's the schedule?" he asked.

There was no point in lying. "Walk with me," she said, and along the way, she told him.

"I figured."

"Figured what? That I was going?"

"No, that you hadn't thought it all through. Do you even know how to find a darkwater pool?"

"No, but I can ask around—"

"You don't ask around in Edgeland. You don't talk to anyone at all."

Suddenly he was the expert? Annoying. "Just because you listened to some stories about the place doesn't mean you know it any better than I do," she said.

He pointed to her backpack. "Check your tablet. I sent you directions."

"To what?"

"To a darkwater pool in Edgeland."

Okay. This was not annoying. This was . . . unexpected. And super cool of him. "Really?"

"The water takes you outside the ridge, into the ocean. Then I guess you just go . . . up."

She smiled. "How did you get the directions?"

"One of my uncles."

Rian's family was enormous. He had several odd uncles. "The one your dad doesn't talk to? The guy who's been to jail?"

"That's the one. He says this pool is out of the way and never too crowded, so someone would probably be able to slip in unnoticed."

"Did you tell him who I—"

"No, and he didn't ask. Well, he asked for money, but . . ."

Rian shrugged, and his words trailed off. They stared at each other. They'd been friends pretty much since they were born. But it was a little weird at times, her best friend being a boy at their age. Especially at moments like this one. If Rian were a girl, Kaya would've hugged him. Instead, she clasped her hands in front of her and bowed slightly. "Thank you."

"What was that?" he asked.

She blushed. "I don't know."

"Kaya?"

"Yes?"

"Just be careful, okay? Really?"

"I'll be careful. Really."

She waited. Was there more to say?

Her friend flicked his hand forward. "Go. You're on a schedule."

The city was divided into quarters, and the nearest entrance to the vacuum train was in a new neighborhood, one that had been hollowed out of the stone only a few years before. Here the buildings were not carved into the walls; this section of the undersea mountains was wide open. The homes were towering palaces of multicolored crystal and glass. Light bounced and glittered off the walls and windows. The streets were paved with stones that were scrubbed nightly. The whole neighborhood gleamed, and the shops carried only the most expensive fashions and technology. Clothes and jewelry, of course. But gadgets, too. In the window of one store, Kaya spotted the latest gravity suit. The beauty supposedly worked for a full day on a single charge. She could drift halfway across Atlantis in one of those!

The entrance to the train platform was several levels below the surface. She was early, but the train floated up from the main tunnel below before too long. Only a few other passengers were waiting. Not many people made the trip from Ridge City to Edgeland. Not on the vacuum train, anyway. Rian was kind of a history expert, and he had explained that the Atlantean government had extended the tunnel out to Edgeland in hopes of reviving the city. Years earlier, it had been a busy seaport. Some of the wealthiest merchants and traders in Atlantis had called Edgeland their home. Then two nearby cities collapsed under the weight of the water above, and Edgeland was cut off for years—the only way to travel there was through the deep sea. This tunnel was an attempt to reconnect the city to the rest of Atlantis and restore its trade. But by the time it was built, Rian said, the battle to save Edgeland was already lost. The city had become a magnet for criminals. No high-speed train was going to change that.

But Kaya would be fine, she reminded herself.

She had a plan.

The doors opened. Her heart started beating faster. Was this fear? Or excitement? She stepped aside as the passengers rushed out, then found her seat quickly. The train drifted down into a connecting tunnel, bobbing slightly as it hovered. Kaya strapped herself in. Once all the air was sucked out of this section of the tunnel, another door would open, and the train would drop into the main tunnel. Then it would shoot forward.

If you weren't sitting at that point, you'd be thrown back against the wall.

Most people hated this part.

Kaya loved it.

As the train accelerated, her whole body was pulled backward. She couldn't even turn her head to look out the window, and in less than a minute, the train reached its top speed. The strange pull on her body eased, and as the train raced forward, she fell into a dreamless slumber. She awoke as her seat swung around to face the rear. That way, your head was pressed back against the seat as the train slowed to a stop.

"Next and final stop, Edgeland," a conductor announced.

Hurriedly, Kaya pulled out her pad and reviewed Rian's directions. Then she was off the train, up the dirty and grimy station stairs, and out into the dank, crowded city. Music blared from different directions, the tunes and drums clashing. Someone was playing the Narwhals. She winced. People shouted from the windows of ash-covered stone homes. A sonic weapon buzzed. Sirens roared.

She could see no glittering glass. No gleaming towers.

This place was vile.

Disgusting.

Loud.

She'd never been anyplace like it in her life, and she absolutely loved it. Even the smells! The people, the homes, the stinking heaps of garbage and clumps of rotting seaweed and fish bars lying in the streets—the smells were horrid. But they were so real and raw. Towering metal columns rose from the city streets to the ceiling high overhead. She'd read about these—they were meant to prevent Edgeland from collapsing in on itself like its former neighbors. She shivered at the thought of all that rock and water dropping down.

This kind of thinking wasn't helpful. Kaya had to look strong and sharp. Like a local. Not some wide-eyed, terrified kid. Her backpack was annoyingly overstuffed. She adjusted the straps, steered her eyes back to the ground, and hustled forward. In a dark alley she stopped to check the directions again. Her heart was racing. Relax, she told herself. Relax.

She strapped into her gravity gear, swung her bag onto her back, activated the drive, and pushed off. But she hadn't risen far when a powerful hand reached out of the darkness and clasped her ankle.

"Get back down here!" a voice roared.

A thick-lipped man had both hands clamped around her ankle now. Whistling, Kaya dialed up the power in the drive and kicked at his hairy knuckles.

"Give me the suit," he growled.

Desperately, Kaya stomped on the man's face. He grabbed his eye and loosened his grip just long enough for her to plant her foot on his head and push off, up and out of his reach. The gravity drive was still on high. She soared away from the alley, nearly smashing into a rusting sign jutting out of a wall. The man was screaming at her. But she was clear. Free. She whistled again, dialing down the power, then pushed off the rock wall.

Hovering over the crowded city square, she slowed her breathing. Focus on the plan, she told herself. Follow the waterway south out of the city: That's what Rian's directions said. But which one? Waterways flowed in from all directions, each one packed with boats and ferries.

The man from the alley was storming through the city square, pointing in her direction.

She had to get out of there fast. One of her gravity gloves had a built-in compass, and after checking the needle, she found a waterway heading south. A thin, jagged divider of dark stone ran down the middle, and the water on either side flowed in opposite directions. She drifted down and through a wide opening in the cavern wall.

The air in the tunnel was warm, thick, and wet. Water fell from the ceiling in steady drops. The passageway narrowed, and soon it was only wide enough to carry one lane of boats in each direction. As Kaya drifted, she passed only a few vessels. Not many people traveled out this far. She was at the border of the city.

The edge of Atlantis.

Before long, the waterway fed into one of the largest aqua-farms she'd ever seen. Mostly kelp and algae, she guessed. But the ripples and waves in some of the pools suggested plenty of fish were raised there, too. The ceiling was hidden behind thick mist. The water below was greenish and still, the air salty, and the distant walls of the wide cavern glittered in the faint blue light. There were some boats, too, and half a dozen farmers scattered around the edges of the pools, tending to their underwater crops. No growling thieves here, thankfully. She hovered in place, breathing, watching the water.

Her nerves calmed.

Her pulse steadied.

The water settled her spirit.

She'd made it this far.

She could make it to the surface.

The waterway crossed the aquafarm, leading into a tunnel at the other end. Rian's directions mentioned a border station at the far side of the waterway. No one could go beyond that point, and his uncle had suggested avoiding the station, anyway. She turned right instead, following a path along the western wall of the enormous farm. A walkway just above the water wrapped around the wall, and scattered trading posts lined the path. Fishermen brought their catches here to be sold and shipped to the cities. The pungent smell of one of the storefronts suggested it was a warehouse for drying kelp. Thankfully, Rian's directions didn't send her to one of those spots. They indicated the post wouldn't be far, and they were right. She could've walked if she'd liked. A small sign overhead read DARKWATER TRADING COMPANY.

This was the place. Kaya drifted to the entrance and dropped down onto the wide path.

In the water behind her, a single small boat was tied to the jagged rock ledge of the walkway. Beneath the sign, a doorway led into a narrow tunnel. She switched off her gravity drive. Her shoulder brushed the wet wall as she walked through the doorway, and after a few steps, she found herself in a low-ceilinged cave. The room was cold—the water from the deep, she guessed. She could feel the chill on her skin.

Inside, a wide darkwater pool took up most of the space, spilling out onto the stone floor. Three small submarines were tied to the edge of the pool, and the walls were lined with wheeled tanks, each one filled with fish of all sizes and shapes. There were some kinds she'd never even seen before.

Two chairs were propped against the wall beside the entrance, facing the cold black water. Both were empty, thankfully. But a blue light glowed beneath a door to her right. Was someone in there singing? Yes, and not very well, either. She probably didn't have long before the owner of that boat outside popped out and demanded a bribe. And sure, she had the coins, but why not save them?

Kaya found a recess in the wall, a kind of hiding place, and slipped inside to change into her dive suit. Carefully, she pulled off her backpack, unrolled the suit, laid it out on the floor, then switched it on. The material hardened and expanded. Kaya kneeled and poked at the sleeves and helmet. Both solid as the stone beneath her feet. Yet once you pulled it on and started moving, the suit was as flexible as a soft shirt. The technology was amazing. She had nothing to worry about. So why were her hands still shaking? Why was her heart hammering?

The inside of the suit was roomy, so she kept her backpack and gravity gear on—that way, she wouldn't leave any evidence that she'd been here. Once she sealed herself into the suit, it quickly filled with oxygen, allowing her to breathe. She jumped in place a few times. No leaks. Everything was working. And the door was still closed.

If she was going to go, now was the time.

Kaya shuffled forward and stood over the black water.

Just another swim, she told herself.

She'd tested this suit a few dozen times.

Only two days before, she'd swum across one of the largest deepwater pools in Atlantis. Sure, she'd never actually been outside the ridge, but was there really such a difference? It was all just water. She knew water. And the suits were built to withstand the pressure and cold.

The door behind her opened.

A vile, large-nosed monster of a man stepped into the cave, adjusting his sagging pants.

Kaya waved with her gloved hand, then turned and dove into the water.

6
DENIZEN OF THE DEEP

THE SUBSPHERE was large, but the living space was tiny. The rooms were spread out and connected by skinny hallways. There was one bedroom with two bunks. Lewis tried to claim the top one, but Hanna said it was hers. Whatever.

While he was very, very happy to find the bathroom, it was so small he couldn't even stretch his arms out all the way. The subsphere also had a kitchen with a tiny fridge, a microwave oven, two short stools, and a table that folded down from the wall. The cabinets were stacked with cans of food. Peaches, pears, beans, soups. All kinds of miniature meals. The insides of the cabinets were magnetized, so once a can of food was empty, you could throw it against the door from the hallway, and it would stick there.

Or that's what he guessed, anyway.

He would never try that.

Of course not.

That would be childish, and he was twelve years old, named after a famous explorer, and on a very serious mission to discover a hidden world. Lewis definitely wouldn't draw targets on the magnetized doors and come up with a game that involved removing three cans from the mix and trying to hit the three separate targets with them in as few tries as possible. He certainly wouldn't pretend to be a circus worker and invite imaginary contestants to play, either.

Nope. Not him. Never.

When he wasn't not playing imaginary games, he explored every inch of the sub.

Mission report? Boredom was unavoidable.

Thankfully, he'd packed the soccer ball. His dad's wristpad had a few decent games. Oh, and he was going to Atlantis! The last he'd heard, they were cruising a mile below the surface of the sea. A mile! The sub was built to withstand the pressure of the deep, and they were going deeper all the time.

After lunch on their first day, he found his dad alone in the cockpit. Something was bothering Lewis, something he wanted to discuss with his father. He moistened the end of his pinky finger and stuck it in his father's ear.

A half-full coffee cup went flying across the cabin.

A few apologies and a quick cleanup later, he got to his question. "So, about Mom. What if she thinks we're . . . you know? We have to send her a message somehow."

"I know, I know," his father said, wiping up the last of the spilled coffee. "It's terrible. I feel horrible. But we can't risk it. Not yet, anyway."

"But—"

"If we dispatch a signal too soon, the Coastal Patrol might be able to track us. And if they find us, they'll stop us." He spread his arms wide. "All this will be for nothing." His father took Lewis's head in both of his giant hands and sighed. "But I understand, Lewis. She needs to know you're safe. She deserves to know. We'll get her a message. We will."

"When?"

"Soon. A few days at most."

His father patted him on the shoulder, smiled, and spun back around. His mom would be okay, right? They'd tell her soon. He had to trust that his father knew best.

Later that afternoon, Lewis was practicing soccer, kicking and receiving with his left foot, when Hanna stopped nearby and leaned against the wall. "I can't believe you actually brought that."

"I always bring a soccer ball with me."

He passed to her. The ball bounced off her foot and rolled to a stop.

"Are you any good?" she asked.

He considered telling her he was the next world superstar, a rare combination of grace and strength. Instead, he opted for the truth. "I'm okay."

"I don't do sports." She pointed at his shirt. "You've been wearing that since yesterday. Did you pack clothes?"

"Some." He had an extra T-shirt, but this one wasn't quite poisonous yet. He had one extra pair of socks, too. He'd already washed the muddy one in the bathroom sink and found a great place to hang it to dry. He was fine on underwear, too. He only had one pair, but if he was careful, that could easily last him a week.

"A toothbrush?"

He had been planning to steal one from his dad. "Well . . ."

"Your dad didn't bring one, either. Lucky for you, I always pack plenty of extras when I travel. I was at a sleepover once a few years ago and three different girls used my toothbrush. Just the thought . . ." She squirmed.

"How do you know three different girls used it?"

"I ran DNA tests on the saliva."

She said this with a shrug, as if it were obvious.

Lewis started kicking the ball against the wall again, switching to his right foot. Hanna didn't leave.

"How do you know my dad?" he asked.

"I listened to one of his lectures online a few years ago. I was finishing college—"

"College? You're my age."

"Three years older than you, and yeah, I'm kind of smart. Weird smart. I started college when I was twelve and finished when I was fourteen. I'm in graduate school now, studying engineering."

"Wow."

"Yeah, nothing's really that hard for me, brain-wise, so I like a challenge. I learned about what your dad wanted to do and figured I could help him."

"Why?"

"Honestly? My parents."

"Your parents?"

"I can never please them. Not even close."

His mom would probably shoot fireworks out of her ears if he were that smart. "But you said you graduated college at fourteen."

"My mom was done at thirteen."

He thought about this for a moment. The thinking got him nowhere. "I don't get it. What does helping my dad have to do with you and your parents?"

"We saw him on-screen one night—some documentary about conspiracy theories. My parents were saying how he was a fool . . ." She stopped herself, then winced. "I'm sorry, I didn't mean to—"

"It's fine." The kids in school had called his father worse names.

"So I heard them talking," Hanna continued, "and even though your dad had already lost his university job, he was way more interesting than my other professors, and I thought, this is what I need to do! You know that feeling when you finally figure out what you're meant for?"

"Nope."

"You'll get there. I decided I needed to help this guy. Granted, I'd already been obsessing over submarines and deep-sea exploration, so our planets kind of aligned. My parents were furious, too, so that was good."

"So you built the subsphere to annoy your parents?"

Hanna paused. "I've never really thought of it quite like that, but yeah, I guess so. Is there a better reason to do anything in life? Anyway, I started working at your dad's lab. Not that shack down by the shore, though. We just put that together recently. I'm talking about the real lab, the one that burned down."

Sure. Totally. The real lab. He'd never been invited to that one, either. And she got to work there? Whenever Lewis asked if he could help, his dad insisted that he had to work alone. Was

Lewis just not good enough? Not smart enough? He kicked the ball hard down the hall. "Why did he let you help him?"

"Well, I had a cool idea for a submarine. And there's one other small matter."

"Yeah? What's that?" Lewis asked.

"I'm rich."

This wasn't a huge surprise. She had a house AI. But she didn't look rich. Her clothes were torn at the knees and elbows. Her shoe was taped together, and she didn't even have a wristpad. The only tech she wore was one of those music rings on her finger, the kind that only played and recorded audio. "How rich?"

"My mom helped invent the wristpad."

Oh. Whoa. "You're serious?"

"I'm serious." Hanna moved closer, lowering her voice. "Listen, this thing with my parents, trying to annoy them and all . . . that's part of the reason I came to find you. I was listening earlier, when you and your dad were talking about waiting to let your mom know you're alive."

The ball rolled back toward Lewis. The submarine was diving gradually, tilting forward. He stopped it under his left foot. "Okay . . ."

"Well, I just want you to know you're idiots."

"Idiots?"

"Emotionally," she said. "No offense."

"None taken?"

"Me, too. I'm an idiot, I mean. What if my parents get back early? The AI's not going to convince them I'm home if they're actually there. They're going to panic. Your mom's probably panicking right now. We can't make them all wait, Lewis. I might have issues with my parents, but they're my parents. I don't want to torture them. Not like this, anyway. We have to get messages to them as soon as possible to let them know we're safe."

Lewis lifted the ball with his right foot and began to juggle. She was probably right.

Of course she was right.

He stopped at five.

"You think we can talk my dad into it?"

"We don't have to. He doesn't have to know," she said. "There's an emergency communications float. We can load a short message on there, then send it to the surface to broadcast. But I'll need you to distract your dad for a little while so he doesn't know I'm sending it."

A distraction? Lewis thought about this for a moment. "I could dance."

"Are you serious?"

Partly. He was a very distracting dancer. The chicken dance was his specialty, with his bent elbows as the wings and his chin jutting forward to the beat of a real or imagined song. But Hanna didn't seem keen on this plan, and he wasn't really in the mood to demonstrate. The chicken dance was difficult to do on command. "No, I don't know. I just said the first thing that popped into my head."

"What's your second idea?"

"Yoga?"

"You know yoga?"

"Not really."

"You're not very good at this."

"No, I'm not."

"How about—"

He held up his hand, interrupting her. An actual plan had occurred to him. A decent one, even. "I've got it."

"Okay . . . I trust you. I probably shouldn't, but I do," Hanna said. "Write down your message for me first. It has to be short. Fifteen words or less. And put something in there so your mom knows it's from you."

He nodded. "When do we start?"

"The sooner, the better."

Hanna turned back toward the bedroom.

Lewis stared down at his soccer ball. Fifteen words? What was he supposed to say? He started juggling again. In his head, he wrote a whole series of messages, counting the words in each. All of them were too long. Finally he settled on something short. He found a notebook in his backpack, tore out a piece of paper, then slipped the notebook into his back pocket. He dashed off the message. Hanna was lying on the top bunk, studying something, when he handed it over.

Quietly, she read his note aloud. "*I'm with Dad. I'm fine. Be home soon. Tell Michael he smells like cheese.*" She squinted at him. "Cheese?"

"They'll know it's from me."

"And the distraction?"

"We're good. Ready when you are."

"All right," she said, swinging her legs down off the bed. "One more thing, though, Lewis."

"Yes?"

She threw a familiar sock at his face. "My bunk is not a clothesline."

Lewis's father was in the cockpit and didn't hear him approach. Lewis coughed. Nothing. Then he clapped once, hard enough that his hands stung, maybe a little too close to his dad's ear. His father nearly leaped out of his seat.

"What the—"

"Hey, Dad, can I ask you something?"

"Why did you . . . I'm busy, here, Lewis. I need to make sure we're on the right course." His dad leaned over his maps.

"Okay, sure, I'm going to head to the kitchen for some food, anyway. I was just wondering . . . I mean, besides the waves and all"—he hesitated, ensuring that his dad was listening—"what makes you think Atlantis is real? No rush. Just wondering. You can tell me later."

Lewis started to walk out of the room.

He began counting.

Three seconds.

That was all it took for his father to switch over to autopilot, ditch his maps, and follow him to the kitchen. He never missed a chance to explain his theories about Atlantis, and during multiple rounds of the can-tossing game, his dad rambled on and on about the hidden world. He explained that the waves were only part of the evidence. There had been sightings throughout history. Stories told by fishermen. Rumors of strange craft washing up on beaches around the world, then being quickly snatched away by various governments. He talked about the ancient texts discovered around the world that mentioned a highly advanced seafaring civilization, one that ruled thousands of years before the ancient Egyptians. His dad was a geophysicist by training, and he referenced scientific ideas about shifting tectonic plates and rising seas that could have caused a giant island to gradually sink into the ocean.

None of this was new to Lewis, but it still fascinated him. He tried to picture this catastrophe—an island slipping beneath the sea. How could the people have survived? Were they already mermaids and mermen when the island sank? And how would that have worked, living both on land and in the ocean? You definitely wouldn't walk too well if you had a big tail instead of legs. Maybe they rolled themselves around on wheeled carts. Or what if they army-crawled everywhere? That would be awkward. And slow. But sort of funny.

"Of course, you'd assume that this civilization would have been wiped out by the rising waters and sinking land," his dad continued. "But I believe they adapted over time—not in an evolutionary sense, but a technological one. They built down into the ground instead of up, effectively sealing themselves off from the water. That's how Atlantis survived, Lewis, and how its people continue to thrive underground, beneath the sea."

His dad was smiling now. But Lewis still had questions. One in particular. "Why would they send all those waves?" he asked. "What did we ever do to them?"

The question injected his dad with new energy. He began pacing in the small kitchen. Lewis sat up on the counter to give him more room. "I wondered that myself, of course!" his dad began. "In the early days of the waves, before the oceans were closed off to travel, I was on the beach one morning, walking at sunrise, watching the water. The tide was out. A fishing trawler was pulling in its nets offshore. The nets were practically empty. A few silvery fish, but little more. I continued walking, picking up bits of plastic and trash as I went. I filled an entire backpack with salt-encrusted garbage before I'd gone fifty meters. Then, farther along, I noticed thousands of dead crabs scattered everywhere, all with brittle, papery shells. Thinking of the empty nets, the dead crustaceans, the plastic, I stopped and stared out at the sea."

His dad was gazing at the wall as if it were the open ocean. "And?" Lewis asked.

"And I thought, 'Of course they'd be furious!'" his father continued. "We're filling the sea with our trash. We're poisoning the atmosphere. Aquatic life is dying out in droves. We're destroying the oceans. Why wouldn't they wage this war?"

That actually made sense. Well, sort of, anyway. Lewis jumped down off the counter. "Wouldn't they try to talk to us first? Maybe ask us to change?"

Again, his dad had an answer. "Ah, but I believe they did try!" he said. "Eight years ago, there was a massive explosion in the water near what used to be the great city of New York. The government called it a submarine accident. But a naval officer contacted me in secret and told me it was really an Atlantean ship that was attacked and destroyed by our own military."

Now he wasn't making sense. "Why would we attack their submarine?"

"The officer said it was a mistake," his dad explained. "The object was traveling as fast as a torpedo, and efforts to make contact with it failed. The navy was left to assume that it actually was a torpedo, since no submarine technology of ours has ever traveled half as fast. We had to destroy it, Lewis, to save the city. But of course, it wasn't a torpedo. It was an Atlantean ship! The craft was decimated, the government covered up its mistake, and the war began."

His dad even said he had evidence, a collection of sonar readouts tracking the craft. At one point, he'd had a few fragments of the exploded ship, too, but these had been lost in his laboratory fire. Of course, his dad blamed the fire on some secret government agency. But no one bought that idea. The officer who had sent him the information had also disappeared. Basically, no one believed his father. Or no one important, anyway. Online? Sure. People loved the story. One site even listed it as one of the top ten Internet conspiracy theories, right after the idea that the last president was actually an alien.

Lewis paused, waiting to see if his father was done. His dad was sitting on one of the tiny kitchen stools. He looked like a giant resting on a mushroom. He seemed exhausted, as if explaining his theory had drained all the energy from his body and mind. Then he cracked his knuckles and straightened his back. "The final question," he continued, "is how to find her. But I won't bore you with my gravitational anomaly theory."

"Thank you," Lewis said.

His dad looked a little disappointed. Was Lewis supposed to ask for more? His brain was already full.

His dad held out his wristpad and projected a three-dimensional map of the ocean floor. "Anyway, all of my research suggests she's right here," he said.

Lewis stared at the projected map. "That's the middle of the Atlantic Ocean. Are you sure?"

Hanna stood in the doorway. "That's why we're going, right? To find out for certain?"

"That's right!" his dad replied.

She winked when his father wasn't looking.

The message had been sent.

Lewis sighed.

At least now his mother would know he was okay. But was he okay? After listening to his father for an hour, he wasn't so sure. Were they actually on an epic adventure, or were they just diving into the dark sea? Was his dad a brilliant explorer, or had he lost his mind somewhere along the way?

Maybe everyone else was right about his dad.

Maybe Lewis should have stayed home.

Three days passed.

The first few times he saw fish outside the window, he was thrilled.

The thrill faded quickly.

He experienced whole new levels of boredom. He slept longer and later.

Being stuck inside your house on a rainy day could be difficult.

Sitting through a really painful movie your mom makes you watch.

Reading one of those books they assigned in school about kids with feelings who feel things all the time, and nothing ever explodes except for their feelings.

All of those things were boring.

But then there was trapped-inside-a-submarine-miles-under-the-surface boredom. He invented a dozen different throw-the-can games. He kicked the soccer ball so many times his feet blistered. But the absolute low was when he started to play hide-and-seek . . . against himself. On the morning of the fourth day of their journey, he'd been crouching underneath the fold-down table in the kitchen for a really, really long time when his dad found him. Explaining himself was embarrassing.

"Did you win?" his dad asked.

"I'm not sure."

"Listen, I already talked to Hanna about this, but . . ."

He could see it on his dad's pale, saddened face. He'd found out about the message.

Lewis felt horribly, completely selfish. They'd risked the whole mission! His dad's work. Everything. He was supposed to trust his father. "I'm sorry, we just thought—"

"No, I'm sorry," his dad replied. "You were right. You were both right. Your mother, Hanna's parents—they needed to know the truth. I guess I just got so caught up . . ."

The subsphere turned suddenly.

Lewis grabbed the edge of the table, but his dad was thrown off his feet. The cans in the cabinet rattled. His dad rubbed the back of his huge head, then called to the cockpit from the floor. "What was that? Did we hit something?"

"I don't know," Hanna yelled back. "Get in here!"

His dad scrambled forward. Lewis raced behind him. Their footsteps clanged on the metal grates. At the controls, Hanna was switching between screens. "Whatever we hit, it was big and it was moving."

A map of the seafloor appeared on the screen. "There are some weird formations up ahead."

His dad pushed a pair of old-fashioned, circular reading glasses up his large nose. He leaned in to study the image. "Weird how?" he asked excitedly. "Buildings?"

"No, more like underwater mountains."

"What bumped us, though?" Lewis asked.

Part of him hoped it was another submarine. A luxury one, owned and operated by a reclusive billionaire. Ideally, this billionaire would invite them aboard and feed them a lavish, delicious dinner. Maybe he'd give them all bathrobes to wear, too. Fancy ones, with little monograms. And slippers. Really soft slippers.

"I don't know," his dad answered. "Nothing big enough to push our sub to the side swims at this depth. We're four miles down."

"That thing might disagree," Hanna said.

Out of the darkness in front of them swam the largest creature Lewis had ever seen—an aquatic monster that looked capable of swallowing their subsphere in two ravenous bites. The beast's nose reminded him of a shark, but its huge eyes popped out like those of a crocodile. An enormous, tightly closed mouth stretched below the snout. The creature didn't have to open wide for Lewis to guess what was inside. He imagined rows and rows of sharp, metal-crunching teeth.

"What is that?!" he asked.

"Hold on!" Hanna shouted. "Strap into your seats, both of you!"

The subsphere steered right, grazing the giant's side.

Lewis was still buckling. "Was that a megalodon?"

"No, they're extinct," his dad answered. "But that creature was gargantuan! Do you know what this means? We might have discovered a new species of megafauna! No one does that anymore!"

A giant prehistoric creature was attacking them miles below the surface, and his dad was thrilled. Lewis leaned to the side as Hanna steered the subsphere to the left.

"We're not going to get any credit if that thing eats us," she said. "The sub isn't built to evade sea monsters. You have any ideas?"

As the huge creature passed in front of them again, circling for another attack, Lewis noticed something strange. The subsphere didn't crank out enough light for him to be sure.

He unbuckled.

"Get back in your seat!" Hanna ordered.

He ignored her and reached for the control panel.

"What are you doing?" his dad demanded.

"Does this ship have headlights?"

"LEDs. Why? You want to startle it?" Hanna asked.

"At this depth, creatures are attracted to light, not startled by it," his dad said. "So that would be a bad idea."

Lewis found the dials on his own and turned them up. Bright white light filled the dark sea in front of them. Hanna reached for the buttons, but he covered them with his hands. "I'm not trying to startle it," he explained. "I'm trying to show you something."

"Show us what?"

"That it's not going to eat us."

"Why not?"

"Because it's not a fish," he said. "It's a machine."

The huge thing swam through the bright white lights, and now Lewis could see them clearly: Seams that stretched across the skin where two metal panels met.

"You're right," Hanna said, almost in a whisper. "He's right."

His dad said nothing. He just stared. "What do we do?" he asked.

Lewis had kind of hoped that his dad would answer that question himself.

The robotic monster turned toward them again, but this time it came no closer. The bright water pulsed and rippled. Lewis felt invisible waves push through his face and chest, as if he were standing next to a giant speaker blasting bass at a concert.

His nose quivered. His ribs and hands, too.

The room around him clouded over.

His jaw tightened, and then everything turned black.

7

BODIES FROM THE DARKNESS

EVERYTHING was going perfectly.

Kaya had made it into the water.

She'd started to rise to the surface.

The suit was amazing. She didn't even feel the cold or the pressure.

Then the water around her started moving. As if some invisible hand had grabbed her around the ankles again, she stopped rising. She was caught in a strange, and strangely powerful, current.

The water spun her faster and faster, in smaller and smaller circles. Had anyone ever thrown up in a dive suit? She really didn't want to be the first.

Now the water pulled her down, still spinning.

She felt like she was falling off a cliff.

Yet she didn't splash down into a pool or an aquafarm. Instead, she was sucked into a small, watery room. A door closed, sealing her off from the surrounding sea, but the space was still flooded. Where was she? At first, she couldn't even tell which way was up. Her legs flipped over her head. Then she steadied, floating between the floor and the ceiling. The water was moving again, draining out of the room through grates in the floor. Kaya tried to calm her rapid breathing. Her stomach had settled. She wasn't going to vomit. That was good, at least.

Once the water was less than half a body length deep, she planted her feet and stood.

There were no windows, but even through the helmet she could hear water rushing past outside. She was in some kind of submarine, and the vessel was dropping fast. She had to stagger her feet, one in front of the other, and hold on to a railing to stop herself from falling forward. Kaya moved downhill, hand over hand, toward what she guessed was the front of the vessel, hoping to find a cockpit. But there were no other rooms or cabins. She'd been swallowed by a submarine, and she was alone. This was . . . good.

Yes, this was good!

Fantastic, even.

Sure, she hadn't made it to the surface, but if no one else was inside the submarine, then no one knew what she'd done, and she could avoid getting in trouble. Maybe the whole thing was automatic. Some kind of Atlantean probe programmed to collect divers who drifted too far from the ridge. This wasn't totally impossible. If Rian was to be believed, Atlantis had all kinds of secret technology that most people knew nothing about. And if she'd been grabbed by some super-smart robot submarine, she could slip back to Ridge City unnoticed.

That was the optimistic version, anyway.

The other possibility? She was about to be thrown in jail. Even erased.

She shivered at the thought.

Soon the submarine slowed and leveled out.

Then it started rising again.

The vessel stopped.

Kaya heard bolts sliding, and a loud hiss as a hatch at the front popped open. A man with long silver hair stared back at her. Right. So the whole nobody-knew-where-she'd-been idea? Not so much. She wasn't getting out of here unnoticed.

But the situation wasn't all bad. Even though he was pointing a large sonic blaster at her stomach, one that could knock down a dozen soldiers with one shot, the man himself didn't look too frightening. He wasn't as ugly as the monster at the trading post that morning. He was probably a few years younger than her dad. His face was round, and he was biting his thin lower lip. Was he nervous? He blinked often, as if his eyes didn't like the light.

"Out of the submarine, and off with the suit," he ordered.

Kaya held her hands up and stepped out slowly.

This wasn't going as planned. And that meant she'd have to make a new plan. First, she needed information. Data. Where was she? She scanned the room. An impressively large cave. Unpolished walls. A colossal darkwater pool large enough to hold at least a dozen submarines. Three times the size of the pool she'd used that morning, at least.

The whirlpool ship that had swallowed her up was the only watercraft tied to the edge. But the space was crowded with machines and workstations and half-built contraptions. This wasn't anything like the other deepwater dock. It reminded her of a mechanic's workshop. Channels carved into the rock carried water from the pool into dark tunnels in the walls.

"The suit," the man said. "Climb out of it now."

She unlatched her helmet and removed it.

The man stammered, so surprised he could barely speak. "You're . . . you're just a kid."

She hated when people said that. "I'm fourteen."

"But you made it out of the ridge! Do you know how dangerous that was?"

"Well, it didn't feel all that dangerous until you sucked me down with that whirlpool. I could've drowned, you know. I mean, what gives you the right—"

"Atlantis!"

"Excuse me?"

"Atlantis gives me the right, young lady. This is my job! Watching our borders. Keeping them safe."

"From fourteen-year-olds?"

He sighed. His thick shoulders slumped. "I'm just following orders, okay? Close the borders, bring back escapees—I don't care for any of that! A smuggler wants to catch illegal fish outside the ridge and sell them in Edgeland? Let him! A girl wants to risk her life and go for a swim in the deepwater? Let her be! I didn't ask for this job." He bit his lip and stared at the ground. Then he held up a finger. "Actually, I did ask for this job, but I didn't think I'd have to do anything. I certainly didn't expect teenagers attempting to escape from Atlantis!"

An alarm startled him. He grabbed his long silver hair. "You're distracting me!"

"I'm distracting you?" The man seemed pretty good at distracting himself.

"Six months of nothing. Glorious, delightful, pleasant nothing. And now, two alerts in one day! A possible invasion, at that. I can't believe . . . this is too much. Too much."

"An invasion?" she asked. "What are you talking about?"

"None of your—"

The alarm was blaring now.

He laid his sonic blaster on a table and rushed over to a workstation. He pressed his hand against a tablet. The surface moved, tiny rods rising and falling. She watched the man's lips move as he read with his hand. Rian did this, too. He couldn't just feel the words when he read. He had to pronounce them, to hear them.

"Are you counting?" she asked.

"Quiet!" He aimed his weaponless hand at her stomach, then stared down at his empty fingers with surprise.

Some guard. She motioned to the blaster on the table. "Don't worry," she said, "I'm not going to grab it. Tell me, though, why are you counting?"

"Two minutes," he mumbled.

"Two minutes until what? What did you mean by invasion?"

He waved toward a door. "Go. Please. Get out of here!"

He'd already moved to another workstation, as if he'd forgotten all about her. She was curious, sure, but she was free. She could get home after all. Everything was going to work out just fine. She moved as fast as she could in the dive suit. The guard was talking to someone through his earpiece as the door closed behind her. She followed a narrow hallway to its end, then pushed through an exit and into a wide tunnel.

A two-lane waterway ended just outside the door.

Kaya stripped off the dive suit, laid it out on the ground, and flicked the power switch. The material softened, and while the suit flattened out, she stared down the tunnel. The waterway led to a wide-open space. An aquafarm. The very same one she'd drifted over earlier that day. Now she was on the opposite side—at the border station. The one place Rian had warned her to avoid. Still, this was good. All she had to do was switch on her gravity suit and drift across. Then she could follow the same path as before. Make the next train. And get home for dinner with her grandmother.

But why had the guard let her go without even a warning? What she'd done was totally illegal. And what was the invasion he had mentioned? Was he talking about people from the Rift? She'd heard horror stories about the Rift, a region east of the main cities of Atlantis, cut off from the rest of their world. Supposedly the people there were hideous. Suggesting someone was from the Rift was a pretty standard insult. But she'd never heard any tales of Rift dwellers invading Atlantis. Maybe it was just another ship. Or a smuggler.

Kaya clicked her earpiece and checked the time. She still had a little while until the vacuum train home. One last glance into the odd workshop wouldn't hurt. She left her suit on the ground and slipped back inside in time to hear something crashing against rock. Something heavy and metal crunching into stone.

Kaya crept quietly through the hall.

The door to the workshop was unlocked.

She heard splashing inside, and stepped through to find

two gigantic submarines docked at the edge of the pool. One reminded her of some kind of prehistoric beast. The other, a gleaming metal ball as large as her entire home, sat heavily in the water alongside it. A hatch was open in the side of the spherical ship, and a long metal ramp reached down to the stone floor. Water splashed onto the rock as the sphere bumped against the edge of the pool. As Kaya watched, the long-haired guard stomped out of the opening and down the ramp, carrying across his shoulders the largest, strangest man she had ever seen.

8

PEOPLE OF THE SUN

LEWIS blinked. The cockpit was dark except for a dim blue glow. His head ached. His ears rang. And he was on the floor. Lying on his back. Had he been napping? He was a very talented sleeper—always had been. He could sleep on floors, stretched out on countertops, sitting in school during Health and Wellness class. One time, he fell asleep in a tree, then tumbled out and broke his arm. But now he didn't even remember—

The monster!

That weird metal monster.

That shock rang through him.

Then he was standing in a dark forest surrounded by low trees, and from the branches of the trees hung socks of every color and thickness, and the socks were all clean and fresh-smelling, and . . .

Wait. That last part was a dream.

The other stuff did happen, though. He jumped to his feet.

His dad was gone.

Hanna was gone.

The air inside the subsphere smelled different. Musty. Like his grandmother's basement. No, worse. Like the old couch tucked away in one of the dark corners of her basement. He'd used it as a hiding spot once (in a game against other people) and had sneezed for hours afterward.

The cockpit was hot, too. Sweat was trickling down the ends of his eyebrows. He wiped his forehead with the bottom of his shirt. Where were Hanna and his dad? The heat, the dim blue light, the lack of power in the cockpit—everything felt weird. Wrong. And why weren't they moving? No water rushed past the glass, so they weren't under the sea anymore. A tall rock wall loomed through the windows. Lights embedded in the rock glowed dimly.

Someone grunted.

The someone was not his father.

Footsteps clanged against metal.

Lewis tiptoed toward the sound.

The sub was rocking slightly, as if it were floating in a calm sea. And the hatch was open. So they had to be back on the surface. But where? Maybe they'd drifted up and floated to the shore of some tropical island. One with coconuts, not cannibals. Maybe they'd have hammocks on the island, too. And treasure! Gold and emeralds and rubies. He'd use it to buy his mom a house with a robotic kitchen and that sweet AI.

He crept closer to the hatch and peeked out.

This was no tropical island.

There was no treasure, and not a hammock in sight.

The subsphere was tied to the edge of a pool in some kind of gigantic cave. The space was three or four times as large as his school gym. The rock wall he'd seen through the window stretched high overhead. The metal monster—he recognized the seams along the side—was docked beside them. Almost everything in the cave was dripping, as if the walls were sweating.

Crystals in the rock glowed blue, and a metal ramp led down from the subsphere to the stone floor, where a small, wide-shouldered man was gently laying Hanna on the ground. His dad was stretched out next to her.

The man's hair was silver and long, his skin gray, almost sickly. He was short, too. A few inches shorter than Lewis, if he had to guess. But he was even wider and thicker than Lewis's dad. His shoulder muscles were huge, as if he'd stuffed small soccer balls into his shirt, and his eyes were too large for his face. They looked like they belonged on a cartoon character Michael would draw. Next to this odd man, leaning over his dad, stood a girl with enormous, moonlike eyes and ghostly pale skin. Her long, straight hair was silvery white, and she was even shorter than the other stranger. She wore a blue-gray suit of some kind, almost like a full-body bathing suit, and a backpack was strapped around her waist and over her shoulders. She could have been dressed for a hike or a war. Lewis's heart started beating faster.

The girl was weirdly pretty.

Both of the strangers turned and stared up at him.

Neither of them offered coconuts. He really hoped they weren't cannibals.

Lewis froze. Should he run? Call for help? Hide under the fold-down kitchen table? Do the chicken dance? No. Too much pressure.

Instead, he shrugged and waved.

The girl did not wave back.

Neither did the man with the soccer-ball shoulders.

Suddenly, Hanna woke with a jolt. She rolled over and accidentally kneed his dad in the ribs. The professor struggled to a crawling position and sat up as Lewis rushed down the ramp.

"What happened?" his dad asked. "Where's Lewis?"

"I'm here," he said.

His dad rubbed his temples. "Where are we?"

The two silver-haired strangers were still watching them. They'd backed away a few steps. Were they afraid of them? Were they even people? They weren't as small as leprechauns, and they didn't have red hair. Lewis kind of hoped they were leprechauns, though, because those Irish fairies were famously skilled shoemakers, and the whole one sneaker thing was getting annoying. He pointed at them. "Maybe we should ask those two," he said. "They might be leprechauns," he added, lowering his voice to a whisper, "or cannibals."

"Cannibals? What are you talking about?"

The moon-eyed girl was staring at him like he was an alien. Did he have food stuck in his teeth? Lewis ran his tongue along the grooves and found nothing. Was it his hair? He'd gotten it cut only a few weeks earlier, and it was kind of long on the top and short at the sides and back. And the unwashed look sort of worked—for pop stars, anyway. His hair should've been good. He swept his hand over his head. The girl copied him.

"Does she think that's a greeting?" Hanna asked.

Lewis's dad waved. "Hello!"

The man reached into his cloak, removed an odd instrument, and pointed it at them.

"Is that a trumpet?" Lewis asked. "Maybe they're musicians!" He noticed for the first time that their feet were bare. Another strike against his leprechaun theory. But barefoot musicians were cool, too. He'd always wanted to be a harmonica player. "Why aren't they wearing shoes?"

"Their footwear is the least of our problems," Hanna said. "I don't think that's a trumpet, Lewis. People don't point trumpets at other people."

"Maybe it's a deadly trumpet," Lewis joked.

No one laughed. Then again, it wasn't very funny.

The man raised his threatening instrument.

"Just be calm," his dad said. "They must be Atlanteans. This is probably strange for them, too."

"Atlanteans?" Hanna said. "Come on, Professor, they're just really weird-looking."

Lewis was doubtful, too. Atlanteans? There was a much better chance that they'd stumbled upon two very pale, short, shoeless musicians who might also be cannibals. "We're probably just in a cave on some deserted island," he said.

His dad turned his wristpad so Lewis could see the screen, which revealed their current depth. "That's right?" Lewis asked.

"We're four miles below the surface. This is a cave, but we're not on an island."

Hanna motioned to the strange pair watching them. "So who are these two?"

"They're Atlanteans," his dad insisted. He held up his hands and faced the man with the weapon. "Do you speak English?"

"Why would they speak English if they're from Atlantis?" Hanna asked.

"Good point," his dad admitted.

The girl tapped her ear, then placed her hand on the man's instrument, forcing him to lower it. Slowly she approached Lewis. He backed up toward the ramp. She tapped her throat, then placed her fingers over her mouth and flung them outward.

Finally, he'd found someone who spoke his unique language. He produced a light, airy little belch. Delicate but clear.

The girl winced and scrunched up her nose.

"What was that?" Hanna asked.

"I thought she wanted me to burp."

"No, imbecile, she wants you to speak," Hanna said.

"Why me?"

"I don't know. Just talk."

Lewis waved to her. "Uh . . . hi?"

"And the first word spoken by the great explorer, Meriwether Lewis Gates, was *Uhhhhhh* . . ."

His dad tapped his wristpad. "We'll strike that from the record," he noted.

"You're recording this, Dad?"

"Of course I'm recording this! This could be first contact! Do you know how important this moment is?"

Now he did. No pressure or anything, though. Just maybe one of the biggest events in the history of both of their civilizations, and he'd started it off by belching. Lewis breathed in slowly through his nose. They were four miles below the surface. There was a decent chance these two might actually be from Atlantis. And one of them wanted to talk to him.

He could do this.

He closed his eyes, then began. "Hi, I'm Lewis?"

The girl watched his lips. Her huge eyes narrowed. She was tapping at her right ear.

"Keep talking, son."

"So I'm Lewis . . . and this is Hanna. This is my dad, Richard. The professor."

"Keep going," Hanna said. "She's listening. Maybe she's trying to recognize our language or something."

"What do I talk about?"

"I don't know. Anything."

Lewis wasn't used to monologuing. In the fifth grade, he'd won a part in the school play, but he'd forgotten most of his lines and done the chicken dance whenever it was his turn to speak. The play was a success. His teacher said *Romeo and Juliet* had never made any audience laugh so hard. The local newspaper even wrote a great review.

But this was different. Now he had to talk. So, with his father's and Hanna's encouragement, he rambled on about anything that entered his mind. He talked about his favorite types of peanut butter and his love of swimming and his odd broken family and the subsphere and his imaginary career as a spy, code name Lefty.

The whole time, the girl's expression hardly changed. She tapped her ear twice while he was blabbering. After a while, he asked, "Can I stop talking now?"

This was meant for his dad, but the girl answered instead.

She touched her throat. "Yes, I understand you."

"What is this peanut butter thing you mentioned?" the long-haired man asked.

Lewis was too shocked to speak.

His dad was stunned. "Wait, you just learned English?"

The girl pointed to her earpiece, then her throat. "We have translators." She motioned to Lewis. "I asked you to speak because your voice has a nice high pitch. It's easier to analyze."

Hanna laughed.

High! That was ridiculous. "My voice is not—"

His voice cracked before he could finish.

"How does it work?" Hanna asked.

"The earpiece turns your language into ours, and this"— she pointed to a clear patch on her throat—"changes our words into ones you'll understand."

"Amazing!" his dad declared.

"Right," Hanna said, slightly annoyed, "but how does it actually work? What kind of processor do you have in there? What sort of algorithms does it run?"

The girl ignored her questions. She turned to stare at Lewis. "Are you . . . People of the Sun?"

"People of the Sun? Of course!" his dad said. "What else would they call us? Yes, yes, that's us." He pointed to the roof of the cave. "We're from up there!"

Way, way up there, Lewis thought. They were in the Earth's basement, really, with four miles of ocean above them. He scanned the huge room again. Water from the pool flowed out through narrow channels in the rocky floor, spilling into tunnels in the walls.

"What's your name?" Hanna asked.

"Kaya." The girl pointed to the white-haired man. "This is—"

"Naxos," the man announced. "My name is Naxos. You . . . you don't look like invaders."

"Invaders? What are you talking about?" Hanna asked.

The girl interrupted them. "I knew it!" she said. "You're real! I can't believe you're here." She reached out and touched Lewis on the shoulder. He felt a chill. She faced Naxos. "Can you believe this?"

The man didn't answer. He looked more confused than surprised.

"Where are we?" Lewis's dad asked. "What is this place?"

"A border station not far from Edgeland," Kaya replied.

"Edgeland?"

"A city known for smugglers and criminals," she added.

"Sure, sure," the professor said. "But what is this place called? This world?"

As if it should have been super obvious, the girl replied, "Atlantis."

Hanna leaned back, away from the girl, or maybe the idea. "Are you joking?"

"She is not joking," Naxos replied.

Lewis shivered slightly. His dad was still for a moment, as if he were paralyzed. Then the professor pulled his arms in tight and began stomping his feet and spinning, performing the weirdest celebratory dance Lewis had ever seen. Hilarious? Yes. Embarrassing? Absolutely. But Lewis couldn't help smiling.

"Everyone says the air up there is poisoned," Kaya said. "They say nothing can survive."

The professor shrugged. "They're wrong."

"There are almost eight billion of us," Hanna added.

"Eight billion?" Kaya asked, astonished.

Naxos was watching them quietly. He was biting his thin lower lip. He looked as if something was bothering him. Or like someone who couldn't decide what to order at a restaurant. And they'd forgotten all about the guy's peanut butter question. Did they have some in the kitchen? Suddenly, Lewis was hungry. Not for canned food, either. Did they have sandwiches in Atlantis? Maybe hot dogs?

His dad was about to add something when Hanna cut him off. "How did that ship knock us out? What kind of weapon is that?"

The thick eyebrows on Naxos's pale face rose and fell. He quickly forgot about whatever was bothering him. "A sonic blaster. Impressive, isn't it? We're masters of nonlethal weapons."

"Nonlethal weapons?" Lewis asked.

"That means they don't kill you," Hanna explained. She motioned to Naxos. "You're going to have to show me how that thing works at some point."

"Your ship," Naxos began, walking toward the subsphere. "I scanned the exterior when you arrived. It doesn't seem to have any weapons. It certainly doesn't seem fit for an invasion."

"Why do you keep talking about invasions?" the professor asked. "We're not invaders. We're more like . . ."

"Tourists," Lewis said, finishing his dad's thought. "Science tourists."

He was about to go on when his dad stopped him. His father wanted another turn, which was understandable. He'd kind of dedicated the last decade of his life to this place. "How many people are in Atlantis?"

"A hundred million or so," Kaya replied.

His dad nearly shouted. "A hundred million people! That's way beyond my estimate!"

"It's crowded," Kaya added. "Very crowded."

Naxos was drawn into the conversation again. "We're constantly forced to expand into new territories," he explained. "We carve and drill out new caves and structures to make space for our people, but the ridge is getting less and less stable. Some years ago, two entire cities collapsed. I can't even say how many Atlanteans were lost, and that was hardly the first time."

They were all silent for a moment.

Only a moment, though. His dad just couldn't wait to ask another question. "That is terribly sad. Terribly sad. How do you feed yourselves?"

"With food," Kaya quipped.

"It's a struggle," Naxos added. "We can't produce food the way we used to, not with the ocean changing so rapidly."

"Yeah," Hanna said, "sorry about the whole climate change thing. That's kind of on us."

"Is that why you're sending the waves?" Lewis asked.

"What waves?" Kaya replied.

Naxos was suspiciously quiet. He cupped a hand over his right ear and leaned away, as if he were listening to a message on a really, really small phone. Hanna and his dad were too wonder-struck to fire off more questions, so Lewis squeezed in a few of his own. He pointed to Kaya. "Why don't you have scales?"

"Why don't you?" Kaya replied.

Fair point. "Can you swim really fast?"

"Faster than you."

"We'll see. Can you talk to fish?"

"No," she said. "We eat them."

"You could still talk to them before you ate them."

"That would be weird."

Another fair point. He looked down at her feet. They were long and wide and bare. "Why aren't you wearing shoes?"

"What are shoes?" Naxos asked.

Lewis pointed to his father's boots and Hanna's taped sneakers.

Kaya's head jerked back slightly. "Why would anyone put clothes on their feet?"

He paused and felt his toes. They were damp and warm and itchy. He'd stopped wearing the one shoe; his back had started to hurt. Now he just wore socks. Stinking, nasty, festering wet rags that hadn't been washed in three days. The smell could probably kill a small animal. He peeled them off in a rush. "How old are you?" he asked Kaya.

"Fourteen."

"So we're pretty much the same age."

"Don't get any ideas, Lewis," Hanna joked.

He felt himself blush, and tried not to look at Kaya. But she wasn't watching him, anyway. She was staring at Naxos, who was still holding one hand to his ear and another to a strange kind of tablet. Her expression darkened. "What's wrong?" she asked. "Who are you messaging?"

Naxos set the tablet on a workstation. "I'm so sorry. Really. You must believe that I'm sorry."

"For what?" Hanna asked.

"Your sensors were bouncing sound waves all over the ridge. Anytime we pick up the signal of a non-government ship so far outside our borders, I'm supposed to bring it in. And since yours is such an unusual one"—he stared at the subsphere—"I concluded that you might be invaders. I had to alert my superiors." He stopped, held his hand to his ear again, and stared at a door in the cave wall. "They're coming."

"Who's coming?" Kaya asked.

"I don't hear anyone," Lewis noted.

"Their hearing could be more sensitive than ours!" his dad suggested. "It could have evolved differently." He wrapped his arm around Lewis's shoulders and pointed to Kaya. "See that, Lewis? Her ears are quite large. The eyes, too." He waved at the glowing cave walls, the scattered blue lights. "Bioluminescence, I believe. Some kind of bio-inspired technology. No sunlight, obviously. Natural selection would favor larger eyes in these dim lighting conditions. It all fits!"

Kaya started to cover her ears, then turned back to Naxos. "Who's coming?" she asked again.

Naxos paused. His eyes darted between the subs and the doorway in the wall. "You have to believe me. I thought this was an invasion. I was following procedure! I didn't think . . ." Now he spun back to face Kaya. "You need to get them out of here."

"What do you mean?" the professor asked. "We just got here!"

"Kaya," Naxos continued, "do you have somewhere you can hide them? Where do you live? Is there someone who can help? Your parents, maybe?"

"I live in Ridge City," she replied. "I guess my father might know what to do, but . . ."

"Yes! That's good. Perfect." A smile stretched across Naxos's pale face, then disappeared almost instantly. "No, no, no. It's too far. Even if you had the money, you couldn't hide these three on the vacuum train." He pointed to Lewis's dad. "Him especially." Naxos held up his hand for them to be quiet. "A cruiser is here."

Lewis's dad whispered into his wristpad. "The people of Atlantis have highly acute hearing. They can detect faint sounds through stone walls."

"Seriously, Professor? You're making notes now?" Hanna asked.

He tapped the wristpad. "My Atlantis journals," he explained. "All my data and evidence is in here. These journals will reveal the truth!"

Lewis felt a small jolt of pride. Any mention of Atlantis used to make him cringe a little. But now they were here. Atlantis was real. Maybe the journals would change everything. Maybe his dad would even write a best seller. How many books did you need to sell to buy a private island for your family?

Naxos tapped his ear. "Our hearing isn't that sensitive," he said, correcting the professor. "I got a notification in my earpiece from my security system."

His dad looked disappointed.

Lewis was stumped, though. What was happening? He didn't understand why they had to run away. Wouldn't the people of Atlantis be excited to see them? Lewis figured they'd plan parties and parades. He had always wanted to be the focus of a big, old-fashioned parade. The kind they used to have at the beginning of the century. The type that snaked through a city as people threw stuff at you from their windows. Light-weight, colorful, festive stuff. Not bricks or pianos.

"Who's coming?" Kaya asked Naxos again. Still he didn't answer. Then her mouth dropped open. "The Erasers! You totally work for the Erasers, don't you? Tell me the truth."

The name jolted Naxos slightly.

"Who are the Erasers?" Lewis's dad asked.

"There's no time to explain," Naxos said.

Lewis imagined the Erasers as a children's musical troupe that sang about school supplies.

Take that colored pencil,

Sharpen it up nice.

Don't get close to Billy,

Last week he had lice.

He was probably a little off target, though.

Naxos stared at the tunnels in the wall. "Can you all swim?"

"Sure," Hanna replied. "Why?"

He pointed to one of the streams that flowed into a hole in the stone. "These tunnels slope downward. The water is slightly cold, but it's shallow, and it spills into a warmer pool. Then it's only a short swim to the edge of the city on the other side. I can hold my visitors here long enough for you to escape."

Lewis studied the tunnels. "So they're like slides?"

"I suppose so," Naxos replied.

Lewis started toward the subsphere's ramp.

"Where are you going?" Kaya asked.

"I'm getting my backpack," he said.

"You need to leave immediately," Naxos insisted.

His dad eyed the subsphere. "My papers. My maps and materials . . ."

"There's no time," Naxos explained.

Lewis watched the rushing water and thought of his canceled trip to the mountains. He and his dad were supposed to hike to where the Blackwater River spilled down out of the canyon. At this time of year, the water was so high that the river overflowed its banks and poured down smooth channels in the rocks. They'd gone once before, when Lewis was nine, and he'd remember that trip forever. They'd spent hours going down the stone slides, hiking back up, then flying down them again. Sure, this adventure to Atlantis wasn't quite the return trip they'd planned. But in a backward, upside-down kind of way, his dad had delivered on his promise. They'd made it to the slides. These slides just happened to be four miles below the surface of the sea. In Atlantis.

"So that's our best way out?" Hanna asked, pointing to the tunnel.

"Precisely."

"Then that's where we're going," Hanna said.

Naxos finally met Kaya's stare. "For now, I need you to trust me. Once you get to the city, find a man named Gogol. He'll be able to rent you a vehicle and help you find your way back to Ridge City. You have gold?"

Kaya nodded. "Some."

Naxos rushed to the metal desk and yanked open a drawer. He reached into the back, then pulled out a small purse. He tossed it to Kaya. "Take that. It should be enough."

Lewis's dad whispered something about currency into his wristpad.

"What about you?" Hanna asked Naxos.

"I'll meet you in Ridge City," he said.

Kaya started toward the tunnel. Lewis turned to follow Kaya when his dad suddenly slapped his neck. "Ouch!" his dad shouted. "What was that?"

Naxos lowered a small pistol. Not the deadly trumpet, though. Something else. He quickly stuffed it back into the desk drawer. "Sorry," he said. "A tracker, to help me find you."

His father scratched at his neck. "Fascinating," he said. "There was an initial pinch, but now I don't even feel it."

Naxos tossed Kaya his weapon. She caught it and pushed it down into her backpack. "Edgeland is not a friendly place," he noted, "but only use that in emergencies." Then he turned to Lewis, Hanna, and the professor. "And you three?"

"Yes?" Lewis answered.

"Good luck! I still can't believe . . . People of the Sun! Now, go!"

Lewis didn't need to be told again. He ran across the stone floor, splashed through the frigid, ankle-deep water in the channel, and crouched as he approached the entrance to the tunnel. Then he threw his hands out in front of him and dove headfirst into the icy-cold water, coasting down the stony slide into the darkness.

9

YOU CAN'T SHRINK A WHALE

THE BOY dove through first. He could have at least waited for some instructions or a warning. Launching himself into the shallow stone tunnel must have hurt. There definitely wasn't enough water to cushion his fall, and she thought she heard him yelp. But then he shouted back to them, his voice resounding through the tunnel, "I'm good!"

His dad, a whale of a man, rushed in next.

The girl, Hanna, waited before sliding after them.

Kaya glanced back at Naxos, but he was already gone. Who was he, really? He seemed so . . . harmless. How could he be an Eraser? She would have to find out more about him later. Now she rushed to the mouth of the tunnel and sat, for a moment, in the cool water.

Sun People! Smiling, she shot forward feetfirst, lying on her back with her arms crossed over her chest. The tunnel swerved and turned as she slid faster and faster. One of the Sun People was whooping and hollering ahead of her. Then the tunnel sloped down. She accelerated. The cool water splashed up onto her legs, her chest, her face. She spat it from her lips.

The tunnel swerved, curved, then dropped again.

Steeper.

Faster.

Whoever had been shouting was silent now. Frightened, she guessed.

But they'd all be fine. The tunnels were safe. The water, too. She heard the first splash.

Then a larger one.

And a few seconds later, a third.

She waited, closing her eyes, then blasted out of the tunnel. She was airborne long enough to spot two of them below her, floundering in the water, hurrying to get out of her way. She backflipped, more for the fun of it than to show off—okay, maybe she was showing off a little—and then straightened out.

Curled her toes.

Flung her arms over her head.

And knifed through the surface between them.

The soaring, the flying over the water, the splashing, wild madness of breaking the surface—she loved it all. But this last bit was her favorite part of any cliff jump or slide: When the water swallowed you and slowed you to a stop, and you hung there, turning, almost free of your body, as much a part of the water as the water itself. She hovered there, feeling it all.

Sometimes she felt like she could hang there forever.

Then she remembered the People of the Sun.

She swam to the surface, smiling.

Yet the others were panicking.

"My dad!"

"The professor is still under!"

She treaded higher in the water. But they were both moving too much, crowding the surface with ripples and splashes. How was she supposed to see anything? "Stop!" she said. "Stay still!"

"What?"

"Stop flailing. I can't read the water if you're splashing it all over the place."

"What do you mean, read—"

"Just do it, Lewis."

Hannah and Lewis calmed their strokes, their kicks. They were still flailing. There was absolutely no way this boy could beat her in a race. He barely even felt the water. But they settled enough for her to see a small boil rise. The water bowled up.

That meant something below was kicking.

Or someone.

A quick, deep breath, and then Kaya dove down head-first. Her eyes adjusted quickly to the darkness. The water was high, so the top of the kelp forest below was several body lengths down. She hadn't felt a single strand when she'd knifed down through the surface. But the professor was bigger. Much bigger. He would've plunged deeper.

Now she could see clearly, and she spotted him tangled in the weeds. His face was full of fear. This kind of thing wouldn't frighten an Atlantean. This was just what happened when you dove into a kelp forest—sometimes aggressive weeds wrapped you in their slimy grip, and you had to cut yourself free. That's why you carried a blade with you whenever you swam in one of these pools. But the whale from the drylands? This was clearly new to him. His face was pale, and he was starting to let all the air out of his lungs in great torrents of bubbles. Was he out of breath already? Seriously? The whole scene would have been almost funny if the poor blubbery giant weren't so obviously terrified.

Kaya dove beneath him. His ankles were wrapped in the thick seaweed.

But that wasn't the only thing holding him under.

A huge sucker fish had swallowed half the man's foot.

Okay. Fine. That might even scare a few Atlanteans.

The fish was truly enormous, but anyone could tell you that these beasts were toothless. Almost harmless, really.

The fish had large side fins, and it was sweeping them furiously, trying to drag the professor lower, deeper into the underwater forest. She'd heard stories about these beasts. They swallowed smaller fish whole. The traders stocked the farms with them, then caught them and sold them illegally at high prices.

The monster had now practically swallowed the professor's calf.

Kaya kicked down and slipped her fingers into its gills. Gently enough so she wouldn't cause any permanent damage, she squeezed.

The beast panicked and spat out the professor's lower leg.

There was still the kelp to deal with, though.

Kaya pulled the knife from her ankle holster and sliced through the leathery seaweed. The professor was pulling desperately. She slipped the knife between his leg and the kelp. He broke free, but her work was hardly finished. She had to get him up to the surface, and he was horribly slow. At least a real whale could move. This man swam like someone who'd never even touched the water before. She jammed her hand into his armpit and kicked hard, pulling with her free arm, hurrying him up.

He breached and began sucking in air.

"Dad!"

"Professor!"

The huge man rolled onto his back, coughed, breathed.

"Is he okay?"

"He'll be fine," Kaya said.

When the professor settled enough to speak, he turned upright and shook a fist in the air. "That was amazing! Thank you!"

He told his son and Hanna what had happened as Kaya led them back to the wall beneath the mouth of the tunnel. Here they could hold on for a moment, catch their breath before the long swim to the other side. She hoped they wouldn't be too slow.

Lewis and Hanna both started watching the water nervously.

"You're fine," Kaya assured them. "The sucker fish stay down low in the kelp."

This was mostly true. And besides, if another one rose up and grabbed them, she'd just jam its gills, too. So there really wasn't anything to worry about.

"Where are we?" the professor asked. "This cave is enormous! It must be the size of several sports arenas."

"Easily," Hanna added.

The professor stared out at the water. "Abundant aquatic plant life. A source of oxygen, presumably, and nutrients." He turned, squinting his tiny eyes. "Is all of Atlantis like this?"

"Like what?"

"Caves. Is it all a network of watery caves, illuminated by bioluminescence?"

"Yes," Kaya said. "What did you expect?"

"The lights"— he continued, pointing at the walls— "are they natural or artificial? How does—"

She stopped him. This was no time for a lesson or a tour. "I'll be happy to tell you all about Atlantis soon enough, but—"

"We're kind of being chased," Hanna finished.

"Exactly."

"So we should hurry."

"Which way?" Lewis asked.

Kaya pointed, and the boy pushed off and started floundering ahead. The other two followed, and she watched them for a moment. The other side of the cave wasn't too far away, but the Sun People were slower than sea slugs. They swam on the surface, not under it. Was that even swimming?

She guessed the distance to the far wall and how long it would take them to reach it. Too long.

Naxos wouldn't be able to hold off the other Erasers forever.

Kaya kicked hard, lifting herself higher out of the water, and spotted the path that wrapped along the cave wall and the Darkwater Trading Company sign in the distance. The drylanders would probably be faster on stone, running instead of swimming. She could hurry them out of sight that way, into the alleys. She swam ahead of them, then made them stop to listen. "Follow me," she said. "And Professor?"

"Yes?"

"Hurry up."

Kaya tried to swim slowly. Really. But after only a dozen kicks underwater, she was at least ten body lengths ahead. The boy and his dad took slightly less than forever to cut across the water. Hanna was a little faster; the two girls were waiting on the path when Lewis and the professor struggled out of the pool.

Thankfully, on solid ground they weren't slow, and Kaya kept glancing back, watching for the Erasers. They were approaching the entrance to the Darkwater Trading Company when she heard the hum of a drifting cruiser in the distance. "Get in, now!" she urged them.

Inside the tunnel, just off the path, they waited until the cruiser passed.

The four of them huddled together in the cramped space, and for the first time, Kaya noticed that the Sun People smelled. Not bad, exactly. Just weird. Almost like an old person's hair. Or was it dried kelp? No. Something else. A scent she couldn't describe. And they were huge! Even the youngest one, Lewis. He was as tall as the tallest person in Atlantis. And he was only twelve years old? Weird. Plus their eyes were so, so small. She tried not to gawk at them, but she couldn't imagine how they could see anything at all with those tiny eyes. Their skin was darker, too. The girl especially. The color was beautiful, though; Kaya was slightly jealous.

The hum of the cruiser's engine faded as it drifted over the aquafarm.

She crept back, closer to the opening and the water. Looked and listened.

The faint blue taillights of the cruiser faded in the mist as the Erasers drifted into the main tunnel, over the waterway heading to Edgeland. "We're safe," she said.

She ushered them back out onto the path. The professor was staring at the side of her neck like some giant fish hoping to latch on and suck out her blood. "What?" she asked.

"He's checking to see if you have gills," Lewis guessed.

"No I'm not."

"Sure you are."

The professor hesitated. "Well . . . do you?"

"Gills?" she asked. "Like a fish? Why would I have gills?"

Hanna explained, "He thought you might be able to breathe underwater."

"That was only one of my theories," he insisted. "I also considered that you might be air-breathers like us. Seven thousand years isn't really enough time for that drastic of an evolutionary adaptation to develop and spread. Size, musculature, the width of your eyes and feet? Sure. But an entirely new way of breathing?"

"Evolution would probably need a few million years for that," Hanna guessed.

"Yeah," Kaya said, "we breathe air, just like you."

The professor tapped at the device on his wrist. A small screen glowed with odd symbols, and he caught her studying it. "This is a wristpad," he said. "It allows me to record everything. Audio, video, temperature. I can scan a rock and tell you the molecular composition within seconds!"

That meant slightly more than nothing to her. But as she listened to the huge man blabber about his little device, she remembered the warning from Naxos. The professor was nearly the size of two Atlanteans stuck together. His hair was oddly thick and dark. His eyes were like tiny little coins, especially compared to his boulder-like head. She'd never be able to sneak this beast through Edgeland. Even the two others would stand out. Not just their faces and eyes—their hair and skin were too dark, their clothes too strange. She could work on the clothes, maybe find a way to cover their faces. But she couldn't shrink a whale.

"What was that?" Hanna whispered.

Voices. Inside the Darkwater Trading Company. The place wasn't empty after all. There were at least a few Atlanteans inside. Kaya started to lead them away, down the path, when someone stepped out of a warehouse far ahead. The man hadn't spotted them. Not yet, anyway. But how was she going to get these three through Edgeland without them being noticed?

Suddenly she had an idea. She ushered them back into the entryway.

"Stay here," she said. "Okay? Don't move."

"Got it," Lewis said.

Kaya followed the small tunnel inside and found the monstrous man from that morning and another dockmaster sitting in busted old chairs near the deepwater pool. The man was sleeping. The other dockmaster, a woman with scraggly hair, picked something out of her teeth with the yellowed nail of her pinkie finger. She watched Kaya through narrowed eyes and scratched a scab on her elbow. The napper chortled and snorted as the woman backhanded him on the shoulder. She stood. He rose uncomfortably.

They were easily two of the two ugliest creatures Kaya had ever seen. Greenish mucous trickled out of the woman's nose. One of the man's eyes was lower than the other. His ears were warped, and there was a huge, swollen bump above one eyebrow. And these were the third and fourth citizens of Atlantis the Sun People would meet? How embarrassing.

The man pointed with a short, stubby finger wrapped in a rag.

But not at her. He didn't recognize her without her dive suit.

Were the People of the Sun hiding, as she'd asked?

Of course not.

All three of them were crouching behind her, staring.

Kaya pulled out the sonic blaster. She'd never used one before, and her hands were shaking. The two dockmasters could see she was nervous, too. They stomped forward, unafraid. Her finger pulled the trigger, and they dropped into crumpled heaps on the stone floor.

"Nonlethal, right?" Hanna asked, hurrying to her side.

Kaya leaned in close and listened to their breathing. "Yes. They're just out."

"It's still a deadly trumpet," Lewis added.

"Did you not hear what I said?"

"About what?"

"About hiding!"

Lewis was leaning closer to the man. "Is that a troll?"

"A what?" Kaya replied.

"You know, trolls? Monstrous creatures. Kind of like

humans. Big noses and ears. Live under bridges, mostly. Usually they have big iron pots to make stew." He started making a stirring motion, prepping something in an imaginary pot.

"I think these two are just ugly," Hanna guessed.

The professor was pointing his wristpad at the fallen dock-masters.

"What are you doing?" Kaya asked.

"Gathering data," he said. The device began beeping. "Oh, no. No, no, no."

"What?"

"It's out of storage."

"You didn't think to clear some memory before we left?" Hanna asked.

"I suppose I could delete some files, but they're all so, so important to me." He stomped his foot like a large, frustrated child. Then he pointed at Hanna's hand. "Your ring records audio, doesn't it?"

"You can't have my ring. It's new."

He pressed his hands together. "Please?"

The girl slipped off the thick metal ring and handed it to him, shaking her head. He could barely fit it over the tip of his pinkie finger. "Don't use up all the storage on that, too," she said. "I have my music on there."

This was ridiculous. Kaya had just knocked out two strangers to help them escape, and they were arguing about jewelry? "Enough," she said. "These two might be dreaming now, but they're not going to be happy with me when they wake up. So hurry up and take off their clothes."

The boy laughed.

Kaya did not.

"Wait. You're serious?" Lewis asked.

Kaya tugged at the sleeve of Hanna's shirt. "The three of you stand out too much. You're all tall, dark, and—"

"Handsome?" the professor cut in.

That was not the word she was going to use. "If we're going to get out of Edgeland, we need to get you into some normal clothes."

Lewis pointed down at the rags the dockmasters were wearing. "Those are normal?"

"For scoundrels and rogues, sure," Kaya said. "And Edgeland is mostly scoundrels and rogues."

She ordered the professor to help her roll the man over onto his stomach. But the huge Sun Person was surprisingly weak. Did the sun destroy their eyes and their muscles, too? She'd just have to do it herself. Kaya dragged the dockmaster into a sitting position, then peeled off his vest. The boy was staring at her, amazed. "What?" she asked.

"Nothing."

"You are surprisingly strong," the professor explained. He squinted at her and bit his lower lip. "Why is that, I wonder?"

"Natural selection?" Hanna guessed.

"Maybe," the professor replied. "Given the hot temperatures, though, you'd think the people here would be tall and lean, to stay cool."

Hanna shrugged. "Or maybe down here in these caves, it's better to be short and strong."

Kaya wasn't short. They were just weirdly tall. "The clothes," she reminded Lewis.

He reached down and pulled the torn gloves off the woman's hands. "Gross! They're all sweaty and they smell like pickles."

"What are pickles?" Kaya asked.

"Crazy-tasty food," Hanna said. "But you don't want your clothes stinking of them."

Hanna unwound a cloth from the woman's head, then borrowed her jacket. She was pinching her nose. "This smells like a cross between old potatoes and a public toilet."

"That's bad?"

"Horrible."

"Well, you're wearing it anyway."

After a few minutes of trading garments, complaining, and some gagging, the People of the Sun were transformed. No costume could disguise their strangeness completely. But the clothes would mask it a little.

"I feel ridiculous," Lewis said.

"You look it, too," Hanna added.

The boy's shirt was loose and wide but short, barely extending past his belly button. The vest fit nicely enough. He had fashioned a kind of headwrap out of some rags, too. That was good. He didn't look quite so alien anymore. Hanna wore the woman's jacket and headwrap. If she leaned over and hunched a little, she'd probably be able to slip past people unnoticed, too. As for the professor . . . well, nothing was going to fit him. He was struggling just to pull a shirt over his shoulders.

"You look like an elephant in a leotard," Hanna quipped.

"Or a hippo in a bikini," Lewis added.

"I'm right here, you know," the professor said.

An elephant? A hippo? Land creatures, Kaya guessed. He really did look ridiculous. She tugged at the shirt, and it promptly split down the huge man's back.

"Next plan?" the professor asked.

"There's no way we'll be able to hide you on the street," Kaya said. "Unless . . ."

"Unless what?"

"How would you feel about being a fish?"

Kaya hurried over to a long row of wheeled tanks. She found the largest one, grabbed the handle, and pulled it toward them, then yanked a brown tarp off the top.

"What's that?" Lewis asked.

"A tank for smuggling rare fish," Kaya said. "Everything we eat is raised in the aquafarms, but some people think the wild fish caught outside our borders are better." She'd learned all about this from listening to one of her dad's news programs.

The thought of her dad stalled her. She whistled quietly to check for new messages. One from Rian, but none from her dad. He was probably busy. She whistled again, switching off the earpiece.

The Sun People were staring at her. Right. What had she been talking about? Smuggling. "The government doesn't want anyone fishing outside the ridge," she continued, "but people sneak around and do it anyway."

Hanna was sitting on the ground, wringing the water out of her strange foot clothing. "It's like smuggling corn into Iowa," Hanna added.

The Sun People laughed. Kaya didn't get it. "Anyway," she said, "my point is that smuggling fish is one of the biggest criminal trades here in Edgeland. Fishermen load their catch into tanks like these, then sell them in town or transport them to the bigger cities." She pointed to the gadget on Lewis's wrist, then his father's wristpad. "They smuggle gear and gadgets, too. Either of those would earn a fortune in Atlantis."

The boy covered the thing with his hand. "I'm not giving this up."

"I'm not asking you to," Kaya said.

One of the dockmasters moved.

"Didn't you say we should hurry?" Hanna asked. "Why the smuggling lesson?"

"Because that's how we're getting him out of here," Kaya said, pointing to the professor. She knocked on the side of the large, wheeled tank. "Climb in, Professor, and we'll throw the tarp over the top. Everyone will think we're just hauling some juicy creature from the deep."

The professor eyed the tank, which was still full of water. "I don't believe I've ever been called juicy before. Am I supposed to hold my breath?" Water rushed out as Kaya opened a drain in the side. "Ah, thank goodness," he said.

The professor stretched from side to side, then climbed clumsily into the tank. He sat upright with his thick legs crossed, wallowing in the little remaining water. Kaya tried not to laugh. Then he pressed his lips to the glass and expanded his cheeks like some giant, human-shaped blowfish. She smiled. Lewis and Hanna shook their heads, embarrassed.

"Come on," Hanna said. "Let's go."

The Sun People were too weak to drag the tank, so Kaya pulled it herself, out of the shop and along the stone ledge that ran along the eastern wall of the huge cave. The aquafarms stretched out into the distance to their right. There were a few other shops and warehouses on their left, but it was near lunchtime now, and everyone must have been tucked away inside their offices napping, because she didn't spot another soul. This was a massive relief. She really didn't want to blast another trader or smuggler. She just wanted to get these visitors to her home as quickly as possible.

Eventually they turned left out of the enormous cave into a small tunnel heading north. The air in the passageway, which was only wide enough for walkers, not cruisers, changed once they left the aquafarms behind them. The temperature rose steadily. Lewis and Hanna were both dripping with sweat. They were blinking and squinting, too, as if they were struggling to see. But the walls were lined with green lights. The path was plenty bright.

"You know where we're going, right?" Hanna asked.

Yes? Mostly. That morning, Kaya had headed south along the waterway. Now they were hurrying in the opposite direction. Along a different path, sure, but hopefully this tunnel would lead them back to the city center. And if not . . . well, she'd figure something out.

They'd been walking for a while when she heard two men stomping toward them. Were they singing? Yes, and mumbling, too. Deep into their drink, she guessed. She tensed. This was their first test. She elbowed the Sun People. "Stay on either side of me," she warned. "And hunch over. You need to look small."

The two men reeked, and they leaned on each other as they

stumbled forward. Their beards were caked with crumbs, and they sniffed at the air as they passed. But they kept walking, hardly noticing Kaya or her new friends. She sighed.

"You were worried?" Lewis asked.

"No," she lied.

Inside the tank, the professor had started talking to himself, or to the thing on his finger. Was this a game to him? Kaya rapped the glass with her knuckles. "Quiet!"

"Sorry," he whispered. "Won't happen again."

But it would happen again. She was certain of that.

They'd passed their first test, sure. But the city would be different, and they were getting closer with each step. The tunnel widened. The ceiling was now higher overhead. Doors began appearing in the walls, too. Homes carved into the rock, she explained in a whisper. More and more people pushed around and past them in the widening space. Lewis and Hanna stayed bent over constantly now, trying to seem smaller. Kaya tapped her earpiece to check the time and her messages. Another one from Rian, asking for an update. He sounded excited and nervous at once; she'd have to respond and tell him what she'd found. Who she'd found. Maybe he'd even be able to help. There were still no messages from her dad, though. And the earpiece's announcement of the time annoyed her. The day was nearly over. Her grandmother would be expecting her home in only a few hours.

That wasn't going to happen.

There were more and more windows carved into the rock overhead as they went along. The two Sun People were glancing all around but trying not to stare. A wave of shouts and music and cries of laughter and roars of anger rumbled toward them through the alleyway. The sounds of Edgeland.

A mix of excitement and fear rushed through her as they stumbled into the large and crowded city square. The smart choice would have been to keep moving. To press ahead and find this Gogol person as quickly as possible. But what if she were visiting their world for the first time? Would she want to be rushed? She couldn't resist letting them stop, even just for a moment, to drink in the scene. Kaya watched their faces as they studied their surroundings, and the Sun People were practically shining with wonder.

10
ESCAPE FROM EDGELAND

LEWIS had to go to the bathroom again. Going in the water back at that aquafarm had felt wrong—maybe they drank that stuff. And sure, he could ask Kaya to find him a toilet, but this didn't really seem like the right time. Plus, this Edgeland place was super cool. He felt like he'd jumped through a wormhole and popped out in some alien city in another galaxy.

Hundreds of small, pale, large-eyed Atlanteans shoved and angled their way through the crowded city center. There weren't any buildings, really. Just rock walls that rose up all around them with doors and windows cut into the stone, balconies and signs sticking out, and stores packed in next to each other, carved into the rock on the ground floor. Rusting metal booths and stalls were spread all over the city center, too. Lewis hadn't been to many cities in his life. His mom and Roberts had taken him and his brother to the new inland U.S. capital once a few years earlier. The buildings there towered so high they disappeared into the clouds. But here in Atlantis, the walls all leaned toward one another near the top and merged to form an arching ceiling. He shook his head. This really was a perfect place for a parade. He could picture the confetti drifting down as people cheered his name. And Hanna's, too. And maybe his dad's. But mostly they'd chant, "Lew-is! Lew-is!"

And the people—well, Lewis couldn't decide if they looked like they were dressed for a medieval movie or a science fiction flick. Or both. He'd guessed Atlanteans would wear sparkly clothes. Sequins. He'd thought they'd be tall and long and beautiful. Or maybe they'd have scales, and shiny little bubbles would drift out of their mouths when they spoke. Nope. More than a few of these Atlanteans were covered with scars and sores and volcanic pimples. An old man walking past him coughed, and Lewis worried about catching some weird Atlantean flu.

Most of the Atlanteans were dressed in brown and gray tattered rags. A few wore the same kind of clothes as Kaya, but in shades of blue and silver. And sure, maybe he was a little stuck on the whole barefoot thing, but none of them wore shoes! All of Atlantis, or all that he'd seen, went barefoot. He pointed to Hanna's squelching-wet sneakers and socks. She crouched down and slipped them off, then tossed them into a garbage bin.

A small woman with a crooked back turned and yelled at them.

Kaya let go of the tank, hurried over to the bin, and fished out Hanna's socks and sneakers. She held them at arm's length. They were dripping and covered in some kind of purple ooze.

"What's wrong?" Hanna asked.

"That was a pot!" Kaya explained. "She's selling soup."

Lewis laughed. "Now with a faint aroma of sock."

Kaya tossed Hanna's foot rags into an actual garbage bin and hurried them forward.

Lewis glanced back. After a quick taste of her soup, the old woman nodded and shrugged. Maybe the sneakers had added a little kick.

The stone floor was warm under his feet, the air thick and humid. The stalls and stores were full of weirdness. Dried strands of green and brown seaweed hung in one window, the bodies of several monstrous, scaly, wide-eyed fish in another. Did Atlanteans eat that stuff? One shop sold all different types and sizes of tablets like the one Naxos had back in his workshop. Lewis had to yank on Hanna's shirt to keep her from rushing inside to check out the Atlantean gadgets.

A few musicians sitting in the middle of the town center banged out rhythms on drumlike instruments, providing a background beat to the shouts and chatter. Behind steamy windows, Lewis could see men and women pressing close to each other, drinking from dull metal cups. Between the shops and stores, wide paths and narrow alleyways snaked through the towering stone walls. He didn't see anyplace that looked like a bathroom, though.

An old lady leaned out of a window above them and tossed a bucket of greenish-brown slop into the alley. It splattered on the ground.

"Gross," Hanna muttered. "Some of that got between my toes."

"People just toss their trash into the street?" Lewis asked.

"Not in my neighborhood," Kaya replied. "We have a

garbage chute. But the slop doesn't stay for long, anyway. Water runs through at night to clean everything. I'll tell you more later. We should move."

Hanna elbowed him and pointed up. High above the highest windows, a man drifted through the air.

"What the—"

A vehicle the size of a hovercar flew in the opposite direction, just below the ceiling of the enormous cave.

No, not flew.

Floated.

The thing had no fans, and it moved without effort. "How is that . . . what are they . . ." Lewis looked at Hanna, but she was so awestruck by the strange floating machine that she couldn't even spit out a response. "Is that magic?" Lewis asked.

"Magic?" Kaya asked. "What's magic? That's a basic gravity drive."

"Sure," Hanna said with a shrug. "No big deal. You've just figured out how to control gravity."

"You haven't?"

"No," Hanna answered. "Kaya, I'm going to need to know . . . well, everything about this gravity drive thing. Okay?"

"Once we're safe. My dad will be able to explain it better than I can, anyway."

Lewis pointed back to the people in the window with the metal cups. He lowered his voice to a whisper.

"What are they drinking?"

"Them? Probably fermented kelp."

"Gross," Hanna said.

But even gross sounded good. Lewis was so parched he'd

drink out of a backwashed water bottle, a bird bath, maybe even the ceramic tank at the back of a toilet. Fermented kelp? Sure. "What does it taste like?"

"Probably nasty," Kaya said. "But we're too young to drink it, anyway. You're thirsty?"

Hanna nodded. "Thoroughly."

Kaya pulled a water bottle out of her backpack and tossed it to Hanna, then stopped at a wheeled cart with several display cases. A woman with different-colored eyes, one blue and the other silver, stood up from her stool. Lewis watched Kaya. What was she doing? Buying jewelry? He wanted a drink and a toilet, not a necklace. He grabbed the bottle from Hanna. The water was cool, with a slight mineral tang, and absolutely delicious. Hanna snatched it back before he finished. "What's she doing?" he asked.

Hanna held her finger to her lips, reminding him to be quiet. The display cases, he realized, were packed with hundreds of earplugs. Kaya haggled with the vendor, pointing to different models and shaking her head. Finally she reached into her pocket, counted out several coins, and passed them to the woman. Then she picked three pairs of earplugs out of the case. She removed them from the packaging and pressed them against her own earplugs, one at a time. Next, she handed a pair to Hanna and another to Lewis, along with small square patches that looked like Band-Aids. She was probably saving the largest earplugs for his dad.

"Pop these in, and stick the patch to your throat."

Hanna was beaming with excitement. "These are translators?"

The earplugs were covered with some kind of crust. Lewis realized too late that Hanna had cleaned hers off first. That would've been smart. Who knew where his earplugs had been, what kinds of strange Atlantean earwax they'd picked up as other shoppers tried them out. But they fit snugly, at least. The patch, too. It briefly vibrated against his skin. "Weird," he whispered.

"Naxos and I trained our translators on you," Kaya explained, "but we can't afford to do that with everyone we meet. I just linked yours with mine, so they have all the latest language updates. This way, you'll understand pretty much everyone you meet in Atlantis, and the patch will alter your speech so everyone can understand you, too."

"Let me guess—you don't know how these work, either?" Hanna asked.

Kaya shrugged. Hanna sighed.

"Where are you from?" the vendor asked.

Her voice was odd, but Lewis understood her.

Whoa.

Wait.

He understood another Atlantean!

He was about to answer, but Kaya pushed Lewis ahead into the crowd. "We're attracting too much attention."

They wound their way across the city center, staying close to Kaya as she pulled the tank.

Ahead of them, Lewis noticed a line of adults and kids outside a shop. A wide, short woman walked out with some kind of wrap in her hands. She peeled back what looked like foil and chomped down. Now he wasn't just thirsty. He was starving. A vision of a chicken burrito stuffed with cheese and slathered in green chili sauce appeared in his mind. He could almost taste the deliciousness. Then he pictured the imaginary burrito, so beautiful in his vision, suddenly sprouting legs and running away, taunting him, shouting in some strange language not even his Atlantean translator could decode.

Apparently he needed to eat. "What about that place? Can we get some food?"

"Lewis, she said we need to move."

"Right, but—"

Kaya stopped and turned to face him. "Please," she said. "We're not safe here. If people start to notice—"

A thump against the glass of the tank. His father could still hear them. And he was, if Lewis had to guess, begging his son to stop talking. But Lewis was starving! And he still needed a bathroom, and his head was bursting with questions. How could he not ask about everything he was seeing, hearing, even smelling? Yes, the place even smelled different. Sort of like the stone wall outside his house after a heavy rain.

His house. Now he thought of his mom. Michael. Roberts.

Had they gotten his message?

Did they know he was safe?

He felt suddenly heavy.

Hanna pulled him along. Ahead, Kaya paused to ask someone a question. Lewis thought he heard the name Gogol. The woman shrugged. The next Atlantean wasn't helpful, either. Finally, Kaya stopped a skinny, brown-toothed man with grimy hair. This time, Lewis was close enough to hear her question: "Do you know where to find Gogol's shop?"

The man pointed to an alley nearby, and they walked in silence toward a wall lined with windows. Lewis stared up and breathed in. The ceiling was a few hundred feet overhead. He pointed to the windows high up in the rock walls. "People really live up there?" he asked.

"Yes," Kaya said, pushing them along the wall, toward the entrance to the alleyway. "He said it's down this alley. Fourth door—"

Kaya whistled quietly and held her hand to her ear.

"What is it?" Lewis asked.

She held up her finger. He waited.

"A message from my grandmother." She pushed them into the alley. "She's just checking in. If I'm late, she's going to be upset. And I am going to be late. Seriously late." She stopped and stared at the ground. Then she looked up again. "Give me a moment, okay?"

Kaya cupped her hands over her mouth, speaking quietly. Then she stopped, breathed in deeply, and smiled. "Okay. I think we're good now. I messaged my friend Rian—I had to tell someone about you! He'll make sure my grandmother doesn't get too worried. You three are going to be a pretty good excuse, anyway," she added with a smile. "I can't wait for you to meet everyone. They're going to be—"

A man with no eyebrows and a face so thin it was skeletal blocked their way. His eyes were black. His teeth were crooked, and one was sharpened to a point. Generally, Lewis tried to avoid people with insidiously curved incisors. Someday, he hoped to be the kind of person who protected his friends from such shady figures. The brave soul who puffed out his chest and clenched his jaw and fists and urged others to get behind him.

He wasn't there yet.

A small burp popped in the back of his throat as he slunk behind Hanna.

"Where are you going?" the man said.

"That way," Kaya said, pointing past him.

"Let's see what's in the tank."

"Let's not."

The man started toward her, reaching for the tarp.

Kaya lifted her weapon and aimed it at his stomach. "I said no."

The man snarled. "You'll need something stronger than that here in Edgeland, girlie."

"It's strong enough," she replied. "I can show you."

The man ran his tongue along his thin, gray lips, then stepped aside to let them pass.

Lewis stared at the guy's teeth and decided he would be better about dental hygiene. He'd bring his toothbrush everywhere from now on, and he'd floss, too. Twice a day. Three times, if needed. As long as he never looked like that Atlantean. The dude's smile would make a kindergartner cry.

They hurried along, faster now.

"That was awesome," Hanna said. "You were awesome! And these earplugs are amazing. I understood everything."

As Hanna pestered her with questions about the gravity drive, Kaya's pace quickened. Lewis could tell she was stressed. Massively. His mom got stressed sometimes, too. That's when Lewis would dance. Mostly the chicken dance, but he had a few other routines in his quiver, too. He was a brilliant fake tap dancer, for example. The key was doing it on a rug. That way, it actually seemed like you knew what you were doing, because no one could hear your missteps. Tap-dancing in Atlantis, though? In this narrow alleyway? It just didn't feel right.

They stopped. "Fourth door on the left," Kaya said.

Once they pushed through and pulled the tank in with them, a series of blue lights in the floor and ceiling began to glow brighter and brighter. The light was so odd; Lewis kept blinking. The room had a single long stone desk at the far end. The walls on either side were crowded with tanks, and there were shelves that reached the ceiling. Fish of all shapes and sizes lazily kicked or hovered inside miniature aquariums. Lewis stepped closer. Most of the fish were about as long as his forearm, but there were a few giants, too. One had to be as big as his little brother. The monster had mottled skin and bulbous lips. Did the Atlanteans eat these things?

He jumped when he heard movement behind him. The tarp was off, and his father was climbing out of the tank, half soaked, crackling with energy and questions. "What did you see? What did it look like? Tell me everything!" Instead of waiting for an answer, he charged over to a tank with a giant fish. He grabbed Lewis, throwing his arm over his shoulders. "Look at that, son! A coelacanth! Amazing. For years, we thought these were extinct. This fish has been swimming around in the oceans since before the dinosaurs! It's living proof of how little we know about what lives down here. You don't eat these, do you, Kaya?"

"I don't think so."

"I hope not." He wiped the sweat off his forehead. "Is it this hot everywhere in Atlantis?"

Lewis was dripping, too. The back of Hanna's shirt was soaked.

"This isn't even that hot," Kaya said. She tapped her belt, and her shirt dried instantly.

Hanna was in awe. "Self-drying clothes, too? You've got to be kidding me."

"Why do you always think I'm joking?" Kaya handed Lewis's dad his earplugs and patch. "Try these. They should fit. But I'll do the talking here, okay?"

His father pulled the ring off his finger and tossed it to Hanna. She slipped it back on. "All set? It worked?"

"Yes, you'll have to send me the file I recorded later. I took a minute to delete some old files from my wristpad and free up memory. There was an old video of you dancing, Lewis, that swallowed up a large chunk of space."

Sure, Lewis thought. That made sense. It stung a little, though. Weren't parents supposed to cherish that stuff?

A heavy man with a nose like a golf ball, dimpled and round, waddled out of a back room and stood behind the desk. The instant he saw the professor, he reached for a small weapon on his belt. This one looked like a flute, but the man didn't look like a flutist.

"Wait," Kaya said. "Please. You're Gogol? We're friends of Naxos."

"What are these things you have with you?"

Lewis glanced behind him. Things? No one had ever called him a thing. He'd been called a bug, a donkey, a motherless goat. That last one he really didn't understand, since he had a mother and there wasn't anything goatlike about him. Someone had called him a walking wedgie once, too. That made a little more sense, though, since he'd been given multiple wedgies in the third grade. But he'd never been referred to as a thing. And especially not by a fake flutist.

"They're from the Rift," Kaya answered.

Gogol studied Lewis's dad as if he were some sort of exotic zoo creature. "I didn't realize they grew them that big in the Rift."

"Naxos said you'd be able to help us get to Ridge City."

The man clasped his hands on the stone surface of the desk. They were swollen and smeared with black grime. "There are many ways to Ridge City. The trains are easiest."

"My friends here don't want to attract too much attention."

"Your friends from the Rift."

"Right."

"I may be able to help." Gogol looked down at his hands, then up at Kaya. "I could rent you a vehicle and show you the way . . . for the right price."

Kaya suggested a number. The man immediately laughed. His breath smelled like smoked fish, and Lewis swallowed a small eruption of vomit. He crossed his legs. This wasn't the right time to ask for directions to a toilet.

She offered another figure.

"I cannot help you."

Kaya removed the purse she'd gotten from Naxos and stacked a dozen gold coins on the desk. "This is all I have."

Lewis's dad snapped photos with his wristpad.

"That is not nearly enough to rent one of my vehicles."

"That's enough to buy one!" Kaya protested.

"Not for an uncharted trip to Ridge City," Gogol replied. "A man like me could get into very, very serious trouble helping you take a trip like that. But you don't have to pay with money. There are other ways."

"Like what?"

"I'll take the big one," he said, pointing to Lewis's dad.

"He wants to buy me? I'm not for sale, sir."

"Not you. The device on your wrist."

Now Lewis's father shook his head. "I'm not giving him my wristpad. All my work is stored in here. My Atlantis journals. This is more valuable than you could possibly imagine—"

Hanna put her hands in her pockets, hiding her ring.

Gogol pointed to Lewis's wrist. "What's that one, then?"

The watch from Roberts. Lewis stared down at the face, the leather band, the tiny compass. When his stepdad had given it to him, Roberts had told him that the compass would make sure Lewis never lost his way. "It's a watch," he said. "It tells you the time of day."

The man leaned over his desk and eyed the timepiece. "Yes, I've seen something like this before. Fetched a very high price. The rumor was that it wasn't from Atlantis at all." He tipped his head up toward the ceiling—or maybe the surface. He motioned to Kaya. "That, my girl, would be worth something."

His dad draped his heavy, sweaty arm over Lewis's shoulder. "It's just an old watch," he whispered. "I'll find you another one."

But it wasn't just a watch. Lewis remembered when

Roberts had given it to him, on his tenth birthday. At first he'd handed it right back. He didn't want any gifts from his stepfather. He didn't want a stepfather. The guy had ruined everything! Every last drop of hope that his parents would get back together had evaporated when his mother had married Roberts, the bald hero from the Coastal Patrol. The guy who was the opposite of his father in every possible way. Then they'd had Michael, and that had pretty much cemented the situation.

Sure, Lewis had wanted a watch. Desperately. But his own dad—his real dad, as he'd reminded Roberts—had already promised him one for his birthday. So he didn't need that one. When he returned the gift, though, his mother was furious. But his stepfather had simply taken the watch, set it on his desk, and told Lewis it would be there waiting for him if he wanted to wear it one day. The guy was almost impossible to hate, and that day arrived sooner than Lewis had expected.

His dad didn't just forget to give Lewis a watch.

He forgot his birthday entirely.

A week passed before Lewis snuck the timepiece off the bookshelf. From then on, he wore it every day, and Roberts never said a thing.

Suddenly, standing there in Gogol's shop, Lewis felt weak. Defeated. The watch, the memory, the thought of his mother—it all sort of pulled him back home. Four miles up and who knew how many hundreds of miles away. He wished he could just blink and be transported back to his little room in his little house.

"Lewis? Son? What are you waiting for?"

Quietly, he unstrapped the watch and laid it on the counter. His chest instantly tightened. He wanted to be back with his mom and Roberts and his drippy-nosed, cheese-stinking brother. His father tried to hug him. Lewis shook off his arm and backed away.

Gogol handled the timepiece carefully, marveling at the tiny gears inside. "I'll take it," he said, sweeping up the coins with one of his grimy hands, "and the gold."

"That's not fair!" Kaya said. "I didn't say—"

"The gold is for the rental," he replied. "But I'm sure these friends of yours attracted some attention on your way here. Nothing in Edgeland goes unnoticed. There will be questions about you four. The watch means I don't give anyone the answers."

Gogol waved them around the counter and through a crowded back room into what looked like a repair shop. Six different vehicles were spread around the space. They were oval-shaped, not quite like hovercars or the old-fashioned autos Lewis had seen pictures of in books. Not a single one had a roof; they reminded Lewis more of metal life rafts than advanced vehicles. One of them had its hood pulled off. Another was missing its windshield. And they were all dented and rusting.

The rust. The dents. For the first time since the wave, Lewis thought of poor Chet. There was no way the old hovercar had survived that tsunami. Good old Chet. He meant well. Told decent jokes, too, for a machine.

"Do any of these things even work?" Kaya asked.

The merchant whistled a series of short, choppy notes.

Inside one of the junkers, a motor began to whirr and spin. The vehicle shook, then rose shakily off the ground, but it soared no higher than an inch or two before crashing back down. Gogol frowned. "That was running beautifully just a few days ago."

"Great," Kaya said. "This place is a real junkyard."

"Heaven is a junkyard," Hanna said, standing with her hands on her hips. "Can I look around?"

Gogol shrugged. "Go ahead. You break it, you buy it."

"Most of this stuff is already broken," Kaya noted.

"That is completely untrue," Gogol replied. The merchant picked up a deadly trumpet and fired at the wall. Nothing happened. "Well, maybe it's slightly true."

Hanna held out her hand. Gogol passed her the broken trumpet. She turned it over and over, inspecting it from every angle. "I'm not even going to bother asking you how this works, because no one around here seems to know anything about your technology, other than what it does."

"Ah, but I know how to fix it!" Gogol replied.

Hanna brightened. "You do? Show me."

Great. She was making friends with a crooked Atlantean mechanic.

Kaya, meanwhile, was focused on Lewis. "Why are you dancing?" she asked.

Was he dancing? Not really.

His father recognized his shuffle. "He has to go . . . you know."

Gogol whistled again, a string of longer notes this time.

A door swung open, and Lewis hurried inside.

His dad and Kaya were still inspecting the vehicles when

he returned. Gogol was showing Hanna how to repair the trumpet.

"All that gold for one of these?" Kaya asked, standing over one of the junkers.

"It certainly doesn't seem equitable," Lewis's dad added.

"These are fine machines!" Gogol protested. "Resilient, too, and beautifully built."

He gently kicked one.

The vehicle's door fell off and clattered to the rocky floor.

"Pristine," Hanna quipped.

"Are they cars?" Lewis asked. "Or boats?"

"Both," Hanna said. She was sitting on the floor, fiddling with the busted trumpet. "Whoa," she added, pointing to a pile of discarded machinery and equipment in the corner. "What's all that?"

"Trash," Gogol said.

Rusting and dented hunks of metal were mixed in with grimy, oil-smeared parts. Hanna knelt before the scraps and picked through them. To Lewis, it looked like an alien spaceship had puked up its insides, but Hanna marveled at every gadget and component and broken part. Lewis's father stood beside her, pointing his wristpad and taking photos. With his other hand, he scratched his neck where Naxos had shot him with the tracker.

Hanna grabbed a cube with wires dangling out the back. "What's this?"

"That connects the car to the soundscape so you can listen to music or stories," Kaya explained. "When it's working."

"So it's like a radio," Hanna said. "Can I take it?"

"I suppose I could sell you a few—"

"She can take all the junk she wants for all the gold I just gave you," Kaya snapped.

"Fine," Gogol grumbled.

Hanna asked for Kaya's backpack, and the girl from Atlantis tossed the half-filled bag across the room. Hanna held up some kind of metal rod in one hand and a cloth case in another. "Sweet! A tool kit!"

Beaming, Hanna continued to pick through the pile. Kaya, meanwhile, was still surveying the vehicles. She walked from one to the next, studying the cabins, kneeling and peering at the underside of each one. The more time she took, though, the more she looked like someone who was trying to appear as if she knew what she was doing but actually had no clue. Finally, she rested her hand on the hood of a low, wide cruiser. "We'll take this one."

"Sorry, that's not working," Gogol said. He pointed to a rusted junker in the corner. "That will be perfect for you."

The vehicle had two wide rows of seats, both facing forward. There was a windshield but no roof, and one of the side panels was crumpled like aluminum foil. How did a vehicle even get that dented? Lewis pictured dozens of gnomes wielding tiny hammers, striking the metal gleefully. They'd be singing, too. Fun, cheerful songs about the joys of destroying machines with their little weapons.

First we bang the doors.
Then we dent the hood.
Next we cut the wires.
Like all gnomes should!

They'd probably eat cupcakes, too. After the singing.

Lewis's dad gently backhanded him. "Are you with us?" he whispered.

"Yep."

He would not mention the gnomes and their song. Ever. To anyone.

Hanna stood with the bag full of tools and scrap parts hanging from her shoulder. "That doesn't even look like it'll start."

"Does it have gravity drive?" Kaya asked.

"Gravity drive?" the professor asked. "What's that?"

"I'll tell you later," Hanna said.

"Yes, it does, but I wouldn't count on it working for very long. Especially given the size of this one," Gogol said, pointing to Lewis's dad. "At your weight, she'll run out of boost in a few minutes. Don't worry, though. You're not going to want to drift into Ridge City, anyway. Not unless you want these people to get noticed. The waterways will be best. She floats beautifully. She's the safest one I've got and faster than you think."

"We'll take it," Kaya announced. "You'll give us directions to Ridge City?"

Gogol nodded. "Of course. No problem. You wouldn't want to get lost in these tunnels."

As Kaya and Hanna jumped into the front seat, Gogol moved to one of the large garage-like doors in the cave wall. He whistled a tune he hadn't used yet. The metal door rolled up, revealing an underground river rushing past on the other side.

Lewis's dad started whispering into his wristpad. "They

control machines by whistling," he said quietly. "New chapter idea: Atlantis as a sonic society. Everything is controlled by sound. Must explore further."

The water smelled like an old, wet shoe. Lewis lifted his shirt to cover his nose and mouth. But the stinking rag he'd peeled off the dockmaster nearly made him hurl. He pulled it down again and breathed deep. The river air was like a fresh mountain breeze compared to the odor-infused shirt.

His father winced slightly and itched his neck again.

The cruiser's engine purred. Not the roar of an old-fashioned engine or the buzz of a battery-powered hovercar, exactly. The sound was smoother, an almost pleasing hum. As Gogol watched, Kaya took the controls, her hands lying flat on two tablets. Suddenly the car was floating on a layer of air.

"Amazing," Lewis's dad said.

Hanna leaned over the side and stared down at the ground. Lewis's dad was on his hands and knees, sweeping his arm beneath the vehicle as if he expected to hit some invisible structure. Again, he spoke into his wristpad. "They've conquered gravity. Gravity! Absolutely incredible. Not to mention that it supports my theory about how they make the waves." He stopped and eyed Gogol. The man's face was pure confusion. "Another possible new chapter on Atlantean gravity technology."

"Are you sure you're from the Rift?" Gogol asked.

"How about those directions?" Kaya pressed.

He nodded and grabbed a tablet. "Yes. Right."

A loud ding sounded. The two Atlanteans eyed the door to the front room.

"What was that?" Hanna asked.

"Probably just a customer," Gogol said. "They'll wait."

Sitting in the driver's seat, Kaya motioned to the tablet. "Directions."

The door to the front room shook as someone tried to push it open from the other side. Gogol reached for the weapon at his waist. "My customers don't try to break through my doors. Are you expecting anyone?"

"Maybe it's Naxos," Hanna suggested. "He said he'd try to meet us."

Now Kaya pointed at Lewis's dad. "Professor, your neck . . . why are you scratching it?"

"Just an odd itch—"

She gasped. "He tricked us."

"What do you mean?" Lewis asked. "Who?"

"Naxos! The tracking device . . . that wasn't for him. That was for the Erasers."

Gogol's face paled. "The Erasers are following you?"

Without waiting for confirmation, he dashed over to the low cruiser Kaya had picked out first. He tried to leap over the side, but his stomach got in his way, and he tumbled over the door and into the passenger seat. This would've been kind of funny, Lewis decided, if the guy hadn't looked so terrified. Gogol shimmied into the driver's seat and switched on the motor.

The motor that was supposed to be broken.

The vehicle quickly rose off the ground.

Sweat beaded on Gogol's huge forehead.

"You said that wasn't working!" Kaya shouted.

"You said they were from the Rift," he replied.

And with a slight shrug, he steered the cruiser forward. Lewis jumped out of the way as Gogol sped through the opening, over the underground river, and away into the darkness.

"So much for directions," Hanna noted.

Panicking, Kaya drummed her hand on the dashboard. "Get in, get in!"

Lewis climbed in first, and when his dad followed, the vehicle dropped to the floor.

The motor hummed louder and louder, but their cruiser wouldn't lift off the ground.

"We're too heavy!" Kaya shouted. "The gravity drive's not strong enough. We need to get rid of some weight."

Lewis tore off his sweaty headwrap and tossed it onto the ground. "How about that?"

"Are you serious?" Hanna asked.

"We need to move," Kaya said.

Yes, he knew that. They all knew that. But how much weight could they ditch?

"We're not separating," Hanna insisted.

"We don't have to," Kaya said. "If a few of us get out, we can push it forward into the river, then jump back in."

"I'll take care of it," Lewis's dad said.

Once he was on the ground, the cruiser immediately rose again.

His dad pushed. The cruiser floated forward through the opening.

The door to the front room shook.

Kaya was still slapping her hand against the dashboard. "Faster, faster!"

"It's remarkably light and easy," Lewis's father said. "I imagine these vehicles require very little thrust." He raised his wristpad to his mouth. "New note: Explore the dynamics of antigravity propulsion."

He was adding to the journals now? Seriously?

The cruiser was finally over the river. "Hey, Professor," Hanna said, "get in!"

But his dad held up his finger. One more note. He just needed to make one more note. He stood at the edge of the underground river with one hand on the side of the cruiser, talking into his wristpad, recording a few last details about the gravity drive. Lewis didn't just want to toss the wristpad into the river. He wanted to smash it with a rock. No, a boulder. Or give it to those hammer-wielding gnomes and tell them to do their very worst. The water was rushing over his dad's boots, and he was holding the wristpad close to his mouth, when the door to the front of the shop burst off its hinges and slammed to the stone floor.

A group of men and women holding deadly trumpets and frightening flutes raced out.

The Erasers had found them.

"Invaders!" one of the women shouted.

Another Eraser dashed across the room with his trumpet raised. His head was gleaming and bald and his wide Atlantean eyes were gray. A thick tangle of green hair hung from his chin, and his crooked teeth were black and brown. Lewis watched the muscles in his fingers tense as he aimed his trumpet at their cruiser.

The Eraser squeezed the trigger.

His dad was the only thing between them and the weapon. A strange sort of cry roared out of him.

Then his dad fell forward, and Kaya pushed the throttle, rocketing the ship into the darkness.

11

FRIENDS OR MONSTERS

THE TUNNEL branched and curved as the water rushed forward. The gravity drive had already died. The cruiser was just a raft now, and Kaya had bumped into the tunnel wall more than she would have liked. But she was finally getting the feel of the steering, and she turned at random each time the tunnel split, choosing left or right without really thinking. Directions? She'd worry about them later. When they had some distance between them and the Erasers. Now she just needed to watch and listen for signs that they were being followed.

There was no chance the Erasers could have tracked them, though. They'd already taken too many turns. Lewis was watching for them, too. Or for his father. The sonic rifle had knocked the poor, huge man out, and Kaya had sped away. Lewis had yelled for her to turn back. Hanna, too. But she'd made the right choice. If she had backed up and tried to haul the professor into the cruiser, the Erasers would have captured all of them. Then what?

She'd recognized the man who'd fired his weapon and the woman who'd called them invaders, too. They'd both been at the theater the night of Elida's show. That proved they were Erasers—normal police wouldn't turn up both in Edgeland and Ridge City. So if she had tried to help the professor, they'd all be gone. Now at least they had a chance. Her father could help them. Maybe her grandmother. Or even Rian's parents.

The Sun People should've thanked her. She'd saved them! Sure, if she had been in Lewis's place and he'd left her father behind, she'd probably be upset, too. But still.

They rode in silence for a while before Lewis finally spoke—and not, thankfully, about his dad. "So who are the Erasers, anyway?"

Happy to talk, she explained what she knew. First of all, she said, they operated in secret, and you couldn't pick them out of a crowd. They didn't wear uniforms or have secret handshakes or special tattoos. Lewis asked if they had their own hats—that was a no, too. "They could be anyone, anywhere, at any time," she added. "I've heard stories about them grabbing people off the street and no one ever hearing from them again. Poof. Just like that. Erased."

"You're sure your dad will be able to help us find the professor?" Hanna asked.

No, she wasn't sure. But she knew one thing: "He'll try." Kaya's dad knew people. Important people. Forget the Erasers. Her dad would find the professor and make sure he was safe. He'd reunite the three of them. He'd make sure that they were treated like honored guests, not criminals, and the Sun People would finally see the beauty of Atlantis. Or that's what she told them, anyway. Was she being naive?

Maybe the Sun People would never be safe in Atlantis.

In a way, Gogol was to blame. He could've taken a few of them in his cruiser. That way, they all would've escaped. Naxos was at fault, too. He'd turned them in! If either of those two fools had only understood, if they'd realized just what a colossal and epic and massively important event this was, then all three of the Sun People would be perfectly safe. Her only mistake had been trusting those two frightened, lying cowards.

Hanna put her hand on Kaya's clenched fist.

The tunnel narrowed. The air was warm and wet as they coasted along, riding the water. Hanna started asking questions about the caverns and the tunnels and how they were built. But Kaya didn't want to talk. All she wanted to do was move. As far away as possible.

Every time the tunnel curved or split, she half expected the Erasers to be there waiting.

She hated that she was scared.

Hanna started working through the junk she'd grabbed from Gogol.

"What are you doing?" Kaya asked.

"Tinkering," Hanna replied. She held up the busted sonic blaster. "If we see those Erasers again, we might as well try to defend ourselves."

"I've already got one of those," Kaya noted.

"Two is better," Hanna said.

Lewis leaned forward. "Where are we, anyway?"

"Remember how I mentioned the water running through

the streets at night to clean up the slop?" Kaya said. "All that water flows out through these tunnels. They run beneath all the cities."

Silence again. Then Lewis muttered something.

"What?" Hanna asked.

"So we're basically in the sewers," he said.

Hanna wiped a few drops of water off her forearm. "Yep," she said. Then she lowered her voice, imitating the professor: "In Atlantis!"

A smile cracked Lewis's stony face. "That was a pretty good impression."

Now Hanna held her wrist just below her chin, speaking into an imaginary device. "The light is dim, but it doesn't seem to bother our guide," she began, using the same deep voice. "Her unusually large eyes are well adjusted to dim lighting conditions. The world she sees—the world we see—is so shockingly beautiful. The walls are soaking wet. Tiny crystals in the rocks glitter as we pass. The air is as steamy as a rainforest."

Lewis was laughing now, and Kaya, too, but what did Hanna mean by large eyes? Kaya's eyes were normal. Small, even. The Sun People were the ones with weird eyes. And the air wasn't hot at all. Wait until she brought them near a vent! Now that was real heat. Get too close, and you'd roast your eyebrows.

Ahead of them, the underground river split again.

Kaya swung the cruiser to the right.

"He'll be fine, Lewis," Hanna said, switching back to her normal voice. "He's one of the smartest people I've ever met.

He will be fine."

"I know," Lewis said. "I know."

As the mood in the cruiser changed, Kaya finally felt herself relaxing. What they needed now was music, and thankfully the soundscape in the old junker still worked. She adjusted the dials on the dashboard, skipping a few story stations and old-fashioned songs.

"This is that radio thing you were talking about earlier?" Hanna asked. She held up the cube she'd grabbed from the junk pile.

"The soundscape," Kaya replied. The first recent song she found was a popular tune by the Narwhals, of course. She quickly switched and found one she liked. The beat was just right.

"What do you think?" she asked.

"I liked that first one better," Lewis said.

Of course he did. Clearly he had no taste.

The water kept racing and swerving, and Hanna started running her hands over the knobs and dials on the dashboard, asking which ones controlled what features. "Where's the gravity drive?" she asked. "Maybe I can try to fix it."

"You literally just learned that there are gravity drives," Lewis said. "Now you're going to try to repair one?"

Hanna shrugged. "Why not?"

Kaya admired her confidence. The Sun People watched closely as Kaya pressed her palm to one of the tablets on the dashboard; Hanna leaned over and tilted her head to the side, focusing on the moving screen, the rise and fall of the tiny rods.

"What are you doing?" Hanna asked.

Wasn't it obvious? "I'm reading." The cruiser's instruction manual was stored in the tablet, and Kaya was scanning through it to figure out how to access the gravity drive. "You don't read like this?"

"We read with our eyes," Hanna said.

"We do that, too," Kaya replied. "But this way is better."

At that point, she didn't need to steer—the cruiser was riding the water. So Kaya climbed into the back and, following the instructions, popped up one of the rear seats to reveal a squat contraption about as long on each side as her forearm. Tubes stretched out to each of the four corners of the cruiser, and there was a single circular panel in the middle. "Your gravity drive, Hanna," Kaya announced.

Hanna made Lewis switch places with her, then popped open the panel with one of her new tools. "It's beautiful," Hanna whispered.

That was not the word Kaya would have used. Waterways and pools could be beautiful. The gleaming buildings in Ridge City. But a motor? Beautiful? No. Yet the girl from the surface was entranced as she picked her way through the tightly packed components. She pulled out more tools and began removing piece after piece of the drive, turning each one over in her hands, then popping it back into place. As she worked, Hanna talked more to herself than either of them, turning the pieces over and around in her hands and narrating in weird, broken speech. "Why is this . . . oh . . . and I don't understand . . . aha, sure . . . never seen anything . . ."

"Are you sure you know what you're doing?" Lewis asked.

"Nope," Hanna admitted. "But I'm learning."

"And she can't break what's already broken," Kaya added.

Lewis nodded, then sat back in his seat and yawned. He seemed more relaxed now. Was he still mad at her for leaving his father behind? She hoped he understood.

At least they were safe. No one could have tracked them. They'd taken so many turns.

Too many, even . . .

She studied the dripping crystalline walls. The dim green and blue lights. The curve of the narrow tunnel. She'd never been in a waterway like this one before.

Were they lost? A little.

But she wasn't going to tell the Sun People.

The river dropped over a small ledge.

Water splashed into the cabin.

In the front seat now, Lewis gripped the handle beside him, but Hanna didn't even look up. "Here," she said, holding up a small metal ball. "Take this."

Kaya reached back and grabbed it; the sphere was warm in her hand and strangely heavy. "What is this?" she asked.

"I thought you could tell me," Hanna replied.

Nope. They didn't exactly learn about the inner workings of gravity drives in school.

"Is it the battery?" Lewis guessed.

"I don't even know if this thing runs on batteries," Hanna replied. Still hunched over, she held out her hand and waved her fingers. "What I do know is that there are four of those little spheres. The other three fit snugly into place, and that one was a little loose." Her fingers kept moving. Oh. Right. She wanted the sphere. Kaya started to pass it back to her.

"So I used those tools Gogol gave me to tighten a few other pieces, and—"

The tunnel dropped sharply, throwing them back against their seats.

They splashed into a huge body of water. An enormous lake.

Hanna stared at Kaya. "Tell me you didn't lose it," she said.

The heavy sphere, thankfully, was still in her hand.

As the cruiser settled into the water, Kaya passed it carefully to Hanna. Lewis cupped his hands around his mouth and yelled, "Echo!" The word bounced back to them off the distant walls. "Wow," he said, scrunching up his nose. "This place smells like a toilet. How big is it? And where are we, anyway?"

"Well," Kaya began, fumbling for an explanation, "I know we're going in the right direction, because there are no other pools this large between Edgeland and the border."

The boy studied her. His eyes narrowed. "You don't know where we are, do you?"

Did they think she ran away from secret organizations often? She stood up in her seat and watched how the water moved. In the distance, streams poured out of tunnels high in the walls. There were dozens of waterfalls, all at different heights. The lake itself was moving oddly, too, not just churning from the spilling water. And he was right. It really did stink.

"We're going in a circle," Lewis said. "It's almost like we're circling a giant drain."

Kaya's stomach suddenly felt sick. She gripped the top of the door and stared out.

No, no, no.

This was a filtering pool.

These pools were the reason every kid in Atlantis was warned to stay out of the tunnels in the first place. How had she not thought about this? All the street water rushed into these pools. Then it was sucked down through filters built into the bottom of the lake, where sharp, churning blades crushed any rocks and waste into sludge.

If they didn't find a way out, they'd be sludge, too.

That would be the end of the Sun People.

The end of Kaya.

"What's wrong?" Lewis asked.

There was no use in lying. She explained everything in a rush. Or mostly everything. They didn't need to know about the spinning blades at the bottom. The thought of drowning was probably frightening enough.

"Try the gravity drive," Hanna said.

"It's broken."

She huffed. "No, not anymore. I fixed it."

Seriously? Kaya swept her hands across the dashboard, found the controls, and dialed up the drive with a long, shrill whistle. But the cruiser didn't float; she could've sworn it sank lower in the water. The girl from the surface wasn't so much disappointed as shocked. She wasn't used to failure, Kaya guessed. And she didn't like it, either.

Hanna mumbled something about giving her a second.

The cruiser was nearing the center of the massive drain.

"What happens when we get sucked down?" Lewis asked.

Kaya didn't answer.

A small square piece of metal bounced off the inside of

the windshield as Hanna tossed it over her shoulder. The girl stared into the drive with her hand on her chin. Then she shrugged and kicked one of the tubes. "Try it now."

Fine. One more time. What else was Kaya supposed to do?

She whistled again, wondering how far they'd get if they tried to swim against the powerful current, or if there was some kind of emergency beacon she could switch on, when . . .

The cruiser freed itself from gravity's grip, rising from the swirling, deadly drain, drifting higher and higher above the water.

Kaya stared at the girl from the surface. Lewis did, too.

"What?" Hanna said with a shrug. "I told you I can fix anything."

Kaya wasn't sure how they celebrated in their world. But she stood for a second and let out a wild, deep scream of delight and relief. Smiling, Hanna followed with some kind of whooping chant, and Lewis . . . well, she wasn't quite sure what he was doing. He stood on the rear seat, pressed his fists to his ribs, underneath his armpits, and started jutting his chin out in jerky, stabbing motions as he leaned forward and turned in place. All she could do was laugh.

Then it was time to focus. Who knew how long the drive would last? Kaya scanned the walls as the cruiser rose higher. There were at least fifty tunnels spouting water into the pool, but she soon spotted the right one. A single dry opening. If she could get them over there, they could push the gravity drive as far as it would carry them, then walk if necessary. She wouldn't have to worry about the water whisking them back. Yes, she thought, that could actually work.

She pointed. "Sit down and hold on."

The boy gripped the rail of one door. Hanna held on to the back of Kaya's seat.

Kaya dialed up the lights. The huge wet wall of the cavern was instantly draped in blue. The Sun People watched silently. The stuff spouting out of the tunnels smelled rancid, fetid, foul enough to make her vomit. Yet the crash and roar of all that water spilling down into the lake below was beautiful. Almost soothing. She switched on the thruster, and they were thrown back in their seats as the junker blasted forward, scraped through the opening of the tunnel, then coasted slowly ahead.

For a moment, no one spoke.

No one even reacted.

Then Lewis looked at her. "Did you just have your eyes closed?" he asked.

"I've never even driven one of these before," Kaya confessed.

The Sun People were silent. Had she shared too much?

Finally Hanna laughed. "I'm starting to like you, Kaya."

12

HOME

AFTER THE GIRL from Atlantis steered them through the opening high above the pool, they drifted through a dark, curving tunnel for hours and hours. This one didn't branch or split; there was only one route. Kaya had studied the manual and learned that the vessel had an autopilot function, so she switched it on, leaned back, and closed her eyes. At some point, Lewis stretched out across the back seat and dropped into a deep and dreamless sleep. When he woke, Hanna was out cold, and Kaya was only just rousing herself, rubbing her eyes. Lewis was dripping with sweat. His hair was so wet it felt like he'd just gone swimming, and his clothes were soaked. Kaya looked perfectly comfortable, though. Her clothes, made of some kind of instantly drying material, weren't even damp.

The light brightened around them as they drifted out of the tunnel and into an enormous open cavern divided into huge pools of water. Hanna yawned and stretched, then climbed into the back seat, pulled out the busted sonic blaster, and got back to work trying to fix it. Lewis stared at her. "What?" she asked.

"You never stop, huh?"

She held up her hands and wiggled the fingers. "They need to stay busy."

"How long did I sleep?" Lewis asked.

"We all slept through the night," Kaya replied.

Hanna stopped what she was doing and stared at the cavern's ceiling. "How can you even tell whether it's night or day?" she asked.

Kaya tapped her earpiece. "This tracks the time."

The water was calm and still in some sections, rippled in others. There were a few people in the distance—some in small boats, others walking along the stone paths between the pools. Drops fell from the ceiling and plunked into the water below. Lewis tilted his head back, trying to catch one in his mouth. Not his best idea. When he finally snagged one, it tasted like rock.

He noticed Kaya's expression change as she stared at a bright light in the distance.

"You're smiling," he said. "Any chance that means you know where we are?"

"We're at the edge of my city. I've been here before on school field trips."

"You have field trips? They have field trips! In Atlantis!" He elbowed Hanna, who accidentally squeezed the trigger on the blaster. His foot exploded with the strangest sensation—a kind of burning, intense vibration. "Owwww!"

"Whoa," Hanna said. "I guess I fixed it. Cool."

"Cool? That hurt!"

Carefully, she placed the blaster on the seat beside her. "Right. Sorry. Are you okay?"

"He's fine," Kaya said. "That version's just painful. It doesn't knock you out like the others. No permanent damage, either."

His foot was tingling, but the feeling came back quickly. Still, a little more sympathy would've been nice. Even fake sympathy.

Leaning over the side of the cruiser, Hanna asked, "What is this place? Another aquafarm?"

Thick strands of rubbery seaweed hung beneath the surface of the water below.

"We grow a thousand different types of kelp and sea grass," Kaya said.

"And you eat that stuff?" Lewis asked.

She searched through her bag, found a rectangular bar wrapped in greenish packaging, and passed it to him. "Baked, dried, fried, boiled . . . any kind of seaweed you could want. This kelp bar has all the nutrients you need for a day's work. Fish bars are popular, too, but I don't have any with me."

Lewis hesitated, sniffing the outside, but his stomach was a mindless, ravenous beast. He would've chewed on a lost-and-found gym sneaker if someone told him it had protein. And so he bit off a chunk. Sure enough, it tasted like cardboard. He stuck out his tongue and tried to scratch it clean with his fingernails. "That's disgusting!" he cried.

Hanna grabbed it from him and tried a small bite. "I disagree. It tastes . . . healthy."

"Exactly," he said. "Gross."

And then he snatched the bar back from her and gobbled it down. Kaya tossed him a bottle of water, then dug through her bag and found another for Hanna. "I'm so sorry," she said. "I didn't even think about whether you'd be hungry. I didn't really pack enough for three people, but we'll be home soon, and you can eat as much as you like."

Home. He still didn't want to think about home.

Or his mother and his little brother.

And he really didn't want to think about his dad. His father was alive. He had to be. The Erasers wouldn't want to hurt him. They'd want to talk to him. Ask him questions. And his dad would be only too happy to chat. A chance to converse with Atlanteans? Maybe even explain his theories? He'd forget all about the blast from the sonic rifle. He'd convince them they weren't invaders. His father and the Erasers were probably sitting around a table together right now, drinking that fermented kelp stuff, already friends.

A low wall with a path through the center cut across the water ahead of them. On the other side, the water churned in places, as if it were boiling. Lewis pointed. "What's that?"

"Fish. I'm not sure which kind. We also have pools for algae, not to mention crabs, clams, lobsters . . ."

"So you pretty much just eat seafood and seaweed," Lewis mumbled. "Weird."

"Really?" Kaya said. "Why? What do you eat?"

"Vegetables," Hanna began, "grains, fruit—"

"And chocolate," Lewis added. "Do you have chocolate here?" Kaya shook her head. "Wow. That's tragic. Really."

"We eat meat, too," Hanna said.

"Meat?"

"You know—from chickens, pigs, cows, goats."

Kaya looked puzzled. Maybe the words didn't translate. "What are they?"

Lewis described each of these land animals, then did his goat impression. He was pretty skilled at imitating farm animals; his cow was stellar, and his pig was perfection. Strangely, though, despite his mastery of the chicken dance, he couldn't quite do a rooster or a hen.

"That was a terrible goat impression," Hanna declared.

She belted out a few bleats herself. Unfortunately, she was good. Really good. He had to try and match her, and soon the two of them were going goat for goat, and laughing hysterically. Kaya? Not so much. The girl from Atlantis looked massively weirded out.

Quieting their inner goats, they cruised onward and over a wide, still square of water. Lewis wiped the sweat from his forehead, swept his hair back, and pointed down. "What about this section?"

"This is a fallow pool," Kaya said. "They'll keep that empty and clean for a few months, then move fish or plant life into it and clean out another one."

"So the water's clean?"

"Very."

"No giant foot-swallowing fish?"

"Not a single one."

"Lewis," Hanna said, "don't!"

But he was already over the side, cannonballing into the water below. His score? Out of modesty, he gave himself a nine and a half, but he probably deserved a ten. The water was cool but not cold. It seeped through his hair and clothes and instantly woke him up. "The water's perfect!" he yelled when he surfaced.

The cruiser dropped slowly, settling without a splash. Immediately Kaya leaped over the side. Hanna took a little more convincing, but she jumped in next. She swam to the edge of the pool and propped herself up on the stone wall, sitting with her feet in the water. "Are you racing?" Hanna asked.

This was an absolutely terrible idea. The girl from Atlantis swam like a dolphin. He was going to get destroyed. "Let's go!"

"There and back?" Kaya suggested.

The other side of the pool was ridiculously far away. "No way. Just here to there."

"Fine," Kaya said.

He was on the other side of Hanna, holding the wall with one hand. Hanna leaned over and whispered, "Just the first race between an Atlantean and a Sun Person. No pressure."

"Right," he said. "Why don't we just wait a few minutes to catch our breath—"

Kaya nodded in agreement, and he dropped down and streamlined off the wall.

Was it cheating? Maybe. But she was from Atlantis. He deserved a head start, and he burst up out of the water and kicked and swung his arms. He felt fast.

Just not fast enough.

He didn't have goggles, so his vision was blurry, but the water was clear enough that he could see Kaya streamlining beneath him. She was a body length or two below the surface, swimming with her arms pressed together over her head, rocketing through the water like a dolphin.

Next time he'd find a pair of fins.

When Lewis finally made it to the other side, she was already rested and relaxed. "I'm more of a distance guy," he lied.

"A bigger pool, and I would have passed you."

Once they'd climbed back inside, Kaya steered over the pools and into a tunnel glowing with lights and crowded with vehicles. They splashed down into the flow of traffic, and Kaya reminded them to crouch so they wouldn't be noticed. Hanna started complaining that Lewis smelled like the armpit of a hibernating bear. He told her she reeked of the crusty crevices behind its ears. Did bears even have those? Michael did. But forest animals? He wasn't sure. Still, it was a good comeback.

At the edge of the city, Kaya switched on the gravity drive again—she said she still couldn't believe Hanna had fixed it— and they drifted above the crowds. She whistled, then cupped her hand over her right ear. Listening to her new messages, Lewis guessed. Then an odd expression formed on her face. Not sad, exactly. Confused.

"What is it?" Lewis asked, leaning into the front seat.

Kaya drummed her fingers on the dashboard. "Well, every-one's worried, obviously. I told Rian and my grandmother I'd be home soon, but my dad . . . he still hasn't messaged me."

Lewis looked at Hanna. "Maybe it just didn't come through yet," she suggested.

"Right," Kaya said. "That's probably it. The signal in those tunnels and waterways can't be good." She sat straighter in her seat. "So," she said, forcing a smile, "what do you think of my city?"

The world below was a sparkling, gleaming wonder. The buildings were all crystal and glass. Hanna said something about how there were none of the straight lines and right angles common to surface cities—how everything was curved.

And sure, that was interesting. But the crowds! There were people everywhere, walking shoulder to shoulder, and waterways jammed with small boats and long, thin ferries flowed in different directions. Atlantis was packed!

As they crossed the city, the buildings and neighborhoods changed. The crystal-lined walls gave way to simple stone. But even these walls were polished smooth, not left jagged and rough, and the windows were made of radiant multicolored glass. Kaya steered into a garage hollowed out of one such stone wall, high off the ground, and they floated gently to the floor.

A dozen other vehicles were parked inside. All of them gleamed, without a single dent or speck of rust. "We're here," she announced.

Hanna gently packed the blaster into the gear-filled bag, slung it over her shoulders, climbed out, and traced her fingers over the roof of one of the other vehicles. "Are these all yours?"

"No, no," Kaya answered. "Twenty other families live in this wall."

Hanna nodded. "So it's like an apartment building. Cool."

Kaya whistled four long, slow notes. A wide metal door slid into the wall, and she led them down stone steps to her level. Someone was playing the drums above them, and Lewis heard a man and a woman arguing. "The Murakis," Kaya explained. "They're always yelling at each other."

At a dark glass door, Kaya whistled again—a different tune this time—and they stepped into a tall, wide-open room. The polished walls rose and curved sharply into a high ceiling. Lights glowed to the right. Windows looking out over the city lined the left side of the room, and a tangle of vines and green leaves grew up out of a shallow pool of clear blue water at the far end.

"Grandmother? Dad?" Kaya called out. "Are you home?"

No response.

Where were they?

"Do you have food?" Lewis asked. "I'm so hungry I'd eat kelp ice cream with kelp sauce and whipped kelp on top."

Kaya checked the other rooms, then returned and began pulling containers out of some kind of fridge. She laid the containers out on a square table. "Sit," she said. "You're going to love this."

His father was the one who would've loved it—and not only because of his fondness for food. He wanted to know everything about Atlanteans. How they lived, what they ate—everything! Lewis felt a kind of pit in his stomach. An emptiness.

Hanna dropped the bag on the floor next to a large couch and stared at the spread of foods on the table. "So, how do we . . ."

"Right," Kaya said. "I'll show you."

She sat with them and unfolded what looked like a seaweed wrap. Then she loaded it with these strange little brownish-green cubes and all different kinds of thick greens. She pinched salt—Lewis hoped—out of a small stone pot and sprinkled it across the top. Next she grabbed a few bottles from the fridge, set them on the table, and dribbled a few dashes of a brownish, syrupy goo onto her food. Lewis leaned forward and sniffed one of the bottles. His nose was instantly on fire.

His sinuses cleared. His whole world had suddenly changed.

Everything was brighter, better, more wonderful.

They had hot sauce in Atlantis.

As he started putting together his own wrap, Kaya pulled two sides of hers together and chomped down. She savored the flavors, closing her eyes as she chewed.

"We're not the only hungry ones," Hanna remarked.

"Go ahead," Kaya said. "It's delicious."

Lewis and Hanna fought over the containers, overloading their wraps with mystery cubes and what looked like crabmeat. Lewis flooded his messy masterpiece with one of the Atlantean hot sauces. He'd beaten his friends Jet and Kwan in hot-sauce-eating contests before. He was still in training, though, and he might never reach the level of mastery of his uncle John, who had once won a hot sauce challenge by pouring the fiery stuff into his eyes.

Kaya held out her hand. "Not too much," she warned.

He dashed on a few drops more, then braved his first bite. The wrap was actually kind of good, and the cube things, although mildly fishy, were way, way better than that kelp bar he'd tasted in the cruiser. And the hot sauce wasn't even that—

The fire rolled in slowly, beginning near his lips.

Then the heat spread back over his tongue and all around the inside of his mouth.

Soon he was burning from the inside out. If he burped, he thought he might actually breathe fire. The girls began laughing as he leaped and jumped around the room, then splashed into the small, ankle-deep pool against the wall. He drank the pool water. He splashed his face and mouth. He even grabbed some of the vines hanging down the wall and rubbed them against his lips—anything to stifle the flames. Between laughs, Kaya raced to the fridge and grabbed a bottle of bluish liquid. She pressed it into his hands and ordered him to drink. He slugged some down, and it tasted like yogurt. He rinsed it around inside his mouth and spat some into the pool at his feet. A bluish-purple cloud spread out. Was he supposed to spit in there? Probably not. He was turning to apologize when the door opened.

An Atlantean boy stepped into the room. His hair was short and silver. He had wide shoulders, wide feet, a flat nose, and his skin was pale. Almost colorless. Kaya rushed across the room but stopped short of hugging him. "Well," she asked, pointing back at Lewis and Hanna, "can you believe it? What do you think?"

The boy's huge eyes widened as he looked from Lewis to Hanna and back. "Whoa," he said at last. "They really are weird! Especially that one," he added, pointing at Lewis.

What? The Atlantean boy was the weird one. Lewis glanced over at Hanna. He tried to see her and himself through Atlantean eyes. She was still at the table, seaweed wrap in her hands. No rags from Edgeland could disguise the fact that she was not from Atlantis. Her dark hair and long, slender frame were probably alien to this kid. And Lewis? Well, he wasn't exactly Captain Normal, either. His height, his hair, his freckles, the shade of his skin. Plus he was standing in the pool with bits of vines dangling out of his mouth and a cloud of blue Atlantean yogurt at his feet. The kid probably thought he was using the pool as a toilet.

He let go of the vines. "Hello," he said. Then he pointed to the blue cloud. "Hot sauce problem. Long story." Thankfully, the supreme, cosmic awkwardness that followed lasted only a second. "This is Rian?" Lewis asked.

"I'm not her grandmother," the boy replied.

A decent comeback, Lewis decided. He'd let the Atlantean have this minor victory. Did they shake hands in Atlantis? Or high-five? Lewis wasn't sure, so he waved, and Hanna did the same. He stepped out of the pool and returned to the table, leaving wet footprints on the floor. Rian remained on the other side of the room. Was he scared of them?

Meanwhile, Hanna had devoured her wrap and was starting to put together another one. Lewis wasn't even halfway through his first. He was hungry, sure, but the wrap was soaked in devil sauce, and for some reason, seeing Kaya relax in her home had flattened his appetite. He was happy for her. Totally. And racing through Atlantis had been amazing. Wild, terrifying at times, but amazing. But now he was done. Now he was ready to find his father and get home. As soon as possible. He wanted to be with his family, in his house, eating his food. Somehow, they had to escape from Atlantis.

Something metal tapped against the floor outside.

"Someone's coming," Kaya whispered.

Hanna scrambled away from the table. The pack with the blaster was on the floor near the couch, and she hurried over to it. She motioned for Lewis to stand next to her, and they both ducked behind the couch, out of sight.

"Relax," Rian said.

An old woman appeared in the doorway. Her skin wasn't wrinkled, but her back was stooped, and she walked with a cane.

"Grandmother!" Kaya exclaimed. She rushed over and embraced the old woman, who broke off the hug quickly.

"You owe me an explanation, child."

Instead of offering an excuse, Kaya signaled for Lewis and Hanna to stand up. "They are my explanation."

The old woman staggered slightly. Rian rushed to grab a chair and set it down near the door. Carefully, Kaya's grandmother sat, then held her cane in front of her and breathed out heavily. "Astounding," she said. "Simply astounding."

Now Lewis heard more footsteps—a group of people rushing down the stairs.

"Is that our friend?" Kaya's grandmother asked Rian.

The boy shook his head. "No, that sounds like a few people."

"What friend?" Kaya asked. "I only messaged the two of you and Dad that I was coming home. I only mentioned the Sun People to Rian."

"And I didn't tell anyone," he insisted. "Honestly."

His response was quick and forceful. Lewis believed him.

"You mentioned these visitors?" her grandmother asked.

"Sure," Kaya said with a shrug. "Why?"

Her grandmother sighed. "They listen to everything, dear. Everything."

"Who?"

Two people burst into the room through the open front door. The woman was slim, had blond hair cut short, and looked like a smaller version of Lewis's third-grade teacher,

Mrs. Finkleman. He recognized her from Gogol's shop. The man, too. The thick green hair growing from his chin looked like a clump of weeds. The Erasers had tracked them again.

"You were at the theater," Rian said to the woman. "You took Elida."

"They were at Gogol's shop, too," Lewis added.

Hanna stood beside the couch. The bag of gear was at her feet.

Mrs. Finkleman aimed a deadly trumpet. "Nobody move."

"Do I look like I'm moving?" Kaya's grandmother replied, still sitting to the right of the unwanted guests. "Whoever you are, this is a private home, and you have no right to be here. You're aiming your weapon at children."

"We're not here to hurt them," Mrs. Finkleman answered. She pointed at Lewis and Hanna. "We're here to take those two with us."

"Absolutely not!" Kaya shouted. "These are my friends!"

"No, child," the woman said quietly. "They are not your friends. They are monsters."

"When my father hears about this—"

"Your father is powerless, Kaya," Mrs. Finkleman said. "Your parents, too, Rian."

"How do you know my name?" the boy asked.

"We know all about each of you," Mrs. Finkleman sneered.

"Lower those weapons," Kaya's grandmother said.

Weed Chin kicked the cane out of her hands. Then he pointed his trumpet at Lewis and Hanna. "We're taking these two invaders with us."

Kaya stomped her foot and leaned forward. "You are not going to take them—"

"No," Hanna said, interrupting her. "We'll go with you."

Lewis breathed in deeply. Was this what being brave felt like? He didn't enjoy it. His stomach was sick. His hands were shaking. "That's right," he said. He pointed to Rian, Kaya, and her grandmother. "Just promise not to hurt them."

"We promise," Finkleman snarled.

This was just about the least believable promise he'd ever heard. Yet Lewis and Hanna stepped forward, and the Erasers grabbed them by the forearms and dragged them out the door.

13
UNUSUAL
CIRCUMSTANCES

KAYA just stood there, frozen, staring at the closed door. Her grandmother started moving toward the table. Rian grabbed her cane off the floor and handed it to her, then sat on the back of the couch.

"We have to do something," Kaya said, starting toward the exit.

"They'll blast us to the floor and take us with them, dear," her grandmother replied.

"We need to get help," Rian added.

He was right. Her grandmother was right. What was she thinking?

She was a kid. She couldn't rescue the Sun People herself. But she couldn't just sit there, either. Waiting, doing nothing. She tapped her earpiece. Still nothing from her dad. Where was he? She messaged him, begging him to respond as soon as possible. Then she noticed that her grandmother was watching her.

In all the madness, Kaya had forgotten that she had betrayed her trust. After guiding the Sun People across half of Atlantis, only to have the Erasers track them to her home, she hadn't thought it was possible to feel worse. But no—there was at least one more level of awful, and she sank there now. "I'm so sorry, Grandmother. I lied. I—"

"Yes," her grandmother replied. "All these things and more." She pointed her cane at the door. "But clearly these are unusual circumstances. Now, dear, before we determine what to do next, please sit down and tell us everything."

Kaya hurried through the details of her trip to Edgeland, the deepwater dive, Naxos, Gogol, right down to the goat impressions and the boy's odd dance routine. Her grandmother occasionally gazed at the ceiling as she spoke, as if she were trying to picture it all. Rian constantly jumped in with comments and exclamations. Kaya finished by saying that she still hadn't been able to reach her father. Her grandmother nodded to herself, as if she were checking the narrative's math.

"I was very worried, you know," her grandmother said in a soft voice.

Someone knocked on their door.

"More Erasers?" her grandmother asked. "I'm not sure I can stand another encounter."

Kaya searched for the bag with the two sonic blasters. She found it stuffed under the couch; Hanna must have kicked it there when the Erasers arrived. Kaya removed one of the weapons just as Rian opened the door. But the Erasers hadn't come back.

Not exactly, anyway. Naxos stood in the doorway.

At first, she was surprised. Then anger raged inside her.

"How could you?" Kaya shouted. "You turned them in! That tracker—"

"He's hurt," her grandmother interrupted.

"He kind of smells, too," Rian added.

Naxos's face was bruised. A cut was swelling over his left eye. And Rian was right. He stank like old seaweed. Was she supposed to feel bad for him, though? He'd betrayed them. Plus, that cut could have been from anything. He could've been celebrating after turning them in. Dancing like Lewis. He could've slipped and fallen. She aimed his own blaster at him.

Her grandmother pointed the cane at her. "Kaya! Put that down!"

"He's dangerous."

"I don't care," she said. "You do not point weapons at people!"

Kaya set the blaster on the table as Naxos stepped inside. "He's the Eraser," Kaya said. "The border guard I told you about." Then, facing Naxos, she continued, "You said you implanted that tracking device so you could find us. But you told the Erasers. They took the professor in Edgeland, and now they've taken Lewis and Hanna!"

"They're gone?" Naxos asked.

"They're gone," Rian confirmed. Then he held up his finger. "So, wait . . . are you really an Eraser? And why do you smell like garbage?"

Naxos pointed his thumb over his shoulder. "I snuck in through your garbage chute. As for your first question . . . am I an Eraser?" Naxos bit his lower lip. "Well, I mean, not in terms of what I believe, but technically? Yes. I suppose so. Still, Kaya, you have to trust me—I didn't tell them anything! They had listening devices all around my lab. They knew all my codes.

I didn't tell them about the tracker. They found out by themselves. That must be how they chased down the professor in Edgeland. Ah, that reminds me . . ."

He pulled a small device out of his pocket and set it on the floor in the center of the room. Then he whistled. A low, horribly annoying buzz played through the speakers around the apartment.

"Cool," Rian said.

"What is that?" Kaya asked.

"Sonic interference," Rian replied. "Jams any listening devices in the area."

"Now we can speak freely," Naxos said.

A thin stream of blood trickled out of the cut above his eye. Fine. He was hurt. And it probably wasn't from celebrating. Kaya tossed him a towel. "Right," she said, her voice flat, "so how did they find us if the tracker didn't lead them here?"

Naxos pressed the balled-up cloth to his cut and looked at Rian, then Kaya. "They must have heard the message you sent your friend from Edgeland," Naxos explained. "The Erasers listen to everything. That's how I found you. I was able to intercept the message."

Kaya thought about this for a moment. Sure, she'd heard this was possible. Supposedly, the government could listen to every message drifting around Atlantis if they wanted. But had she really given up any important information? "I didn't say where I lived."

Rian was at the window, looking out over the city. He turned and winced as he looked at Kaya. "Yeah, but each earpiece has its own signature. So, with access to the communications system, they probably could've used the signatures to figure out our names, and if they knew our names—"

"Then they knew where we live," Kaya finished.

"Precisely," Naxos answered.

Kaya felt as if a powerful force were pulling her down, as if the strength of gravity had doubled. She held on to the back of the couch.

This meant Naxos wasn't to blame.

She hadn't protected her friends from the surface.

"This is all my fault. I led them here."

Kaya had doomed them.

"There's still hope," Naxos said. "We can save them."

We? Kaya glanced at the Atlantean Eraser, her undersized best friend, and her exhausted grandmother. Not exactly the ideal rescue squad.

"Don't look at me, love," her grandmother said. "I'm too old for adventures."

Kaya turned back to Rian and Naxos. Her friend was bringing Naxos a glass of water.

"Why should we trust you?" Rian asked. "You're one of them."

As Rian moved back to one side of the window, looking out, Naxos shuffled painfully across the room and sat on the edge of the pool. He breathed deep. Then he looked up at them. "Yes, but I didn't join them to . . . well . . . erase anyone. I just wanted to build." He turned to Kaya's grandmother. "I'm an engineer and inventor. I joined when I was just out of school. I grew up poor." He waved his hand around the room. "Not like this. But I dreamed of building beautiful vehicles. The Erasers offered me the resources to turn my dreams into reality."

"Like the ship in your lab?" Kaya asked.

"A minor plaything," he said. "My crowning achievement is a new kind of transport, a beautiful vehicle that's as comfortable in the deep ocean as it will be in the sky. My hope was that it would be used for exploration, to see the surface, but then I learned it was going to be transformed into a warship. I refused to work on it anymore and asked to be transferred. I'll admit this wasn't a powerful protest. The design was done. They could already build all the ships they wanted without my help. So they agreed to my request and sent me to the border. I was hoping to spend the rest of my career in peace. Then a few People of the Sun appeared on my scanner, invaders—an accidental invasion, as I've since learned—and some wildly adventurous girl . . . and everything changed."

A fairly convincing story. Sure. But if he expected Kaya to feel sorry for him, well, that just wasn't going to happen. The man was a coward. A liar. Kaya flopped down in a chair at the table. She glanced at her grandmother, who was stone-faced as she stared at Naxos, then Rian.

"Why are you even helping us?" Rian asked.

The inventor's head jerked back slightly, as if the answer were obvious. "Because the People of the Sun are real!" He sprang to his feet, then winced slightly. He looked at each of them in turn. "In my childhood, I heard the stories. When I joined the Erasers, they confirmed that the rumors were true, but we were told the surface people were murderous barbarians determined to destroy Atlantis. Then your three friends appeared, and . . . well, they did not seem like barbarians." He moved to the window and stared out at the city. "They should not be imprisoned." He shrugged. "I'm helping you because it's the right thing to do. We need to free them."

"And how are we supposed to do that?" Kaya asked.

Naxos sipped his water. "The professor is being held near the Erasers' headquarters," he started. His voice had new energy to it now, new life. "The tracking device is still active—or at least it was sending out signals until recently. The two kids . . . I don't know. But I imagine they'll be taken to the same place."

Rian asked, "So what do we do?"

Naxos reached into one of his pockets. A half dozen writing instruments fell out. He grabbed one off the floor, then leaned over the table. "Would you mind?"

"Go ahead," Kaya's grandmother said. "Kaya used to draw all over that when she was young." She joined them, leaning on her cane as Naxos sketched out a rough map of northern Atlantis. He actually wasn't a bad artist; Kaya was impressed. "The headquarters of the Erasers lies far from Ridge City, in the Stone Barrens, along the western edge of Atlantis."

"The Stone Barrens are abandoned," Rian noted.

He was right; they'd learned about the area in school. All you'd find up there were the scattered remains of cities that had collapsed hundreds of years before. Maybe a few waterways and vacuum tunnels for people venturing to and from the far north, up near the Rift. But that was it. "There aren't even any buildings there," Kaya added.

"Not on any official map," Naxos said. "But I can assure you that it's far from abandoned." He started adding details, marking out what looked like tunnels, and a series of buildings along the ridge.

"What's that?" Kaya asked, pointing to one of the larger structures he'd outlined.

"The headquarters," he explained. "I tracked the professor to this area here"—he pointed to a spot just south of the headquarters—"and I imagine the others will be taken there as well."

Rian joined them around the table. "You're sure of that?" he asked.

"Well, no, but—"

"Go on," Kaya's grandmother interjected. She tapped the map with the tip of her cane. "Once you find them, then what?"

"We'll travel through the tunnels and take the shuttle across the seafloor"—he traced a line away from the edge of Atlantis, then pointed to a circle—"to this factory. There should be hundreds of ships inside. Maybe more. My understanding is that their factory machines have been building constantly, using my design, ever since I was stationed in Edgeland. We'll take one of the ships and speed our friends to the surface."

Proudly, he stood back, allowing them a closer look at his sketch.

"This sounds rather dangerous," Kaya's grandmother noted.

"Not too certain to work, either," Rian added.

"But we have to do it," Kaya declared. "Right?"

"The People of the Sun will never be safe here in Atlantis," Naxos replied. "Not as long as the Erasers exist. We need to help them get home."

Her grandmother tapped her cane on the floor. "You keep saying *we*. Does this mean you want these two to steal one of the vehicles with you?"

Naxos paused, then swallowed. "Yes?"

Kaya began, "Grandmother, I—"

A cough from the other side of the room. Rian was standing to one side of the window, looking down. "I'm not going," he said.

"What? Why not?"

He pointed to the street. "Don't look now, but two people have been hanging around in front of the building across the street, watching your wall the whole time we've been here."

"Erasers," Naxos guessed. "Naturally they'd station a few people here to make sure you don't leave, Kaya."

"How do we ditch them?" she asked.

"I'll lead them away," Rian said. "I've got an idea. Then you two can go."

Kaya glanced at her grandmother. Did she need her permission? "I know what you're going to say—"

"Do you?" her grandmother replied. "Young people always think they know everything, and I imagine you expect I'll try to stop you. But it is quite clear to me that you would find a way to join this misguided inventor on his misguided mission whether I gave you my permission or not."

What was she supposed to say? Kaya shrugged. "Sorry?"

"No, you're not," her grandmother said with a laugh. "Of course you're going. You must go."

Excited, Kaya added, "I'll be safe."

"Good," her grandmother said. "And one more thing."

"Yes?"

"Make me—and your mother—proud."

Kaya rushed to hug her, and held the embrace longer than she'd planned. Her grandmother pushed her away, wiping at her eyes with the backs of her hands.

The mention of her mother reminded Kaya of her father. Was he really going to approve of this plan? Not a chance. She tapped her earpiece, checking her messages again. Nothing. "What about my dad?" she asked. "What will you tell him when he gets home?"

Her grandmother clasped the top of her cane with both hands. "That's where we have a problem, Kaya."

A problem? What problem? Her grandmother wasn't even looking at her. "What do you mean?" Kaya asked. "Did something happen to him? Where is he?"

"A more appropriate question would be, 'Who is he?'"

"I don't understand."

"Well, Kaya, I'm not sure exactly how to tell you this, so I will simply tell you directly. Your father, my son-in-law, is a member of the Erasers."

14

THE NATURE OF WAR

WHAT was wrong with these Atlanteans? First of all, they'd called him a monster, and Lewis wasn't even close to being monstrous. If he was going to be a beast, he'd want to be at least nine feet tall. He'd want snake hair, too, like that woman in the myth. Spit that could melt through metal. Razor-sharp claws. Maybe a third eye in the middle of his forehead for seeing in the dark. Oh, and webbed hands and feet, too, since they were in Atlantis.

Actually, forget the extra eye. Forget all of it! He wasn't monstrous at all. He was skinny. Clumsy. Freckled. He'd been in five fights in his life and lost them all. And Hanna? She wasn't a monster, either. He'd never admit this to anyone, especially not her, but she was sort of pretty.

The Erasers were the monsters. After dragging them out of Kaya's home, they'd thrown them into the back of some weird floating van. Then they'd driven—or floated, or drifted, he wasn't even sure anymore—for hours without stopping one single time to grab food or water. The trip did give them a chance to see more of Atlantis, or at least Ridge City. Down below them in the crowded streets, he saw kids his age playing some kind of ball game, laughing and joking like him and his friends. What would they do if they knew there was a whole world up on the surface?

When they arrived at their destination, Lewis and Hanna were dragged out of the cruiser and locked in a windowless room. Weed Chin and Mrs. Finkleman finally did bring them something to eat and drink, but the water was warm and minerally, and the bowl of mush looked like oatmeal but tasted kind of like celery. Not a good combo.

Mrs. Finkleman watched them with curiosity. She squinted at Lewis. "They don't look like invaders," she noted to Weed Chin.

"Because we're not!" Lewis replied. "We're more like tourists. And you're not being very good hosts."

Hanna held up her bowl. "This is vile," she protested. "Why are you even locking us in here?"

Finkleman didn't answer.

"It's for your own good," Weed Chin replied.

People only told you that when the opposite was true. Like when Mrs. Reilly gave Lewis a terrible grade at the end of the year because he'd forgotten to study for his math final and flunked. She said it was for his own good, but his mom and Roberts were furious with him, and decided not to get him a new wristpad as an end-of-the-year present. He had no choice but to give the thank-you gift card meant for Mrs. Reilly to Jeff, the school custodian. Everybody lost! Except Jeff.

"When are we getting out of here?" Lewis asked.

Neither of them answered.

Lewis pointed at Weed Chin. "What's that stuff growing from your face?"

The man fingered the greenish hairs. His voice softened. "It's my beard."

"It looks like seaweed," Lewis said.

"No it doesn't."

In the doorway, Finkleman shrugged. "It does a little."

"Why does that even matter?" Weed Chin asked.

"I figured maybe you Atlanteans had developed some way to grow seaweed from your chins," Lewis suggested. "Then you could snip some off whenever you got hungry."

"Wouldn't that be self-cannibalism or something?" Hanna asked.

Weed Chin stomped his foot. "QUIET! Or I will dial up this weapon and send you both into a world of complete and total pain."

"Okay. Sorry."

The man covered his chin. "You're still looking at it."

"It's just really—"

Weed Chin leaned forward menacingly, looking very ready and willing to fire. Lewis stopped talking. Mrs. Finkleman backed out of the room, still studying them, and Weed Chin slammed the door behind him as they left. Only a few minutes later, it opened again, and a different man stood in the doorway.

The lights in their room brightened as the man whistled, and he stepped inside. His hair was short, and there wasn't much of it, either. He was skinnier than the other Atlanteans, and his chin jutted out sharply. His lips were almost purple, and he held his hands behind his back. "Welcome," he said.

"Are we really welcome?" Hanna asked.

"Where's my dad?" Lewis asked.

The man moved slowly; Lewis realized he was old. The skin around his high cheekbones sagged slightly. He sat across from them on a thin chair. "Your father is fine," he said. "No harm has come to him."

Hanna sighed, and Lewis felt a wave of relief pass through him. He didn't feel better for long, though. The man's gaze was creepy. He was watching them like they were zoo animals. Or patients—Lewis felt like he was getting a physical exam at the doctor's office. The guy wasn't sticking an otoscope in his ear, exactly, but his huge eyes squinted, then widened as if he were recording everything about them in his memory. Was this what Kaya had felt like when his own dad checked her neck for gills? He didn't like it. Not at all.

"What do you want?" Hanna asked.

"What is important is what you invaders want and why you're here."

"Why does everyone keep calling us invaders?" Hanna asked. "We're explorers! We're scientists and engineers and . . . well, and Lewis."

"Lies," the old man said. "What do you want?"

"Well," Lewis said, "I want to see my dad. And I want to go home. Soon, if possible. I'd also like some clothes that don't smell like feet. Maybe a little seltzer, too. My stomach feels weird."

"Seltzer?"

"Water with bubbles," Lewis explained.

"No, we don't have that," the man replied, "and I think you misunderstood my question. I would like to know why you're here in Atlantis."

"To learn," Hanna said. "We want to know about your history, your society, your technology. I mean, how did you figure out how to control gravity?"

Lewis pointed at the door. "Also, are you sure that's not edible seaweed growing out of that guy's chin?"

The old man ignored him and pointed to Hanna. "I admire your curiosity."

"Who are you?" she asked.

"My name is Demos, and I represent a very powerful group."

"Yeah, we know," Hanna said. "The Erasers."

"Slang. I detest that name. I am a member of the High Council of Atlantis. The ones you call the Erasers are, I suppose, our agents. You see, our world is fragile. Cities collapse with little notice. Down here under the ocean, clean air, water, and food are all very difficult to provide." He breathed deeply. "Even the presence of this wondrous oxygen we're breathing is a fantastic technological feat. It takes work to keep Atlantis stable and peaceful. So when troublesome individuals or groups arise in our society, the High Council deploys its agents."

"And erases them?" Hanna replied.

Demos waved his hand in the air dismissively. "Don't be dramatic. We're not murderers. Not like you Sun People. Our solutions are far more civilized." The man stood and moved closer to Lewis, then reached out and grabbed his forearms, checking each of his wrists. His hands were cold, and he smelled like mushrooms. Lewis wrinkled his nose.

Demos backed away. "Are you smelling me?" he asked.

"No, I was listening. We listen through our noses on the surface."

"We drink through our ears, too," Hanna added.

"You're lying."

"Why were you checking my wrists?"

Demos inspected Hanna's forearm. "I was looking for a device your friend Gogol mentioned when we spoke with him. Something your father had on his wrist. But the Sun Person didn't have it with him. Still, I'll admit, your technology is intriguing." He motioned to Hanna. "I'm impressed you were able to fix the gravity drive in that old cruiser, too, and your submarine has already provided us with a wealth of knowledge. I imagine we'll be studying it for years."

"You better not mess it up," Hanna said.

Demos didn't respond; he was staring at Lewis's nose. Lewis really, really hoped the guy believed the listening thing. "So where is my dad?"

"You'll see him shortly," Demos answered.

Hanna scratched her chin. "So, the professor probably asked you this already—"

"He asks a lot of questions," Demos replied.

Lewis smiled. The man was clearly annoyed. That confirmed his dad was okay.

"Right, but I'm burning to know," Hanna continued, "do you generate the waves? Atlantis, I mean."

Demos shrugged. "Yes. Of course we do. Most people here

in Atlantis have no idea, though. Personally, I'm not fond of the approach."

"Because your waves kill people?" Hanna said.

"No, because the waves are ineffective," he said. "You continue to poison and pollute the oceans no matter how frequently we pound your coasts."

"So you don't even care that people have died?" Lewis asked.

"Those waves ruined homes, towns, entire cities!" Hanna added.

Demos waved his hand again. "We're doing it to protect the hundred million people here in Atlantis. Leaders must make difficult choices. This is the nature of war."

"War?" Lewis asked. "Who's at war?"

"Our two worlds, of course."

"But that's crazy," Hanna answered. "No one on the surface even knows Atlantis exists!"

"Of course they do. It appears the secret is well kept."

Wait. What?

This was huge news.

Enormous.

"Really?" Lewis asked. "Who knows? The government? The military? Circus clowns?" Lewis had a theory about them: The reason they danced around acting goofy and silly all the time was that they were secretly spies. The greatest clowns in history were all Russian. Coincidence? Nope. And the clowns probably knew all about Atlantis, too.

"I can assure you that powerful forces on the surface are very well aware of our existence," Demos said. "They've failed to locate us so far, but your underwater probes constantly scour the oceans in search of Atlantis. Thankfully, while some of your technology is far beyond ours, your tools for exploring the seas are primitive. We can dispense with those robotic submarines of yours easily. We're lucky none of your warmakers are as resourceful as your father, boy. There would be no Atlantis if they were."

"I'm the one who designed the sub," Hanna noted. "Funded it, too."

Lewis was stuck on the man's last point. No Atlantis? What was he talking about? "I don't understand," he said. "What do you mean?"

"The moment your leaders find Atlantis, we're doomed."

What? Lewis thought of the kids in his grade. His little brother. Even Roberts. Everyone would be thrilled. They'd probably put together real, actual parades. Huge ones, with marching bands and colorful paper tossed out of windows and good, hot food spread out on giant buffet tables, not cold fish wraps. Maybe they'd play music, too. Everyone could dance in the streets. Or on the beach, if that made the Atlanteans more comfortable. "People would be amazed!"

Demos laughed coldly. "Amazed? Have you studied the history of your civilization, child? When new lands and peoples are discovered, they are conquered, slaughtered, and destroyed."

Christopher Columbus, the conquistadors, the Pilgrims, the settlers of the Old West, even his namesake . . . not exactly a string of saints. Okay, maybe the Atlantean had a point.

But that was a long time ago!

"How do you even know our history?" Hanna asked.

"We're very good listeners," Demos replied with a smirk. He

tapped his earpiece. "As you've learned, our audio technology is very advanced. We have probes on the surface and microphones and recording devices placed throughout your world."

"We? You mean Atlantis?" asked Lewis.

"The Erasers," Hanna snapped.

"The High Council," Demos said, correcting her. "Our goal is to ensure that Atlantis survives and flourishes, and for that to happen, we must do the work that others are too timid or cowardly to do themselves. You Sun People are poisoning the oceans with your plastics and chemicals. Soon, the oceans will be so ruined that we won't be able to feed ourselves. Atlantis will die. The waves were our first attempt to urge you to leave the seas alone, a warning meant to push you back. But they have failed, and we fear the oceans may need decades to recover, so we have been forced to implement the next phase."

"The next phase?" Hanna asked.

"A more complete approach to securing the future of Atlantis and her people. You're the engineer, right?" he said to Hanna. "From a technology standpoint, I think you'd find it brilliant, Hanna. I'm incredibly proud of the work our team has done. Our original hope was simple: That you would leave us the sea, since you have the sky. But your factories and vehicles are destroying the oceans and the skies. For so long, we've told our people that the air above is poisoned. Now the lie is becoming truth."

"I'm sure there's another way," Hanna said. "We could have a truce, or . . ."

She let her words trail off as Demos began laughing. "A truce? There is no hope for peace now. We tried that once."

"What do you mean?" Lewis asked.

Demos didn't answer. "My point is that we in the High Council know the difficult truth. War is the only path to peace and security."

Now Lewis's brain hurt. The only way to peace was through war? That would be like settling an argument with a kid in his grade by punching him in the face. That was a terrible strategy! His hand would hurt. The kid would probably hit him back, harder. And they'd both get suspended.

"What are you going to do with us?" Hanna asked. "We're obviously not invaders." She motioned toward Lewis for emphasis. "I mean, look at him. Why can't you just let us go?"

"Because there is so much more we can learn from you," Demos said. He looked over his shoulder. An unfamiliar woman stood in the doorway. Her nose and eyebrows were thin, and her hair was short on the sides. She reminded Lewis of a school principal. A coldhearted, evil school principal who slept in a coffin under her desk.

"Everything is ready for them," she said.

With Weed Chin and Mrs. Finkleman walking a few steps behind, Demos led them down a series of hallways, past closed doors and the occasional startled Atlantean, until they entered a room the size of the small auditorium at Lewis's school. Long desks were lined with speakers, knobs, dials, and those strange tablets. The surface of each one moved constantly. A woman standing at one of the workstations glanced up when they arrived. Her already large eyes widened. Then she looked away, refocusing on her work.

The vampire principal activated some kind of speaker.

A strange, low tune played, and the whole room vibrated.

The wall across from the door began to change and shift, the stones rearranging themselves until they revealed an enormous metal hatch. Two semicircles opened like eyelids, unveiling a large glass window that looked out over a vast undersea pool. Lewis moved forward. No one stopped him. The water was dark and stretched on forever. "Is that the ocean?" he asked.

"No, an enclosed pool," Demos answered, "but a large one."

Hanna stood at his side. She pointed. Dots of blue-white light moved past the window from right to left, coasting through the darkness like slow shooting stars. The water was moving like an enormous, swollen underground river. Lewis felt cold. The darkness reminded him of the ocean before that tsunami had struck. One of the lights was closer, and larger. "What are those things?" he asked.

"You'll see," Demos said.

The water to his right brightened and glowed as something swept into view with the current. Something the shape of their own submarine but smaller, and made of clear glass. Inside, the space was divided into three floors. There were tables and chairs. A couch. Even a bed. Vines were growing up the back wall. "That looks like a little house," Lewis said.

"Something like that," Demos replied. "Our residents are criminals, revolutionaries, and disruptors of the peace. We remove all of the most unfavorable elements from society."

"So what is this place? Some kind of underwater jail?" Hanna asked.

"A highly civilized and inescapable prison," the vampire principal replied. "Each of the spheres has everything one needs to lead a long and healthy life. I would venture to say that many of our guests are healthier now than when they arrived."

"But they're in prison," Hanna noted.

"Where . . ." Lewis struggled to speak. His voice was low and weak. "Where's my dad?"

A glass cell drifted closer, then attached itself to the wall with a heavy thunk. The viewing window slid into the stone and a circular glass hatch swung open. Warm air rushed out of the cell, as if it were exhaling a long-held breath. Lewis felt the air sweep past the tiny hairs on his face. He shivered, despite the warmth. His father was standing inside the cell, looking out, and any joy or relief Lewis might have felt upon finding him disappeared immediately. His father turned ghostly pale. The principal raised a weapon, on the off chance he was considering rushing out.

"What are they doing here?" his dad asked Demos.

"Why is the professor in there?" Hanna pressed. "What are you doing to him?"

"I assure you, he's quite comfortable," Demos said. "But there is no hope of escape. The water is only a notch above freezing, and it is laced with toxins. Even if he were stupid enough to try to swim to safety, he'd die within minutes from the cold and the poison."

Hanna gulped. "That's . . . evil."

"It's necessary."

If he was trying to scare them, it was working. Lewis shivered again. "Why are you telling us all this?" he asked.

Demos walked to the hatch and pointed inside. "My apologies. I thought that was obvious. I'm telling you this because this cell is going to be your new home. This is where the three of you will spend the rest of your lives."

15
AN ELABORATE SCHEME

A WHIRLPOOL of thoughts and questions and emotions roiled in Kaya's brain. Her father was an Eraser? Impossible! Ridiculous. Absurd, even. She wouldn't have considered the idea if someone else had suggested it. She would have laughed. But this had come from her grandmother. She'd even sworn to Kaya that it was true. Still, it didn't make sense. Sure, her father went away for long stretches of time. He was absolutely devoted to Atlantis and its people. But she thought he was just an engineer. How could her gentle, loving dad be part of such a brutal, heartless group? And why would he lie to his own daughter? The idea was preposterous.

Right?

A question popped into her head. One that it hurt to even ask. And one she definitely didn't expect her grandmother to answer. "What would my mom have thought?"

Her mother was the one who had introduced Kaya to Elida's stories of the surface.

Her mother had believed in the People of the Sun.

She had thought the stories were true.

"Kaya, dear," her grandmother replied, "she was the reason your father joined the Erasers."

This one really mangled her mind.

She couldn't even respond.

Rian was the one who asked her grandmother to explain. "What do you mean?" he pressed.

Her grandmother pointed to the device Naxos had set on the floor. "That is still working, yes?" she asked. "We can speak freely?" He nodded. "Very well. So, Kaya, your mother was chosen for a mission to the surface—"

Kaya interrupted her. "Excuse me," she said. "What?"

Her grandmother turned to Naxos. "My daughter, Kaya's mother, was something of a bright light in the political world, you see." She faced Kaya again. "She was no great force at the time, but she had a wonderful career ahead of her. There were some who thought she might one day be the leader of the High Council. Anyway, she was part of a small group of prominent Atlanteans—politicians, scientists, and storytellers—chosen for a mission to the surface. Their goal was to attempt to meet the leaders of the People of the Sun."

"So she did know they were real," Kaya said, as much to herself as to anyone else.

"She did, yes," her grandmother answered. "But I'm not sure she ever had the chance to see them for herself." Her tone darkened. "We were never told the exact details, but evidence suggests their ship was destroyed before they made it to land. Some believed there had been an accident. Others—your father included—believed it was intentional. They thought the People of the Sun had struck out against us, and they took this as a declaration of war."

Both Rian and Kaya barraged her with questions. Unfortunately, this was all her grandmother knew, and Naxos had little to add. He was merely an inventor, he insisted. But Kaya was already overwhelmed anyway. The story of her mother's disappearance, the truth about her dad, Naxos and Rian and her grandmother all watching her as she tried to make sense of this information—it was too much. She rushed out of the kitchen and into her room. The Narwhals flag was hanging over her bed; she tore it down and tossed it into the corner. Now more than ever, she needed to talk to her father. Not through her earpiece, either. Face-to-face.

She was circling her room when Rian whistled at the door, then leaned inside. "Look, I'm sorry and all, but . . ."

"But what?" she asked.

"Your friends need you," he said, his tone urgent. "Hanna, Lewis, and the professor you were telling us about. I know this is a lot to handle. That stuff about your dad, your mom . . . I can't even imagine. But those Sun People—they need you, Kaya. This Naxos guy"—lowering his voice, he pointed his thumb toward the living room—"he clearly can't do this alone. He'll probably end up in another garbage chute. He needs your help, too. So pick yourself up, snap your heart back together or whatever, and get out of here."

She was about to argue, more due to reflex than reason. He was right, though. Convincing, too. She smiled crookedly.

"What?" he asked.

"That was pretty good," Kaya replied.

"What was?"

"Your speech. Did you practice?"

He shrugged. "Totally. I always knew you'd have to over-come personal heartache to rescue a bunch of accidental invaders from the clutches of a secretive police force. I've been planning that for years."

She paused. "Right, but how do you snap a heart—"

"Oh, quiet down and pack your gear. Leave your gravity suit, though."

"Really?"

"I'm going to need to borrow it."

"Rian, this isn't the—"

He cut her off. "I'm serious this time, Kaya. There are two Erasers outside, remember? Someone needs to draw them away so you and Naxos can sneak out in the cruiser. They're watching the garage. They're watching you. So I figure I'll strap on your gravity gear and use your balcony trick."

She stopped herself from replying. Thought for a moment. His plan might actually work. "Are you sure this isn't just some elaborate scheme to finally borrow my favorite possession?"

"That's exactly right," he said. "I'm risking my life to test-drive your toys."

He was joking, of course. But he really was about to risk his life. Or his safety, anyway. He was planning to trick a pair of Erasers. And he was doing it for her.

They turned quiet. She didn't know what to say.

Thankfully, Naxos hurried into the room. "Approved?" he asked Rian.

"Approved," Rian replied.

After an awkward half hug, half handshake with Rian, she grabbed a change of clothes, packed some more food, and stuffed it all into her backpack with some of Hanna's scraps. Rian emerged from her room buckled into her gravity gear . . . and wearing one of her jumpsuits, too.

"What are you—"

"Your grandmother's idea," he snapped. "Get over it. I'm not happy about it, either. But we need them to think it's you." He wrapped a scarf around his head as a finishing touch, to hide his shorter hair. Then he rolled his shoulders and jumped up and down a few times. "Surprisingly comfortable," he added with a shrug. "They should make these jumpsuits for boys, too. Naxos, are they still in position?"

Pressed against the wall, Kaya peered over Naxos's shoulder. The two Erasers remained in place. "Still in position," Naxos responded. "Whenever you're ready."

"Straight home, Rian. Understood?" her grandmother asked. "Straight to your parents, please."

"Well, I might tour the city a little first, or—"

"Straight home."

"Straight home," he repeated. "And Kaya?"

"Yes?"

"Good luck. Tell me all about it when you get back."

Her friend hurried into her room before she could reply. He wasted no time. The two Erasers stood against the wall across the street, to the right. Inside, Kaya, her grandmother, and Naxos watched as Rian leaped off the balcony and, with his back to the Erasers, soared straight past their window toward the city center. The Erasers panicked. They rushed for their cruiser and hurried inside, already too far behind.

Kaya's grandmother watched Rian drift into the distance. "That's not the way to his house, is it, dear?"

"No, definitely not," Kaya laughed.

The three of them hurried up the stairs to the garage. Her grandmother was slightly out of breath by the time they reached Gogol's dented cruiser. She shook her head at the sorry sight. "We'll have to do better than that," she said. She whistled, and a shining luxury transport drifted out of its parking spot.

"That's your new cruiser," Kaya noted. "Grandmother, I—"

"Take it," she said. "You have a long journey."

After Kaya climbed inside, her grandmother leaned over the door and stared deep into her eyes. She took Kaya's hands in hers. "My curious, impatient, adventurous girl. So much like your mother in so many ways. I knew these walls wouldn't confine you for long. Now go!"

16

THE PRISON BENEATH THE SEA

LEWIS definitely didn't want to spend the rest of his life in jail. Still, if he had to pick a cell, this one wasn't all bad. The view was interesting—all the water everywhere. On the third level, each of them had their own bed, and the mattresses were surprisingly comfortable. The bathroom, thankfully, was made of darkened glass, so he had a little privacy. The floors were dark, too, so you couldn't see through from one level to the next. Ladders connected each level of the cell, and there were hatches you could close over them for privacy. Well, and safety, too. Lewis nearly fell through one of the openings when he was first touring the place.

The center of the cell had the largest room, a living area with a table and chairs, a few couches, and a kitchen of some sort. He asked if they could order takeout, but no one thought that was funny. There was some exercise equipment, too, but the weights were meant for Atlanteans. Even his dad could barely budge them.

The lowest level had giant tanks for fish and kelp, plus

smaller ones growing different sea greens, and a whole bunch of machines and pumps for keeping the air clean and the water filtered. Lewis found some kind of washing machine, too, which was good, because his clothes were starting to smell like compost. Whole colonies of tiny creatures were probably growing in his armpits. Then again, if he waited long enough, maybe these little beasts would evolve and grow, and he'd have an armpit army under his command.

Eventually, if he trained himself to lift those heavy weights, maybe he could even lead these tiny warriors into battle against their jailers.

Now that was an escape plan.

Negatives? Sure, there were plenty. No soccer ball. No gaming setup. Some weird bathtub thing instead of a shower. No real food—fish and seaweed were going to get old fast. Oh, and then there was the fact that they were imprisoned in an inescapable underwater jail.

Yep. That was the real bug in the code.

He was trying to stay positive. Optimistic. Hopeful. But he felt like he'd been lowered into a thousand-foot-deep hole in the ground.

They had to escape.

Or call for help.

Or something.

Overall, his dad had been pretty weird since they'd reunited. Sure, he'd been happy at first. But then he'd changed. He'd become quiet. Not cold, exactly, and not the way he used to get when Lewis was looking for attention—a hug or even just a smile—and his dad's mind was clearly elsewhere, drifting in search of Atlantis. No, this was a different kind of distance. Sometimes he caught his dad smiling at him sadly. At other times, his father unexpectedly wrapped him in quick but very real hugs.

They'd been in the cell for half a day, maybe more, when Lewis went looking for him. He was hoping they could discuss an escape plan. His only knowledge of jailbreaks came from movies. Mostly, people dug tunnels. That wouldn't really work here.

His dad was on the third floor, sitting on the ground between the beds with his legs crossed, staring out into the water.

"What are you doing?" Lewis asked.

His father held up his hand. Was he meditating? His lips were moving slightly. Lewis waited. His father whispered a number into his wristpad. "Give me a few more minutes, son."

Research. He was doing more research.

All for the ridiculous Atlantis journals.

Lewis nearly exploded with frustration. Couldn't his dad just pause his curiosity for a few hours? Even a few minutes? They needed his help! They had to find a way out of this cell, not waste their time gathering data for some book his dad would never have a chance to publish. Lewis had risked his life to be with his dad. They'd found Atlantis. Together! But nothing had changed. They were trapped in the same jail cell, and he still felt like his dad lived on the moon.

Nothing was more important to his father than Atlantis.

Not even his son.

Lewis hurried down the ladder to the second floor.

He sat for a minute, letting his eyes dry, but he didn't want to be alone.

Hanna was on the lowest level, watching the two floor-to-ceiling tanks—one filled with kelp, the other with swimmers. Hundreds of fish swirled inside, kicking in a circle as if they were trapped inside a slow-motion blender. The miserable lives of those fish made Lewis feel slightly better about his situation. At least no one was going to eat him. Right?

"Hey, check this out," Hanna said, waving him over to the clear wall. She was crouching and pointing to something in the water outside of the cell.

Lewis pressed the side of his face against the cool glass. "What am I looking for?"

"Okay, so I've scoured this cell, right? Every square centimeter. Every hinge and bolt. None of the controls are on the inside. But the professor and I were talking . . . by the way, what is your dad doing?"

Lewis shrugged. "Meditating? Or counting. I don't know."

His dad lowered his huge head through the hatch. "Counting," he said. "Based on our estimated speed, and how long it takes this cell to complete one loop, this pool must be the size of a small city. There are probably hundreds of cells in here." His words trailed off into a mumble; the excitement faded from his voice. He started climbing down to join them.

"How do you still have that?" Lewis asked, pointing to the wristpad. "Didn't they search you? Demos was—"

His father shushed him, then pointed to the ceiling.

Right. They'd be listening. His father mimed taking off the wristpad and slipping it into his shoe. Then he removed the other shoe and winced. "When they frisked me, I took off the first shoe," he whispered, "and they kindly asked me not to remove the second. So, tell me—what were you two talking about before I interrupted?"

Hanna pushed up close to the glass again, pointing. "See that ring around the outside?" She showed Lewis, then hurried across the room and showed his father the same thing. "It's some kind of gigantic magnet circling the whole cell. But I can't figure out how they activate it."

"Sound," his dad answered.

Hanna jumped back. "Of course!"

"I don't understand," Lewis said.

"When they want to bring a cell back to the control room," Hanna explained, "they must play a particular sound."

"Each cell has its own combination of tones," his father added.

"When the cell picks up those sounds, this magnetic ring activates . . ."

She was guessing, Lewis realized, and waiting for his dad to finish the thought.

"As the cell in question circles our aquatic prison," his father explained, "it is pulled toward the control room."

Hanna held one hand upright, flat and still, then slowly brought the other one, balled into a fist, closer and closer, until it smacked into her palm. "The magnets connect, the cell is locked into place, and the doors open."

"Exactly."

Hanna was bouncing on her toes. "So if you could play the right tones . . ."

His dad's expression didn't change. He didn't share her excitement.

"What's the problem?" Lewis asked.

His dad knocked on the glass. Hanna's shoulders fell. "The walls are soundproof," she said. "So even if you could play the right tones, you'd have to get into the water to do it."

"And the water's cold enough to kill you," Lewis added.

"Poisoned with toxins, too."

The three of them were silent. The walls seemed to grow thicker, the light dimmer.

Then his dad clapped his hands together. "Don't worry. They'll come to their senses! They'll realize this is all a big mistake. They'll release us. Before long, they'll release us."

"What if they don't?" Lewis asked.

"They will. Not to worry."

"Okay, sure," Hanna said, "but what if—"

"Let's not think that way, Hanna."

"So you just expect us to sit here and hope?" Lewis asked.

His father smiled weakly and dropped one of his huge hands onto Lewis's shoulder. "I wouldn't discount hope. It is a powerful force."

His dad ended the conversation and climbed back to his perch on the third floor.

Hope? That was his solution?

For a while, Lewis stared out into the water. Other cells drifted past in the distance, above and below them. How long had those other prisoners been there? Years? Decades? He wondered if he would get old in the cell. Maybe he'd grow a really long white beard. No—he'd probably lose his hair. His teeth would fall out, too, because he'd miss all his trips to the dentist. He'd probably grow a wart or two. Maybe his back would end up all twisted and hunched, and his fingernails would get long and yellow. And he wouldn't just be ugly. He'd be broken. He'd never see his mom again. He'd never hear her whisper good night to him in bed. And his brother . . . his little brother would grow up without him. Alone. With better teeth and no warts. And no one to teach him things like the chicken dance.

Something clattered to the floor behind him.

Hanna had opened a panel below the fish tank. He watched her study the tangle of tubes and pipes. "What are you doing now?" he asked. "I wouldn't mess with that too much. It's kind of our food."

"I was trying to see if there's anything in here that could send a signal. So much of the technology in Atlantis is based on sound. It's like their tech took a completely different direction from ours. We went visual. Screens and light. But their audio stuff is just ridiculous. When we were back in the cruiser with Kaya, I was thinking that if I could put together a radio, then use one of those sonic weapon things as an amplifier, we could signal for help."

This was a good idea. A fantastic one.

Genius, really.

And yet she didn't look all that excited. "So what's wrong?"

"I don't have the radio equipment. It's all in the bag back at Kaya's house."

"No deadly trumpet, either," Lewis added.

"Yeah, and we're in a soundproof jail cell, anyway."

Okay, so maybe her plan wasn't pure genius.

Seated on the floor, she leaned back against the base of the tank and exhaled. "This wasn't supposed to happen."

"Jail? Yeah, I didn't—"

"No, Atlantis! This wasn't supposed to be real."

Her eyes were bloodshot and teary. Lewis didn't know what to say. So he sat beside her on the floor. She inched closer, and the two of them watched the water and the distant passing cells. She held his hand. Not in a weird way, though. Now she seemed more like the sister he'd never had. A frustratingly smart, occasionally annoying one, but a sister nonetheless.

At some point, Hanna moved upstairs, and Lewis found himself yawning. His father was still on the third floor, trapped in his trance. Or thinking about the next chapter in his Atlantis journals. Lewis was still too annoyed to talk to him, and since lying down in an actual bed felt like giving up, admitting that this was their new home, he dropped onto the other couch, across from a snoring Hanna. A massive yawn shook his whole tired body, and he was asleep within seconds.

In his dream, he was back home, outside his house. His brother was there. Roberts, too. And his mother. They were all looking for him, calling his name. He could see them and touch them, but they couldn't see or feel him. To them, he was invisible. There were goats in the dream, too, and they were wearing tuxedos, serving tiny hot dogs as appetizers.

Next he was at the edge of some dreamworld version of the cliff near his home, and the ocean wasn't miles away, as it was in reality. The sea was roiling right below him. A dark sea churning angrily with wild, whitecapped waves.

He awoke shivering.

The room was dark.

On the other couch, Hanna was on her side, drooling.

A feeling of dread spread through Lewis. The dreamworld hadn't faded yet. He thought of the goats in their tuxedos. At least they had been funny.

He stood and walked to the ladder. The glass hatch between the second and third floors had been removed from its hinges. A light on the third floor was still shining. He climbed up, but his father wasn't there. The dread from his dream wasn't all gone; it clung to his chest. Where was his dad?

He hurried back down. Hanna was snoring—a light, fluttering snore. His father wasn't on the second floor, either.

Lewis rushed down to the lowest level of the cell.

Still no sign.

"Hanna," he called out. "My dad. Where is he?"

She mumbled as he rushed back up. He grabbed her by the shoulders and shook her lightly. She sat upright. "Your dad? What do you mean?"

"He's gone."

"He can't be gone," Hanna said.

Then her eyes bulged. She raced for the entrance. Lewis followed. They'd first stepped into the cell this way; the entrance had connected to the Erasers' control room. But Lewis had paid little attention to it since then. There was an inner door, a small, enclosed entryway, almost like a mudroom in a normal house, and then another door in the outer wall of the giant cell. His dad was inside the entryway. Pumps churned below them, and water was filling the space. His father stood with his back to them, staring out into the huge pool.

The water was already up to his waist.

Hanna was pounding on the glass. "Professor!"

"What's he doing?" Lewis asked. He was too frightened to think.

"Professor! Stop!"

"What's happening? Hanna?"

"He's trying to get outside the cell, into the water."

"W-why?" Lewis stammered, barely able to get the word out.

The water was rising faster.

Hanna was shouting now, slamming her fists against the inner door. "Professor! Professor!"

Could he even hear them?

As the water reached his shoulders, his dad turned, smiled, and raised both of his thumbs.

Everything was okay? Was that what he was saying? No. No, no, no.

Everything was absolutely not okay.

His dad turned again, then leaned back, so they could see the top of his head, and sucked in a huge breath. The water rose faster now, climbing over his head and up to the ceiling. Then the outer door opened, and his dad pressed his hands and feet against the interior walls. He braced himself there, like someone scaling the walls of a narrow alley.

"What is he doing?" Lewis asked. "I don't understand what he's doing."

"I don't know," Hanna admitted. "Wait," she continued. "Look!"

His dad held himself in place with his legs and one arm, then reached into his pocket and pulled out his wristpad. Lewis yelled his father's name over and over. His calls bounced back off the soundproof walls. His father held out the wristpad. "Is he recording something?" Lewis asked.

"Or playing something," Hanna said.

The entire cell started moving differently, as if pulled by some outside force.

The pumps began churning again. The outer door slid closed, and then the water began to drain out of the entryway. His dad was trying to get back inside. But what was he doing out there in the first place? Had he risked his life to collect more data?

Lewis pounded his fists against the door. Hanna grabbed him, holding his wrists, pulling him away. They fell to the floor in front of the entryway as the door opened. The last of the water spilled out, and his father collapsed forward. Lewis crawled to him. His father was icy cold and soaked. His skin was gray and white. He mumbled something about the hatch.

"What?" Lewis asked. "What about the hatch?"

"A shield," he said. "When the door opens, they'll come for you. Use it as a shield."

"Who's coming for us, Dad? What are you talking about?" Lewis turned to Hanna. "What does he mean?"

The wristpad was playing the same notes over and over.

"I know that tune," Hanna said.

His father closed his eyes and gently sealed his lips, breathing only through his nose.

Hanna sat back with her hands clasped behind her head, thinking.

"What was he doing?" Lewis said. "Why did he do that?"

She still didn't answer. She squinted at the wristpad. "That song . . ."

The same simple tune continued to play.

His father was breathing, but he was barely moving.

Hanna raced to the couches, pulled off two blankets, and tossed them to Lewis. "I've got it! That was brilliant, Professor."

Lewis started wrapping his dad in the blankets. What was so brilliant about swimming in toxic, frigid water? "I don't understand."

"He records everything, right?"

"Right."

"So he must have recorded what happened when he was in the control room on his wristpad. They played that tune when we were there, too. It must control this cell. The wristpad is waterproof, and the speaker's powerful. Not powerful enough to carry through these walls, though. So he played it outside, in the water. He tricked the cell into thinking it was being called back!"

Lewis looked at his dad. His eyes were still closed.

So that's what his father had been thinking about.

He wasn't doing research. When Lewis had thought he was collecting more of his stupid data, his dad was plotting a way to save them.

He held his hand to his dad's face. His skin was frigid. Hanna helped Lewis strip off his dad's soaking-wet shirt. She rushed upstairs and pulled all the blankets and sheets off the beds, then tossed them down through the hatch. Lewis draped them over his dad; he needed Hanna's help to roll him onto his side. The weight of him was tremendous, especially since he was limp. Dead weight, Lewis thought.

No—his dad was alive. And he was going to stay that way.

"What did he say about the hatch?" Hanna asked.

"Something about using it as a shield," he said. "When the door opens."

Hanna pointed through the glass as the cell moved closer to the outer wall of their watery prison. The window of the control room came into view. She looked down at his dad. "That might be the craziest idea you've ever had, Professor Gates," she said. "But it's actually working."

≋ 17 ≋
A DIFFERENT KIND OF LOSS

KAYA AND NAXOS had been traveling for what felt like forever when the cruiser finally lifted out of the water and turned into a dry tunnel. They could've moved so, so much faster, but Naxos insisted on saving the power. She had tried to remind him that this was a newer model of cruiser. The power practically lasted forever. Had he listened? No.

Now he leaned forward, concentrating. For the first part of their journey, he'd rambled on and on about his marvelous vehicles and his plan to help the People of the Sun escape. But she was only half listening. She couldn't stop thinking about her parents. Had the Sun People really destroyed her mother's ship? And was her dad really an Eraser?

Naxos brightened the cruiser's lights.

"Are you sure this is the right way?" Kaya asked.

"Ah, she's alive! Those are the first words you've spoken in some time."

"I've been thinking," she said.

"Well, this is the right way, I can assure you. The last signal the Sun Man's tracker sent out was from right here. We're very close to the headquarters of the Erasers."

The tunnel ended in an empty cavern. Three small cruisers rested on the floor. Two guards sitting on either side of a single steel door leaped to their feet. The smaller of the two rubbed his eyes with his fists and sneered as they approached. Both of them raised sonic rifles.

"Stay calm," Naxos whispered to Kaya.

"They're holding blasters," she pointed out. "I'm getting mine—"

"No," he insisted. "We won't need weapons."

He hunched over and limped as they walked from the cruiser. "Greetings, friends," he grumbled in a weak voice.

The guards lowered their weapons. The sneers disappeared. "This is a private tunnel," the smaller guard said. "Turn yourselves around and head back."

"But we're a bit lost, you see, and I—"

The guard raised his hand to his earpiece. "Quiet," he barked. Someone was calling him. He leaned his head to the side as he replied. "What's that? What's wrong?"

Both guards crumpled to the floor.

Naxos lowered his sonic pistol.

"I thought you said we wouldn't need weapons," Kaya said.

"The situation has changed."

She grabbed the backpack stuffed with Hanna's cords and cables and gadgets. Naxos hurried over and pressed his ear to the door, then gestured for her to do the same. The metal was cool against her cheek. She cupped her hand over her other ear. She heard alarms. Shouting. "What's happening?" she asked.

"I don't know."

Naxos reached down and grabbed a small square device attached to one of the guards' belts. He clicked a button in the center, and a tune played. The door swung open, and Kaya's ears rang from the sound of the alarm.

Inside, lights flashed in a long hallway, but she saw no other guards.

The place was almost empty.

Then she heard voices. "This way," she said.

Naxos and Kaya raced around a corner and into a large room. Two women were standing at their desks, frantically working on their pads. One of them swung a weapon in Kaya's direction. "Who are you?" she demanded.

"Look!" the other called out.

The stones in the far wall were shifting and moving. A sealed metal hatch was hidden behind them. The alarm continued to wail, and Kaya watched as the hatch opened. She was looking into some kind of glass-walled room. No—there were several rooms, and an enormous pool of water behind them. There were people inside, too.

Not just any people.

Sun People.

Or Lewis and Hanna, at least. But where was the professor?

The two women rushed across the room, weapons raised, as the door popped open.

Kaya yelled to her friends as they hurried through the opening, crouching behind some kind of circular glass shield.

Naxos tackled Kaya to the ground, then pulled her behind a desk.

The first woman fired as the other called out for her to stop.

A pulse rushed through Kaya, a vibration that rang in her bones. She was shaken but awake. Naxos, too. He shifted his jaw from side to side as if he'd been punched in the chin. She heard bodies drop heavily to the floor.

"Help! Please!"

That voice—Lewis.

Off-balance, her ears ringing, Kaya stood. The Atlantean women were down, but the Sun People were still standing. The shield must have deflected the blast and sent it right back at the women. But where was the professor?

Kaya and Naxos sprinted across the room as Hanna tossed aside the glass shield. Finally, Kaya spotted the enormous man; Hanna and Lewis were struggling to drag the professor out of the cell. He was lying on his back, looking like some huge, exhausted fish reeled out of the deep. His thick hair was sopping wet. The blankets wrapped around him were soaked, and his skin was blue.

Naxos stood before the cell, staring into the water beyond. "I've heard of this place. This is the High Council's secret prison. No one has ever escaped."

"Yeah, well, we're trying to change that," Hanna snapped.

"What happened to him?" Kaya asked.

Lewis was holding one of his father's large hands. "He swam out of the cell to save us."

Naxos paled. "I've been told that the water is filled with toxins. It's impossible to swim out of one of these cells and—"

"That's enough," Hanna said, cutting him off. "Are you going to help or not?"

Survive, Kaya guessed. That was the word he was going to use. No one had ever swum out of a cell and survived.

At Hanna's orders, Naxos helped drag the professor farther into the room. The alarms were still ringing.

"Can we find a doctor?" Lewis asked.

Naxos pressed his ear to the professor's chest. "His heartbeat is weak."

"How do we shut off these alarms?" Hanna asked. "This place will be swarming with Erasers soon." She pointed to Naxos. "Figure it out."

He started to say something, then simply followed her orders, rushing over to one of the workstations. Apparently Hanna was in charge now. And Kaya was fine with that.

One of the women—one of the Erasers—rolled onto her side. She'd wake soon.

Hanna grabbed the sonic pistol from her, prying it out of her sweaty fingers. Then she did the same with the other woman's weapon.

"What should we do with them?" Kaya asked.

The alarms stopped. Naxos smiled proudly.

"Good work," Hanna said. "As for these two . . ." She glanced at the still-open cell, then shrugged. Naxos needed no further instructions. He dragged the two Erasers into the glass prison. Kaya helped him carry in the guards from outside the entrance as well, and then they sealed the door. Finally, Hanna played the tune stored on the professor's wristpad, and the strange glass sphere drifted out into the water.

As the cell floated away, Kaya stood at the window, staring out into the prison. Who else was trapped inside? And did any of them actually deserve to be there? The Erasers had grabbed Elida at the theater. A harmless old storyteller—or harmless in Kaya's mind, anyway. Was she in there, too, trapped in one of those cells? Kaya rushed over to the tablet, scanned the list of prisoners, and found the storyteller's name.

"What are you doing?" Hanna asked. "We need to leave."

"I'm retrieving another prisoner," she explained. "Someone who shouldn't be in here."

A new tune played.

"We can't wait," Hanna insisted. "Let's go."

Lewis was crouched over his dad. "He's still not responding."

Hanna motioned to Naxos. "You brought a cruiser, right?" she asked.

Kaya nodded to the doorway. "It's out front."

"Carry him to it now," Hanna said. Then she pointed to Kaya. "Your friend will have to make his own way out."

Her way, Kaya thought, but she didn't bother correcting Hanna.

Naxos grabbed the professor under the arms, dragged him to the door and down the hall. At the exit, Kaya grabbed him at the ankles so they could carry him down the few steps.

Two guards appeared from around a corner.

They stopped a quick sprint away.

Kaya hadn't seen them before, and the two men had clearly never seen People of the Sun. Neither man even reached for the pistol at his side. Instead, they stood motionless, mouths open, staring at the giant Sun Person as Kaya and Naxos held him.

The guards fell.

Hanna calmly lowered her sonic pistols. "Hurry," she reminded them.

Outside, Kaya and Naxos lifted the professor into the waiting cruiser. Lewis was holding his hands to the sides of his head. The boy's face was flat, cold, expressionless. With a pistol still in each hand, Hanna swung her arm over his shoulders. "It's okay, Lewis. He's going to be okay."

"He's shaking," Lewis said.

Naxos said nothing. The boy was staring up at Kaya now. Did he expect her to have an answer? A solution? What was she supposed to say?

"Shaking is good," Hanna said. Her voice was calm, strong, reassuring. "Shivering is the body's way of trying to warm up."

Good? His eyes were still closed, and his breaths were shallow and weak, as if someone were squeezing his lungs tight from the inside. Lewis leaned over his shivering father, running his hand over his wet hair, whispering to him, pleading with him to stay alive. What was he feeling? She could hardly imagine. Sure, she'd lost someone once. But she had been so young at the time. This had to be a different kind of loss.

No. This wasn't a loss. Not yet.

They weren't going to lose him.

They couldn't lose him.

"We need to get him to a doctor," Naxos said.

"Yeah, I know, but how?" Hanna asked. "We're at the bottom of the Atlantic Ocean. The nearest doctor is a day's journey at least."

"Not one of your doctors," Naxos said. "One of ours."

Lewis rubbed one of his father's hands between his palms. "Really? Will they treat him?"

Hanna was watching the door. "I don't like being here. We really need to go."

Lewis looked at Kaya again, quietly pleading. For what, though? Reluctantly, she reached into the cruiser and clasped the professor's other hand. His skin was frigid and damp. The cold leached into her. She wanted to pull away. But Lewis was almost smiling now, watching her hold his father's hand. She pressed it tighter.

"I know someone in Evenor who would help," Naxos said.

"Evenor?" Kaya replied. "The flooded city?"

"Yes. She's a healer," Naxos added. "I'd trust her with my own life."

Hanna turned to Kaya, then pointed to Naxos. "Sure, but can we trust you?"

Right. The last the Sun People had seen of Naxos was when they were fleeing the border station. After the Erasers had turned up at Gogol's shop, they'd blamed him. So this was a fair question. "Yes, we can trust him," Kaya said. "Plus we don't really have a choice."

Suddenly the professor coughed and blinked.

Lewis jumped back, startled. "Dad?"

The huge man coughed again. His teeth were chattering. He was struggling to speak. "Just relax, Dad," Lewis said. "Relax."

"But stay awake," Hanna said, still watching the door. "Keep him awake, okay?"

Kaya studied the professor's neck. "Even if we do get him to a doctor, won't they track us? Can you turn that thing off?"

Naxos sat back. "I could destroy it, but . . ."

"But?" Hanna asked, skeptical.

"But I don't think we should. It could prove helpful."

"Helpful?" Kaya replied. "How?"

While Lewis stayed at his dad's side, the three of them gathered at the front of the cruiser. Hanna grabbed the backpack full of gadgets and scraps, stuffed one of the pistols inside, and pulled the straps over her shoulders. The bag did belong to Kaya. But this didn't really feel like the time to point that out.

"We split up," Naxos suggested. "Kaya can get you two back to the surface."

"Us two? What about the professor?"

"He stays here in Atlantis."

"No," Lewis answered. He was still trying to hold his shivering father.

Hanna, so vocal until that point, was listening quietly now. Thinking.

"The cruiser will be much faster without all of you in it," Naxos said. "The vehicle has plenty of power left"—Kaya had to credit him for riding the waterways instead of drifting—"and with this model, I can get to Evenor long before they find us. I'll draw them away and give you time to escape. Then I can destroy the tracker and rush him to the healer."

"They'll know where you are," Kaya noted.

"Evenor is an easy place to hide," he replied.

"Even with a giant?" Kaya asked.

"Even with a giant."

Now Hanna jumped into the debate. "And if we all stay together?" she asked.

"I told you—we'll be too slow with the added mass. They'll catch us. They'll be everywhere soon."

"We are not leaving my dad."

Hanna pointed her pistol at the closed door, in the direction of the control room and the pool beyond. "Then we'll all spend the rest of our lives in that watery prison," she said. "I'm sorry, Lewis. But Naxos is right. This is the best plan. This is our only chance."

"We can't leave him, Hanna," Lewis replied, his voice shaking. "We can't."

The girl from the surface placed her arm around his shoulder.

Lewis looked at Hanna, waiting for a reply.

Her silence said everything.

"I'm sorry, Lewis," Naxos said, "but the Erasers will never stop searching for you as long as you're in Atlantis. If we split now, we all have a better chance of surviving, including your father. I've given Kaya instructions on how to get you safely to the surface. The tunnels leading to the factory are just below us—"

"What factory?" Hanna asked.

"I'll explain on the way," Kaya said.

"Here," Naxos said, handing Kaya his tablet. "All the information you need is in this—maps, instructions, controls, everything."

The tablet felt suddenly heavy in her hands. During the trip from Ridge City, when Kaya had talked about this plan with Naxos, she'd imagined him leading. He knew the ships, the factory. He knew his way around headquarters. Now everything was her responsibility?

She'd let the Sun People down once before.

She wasn't going to let that happen again.

The door started to open.

The four of them turned and stared.

"We need to go. Now," Hanna insisted.

Lewis crouched by his father. "I'm not going anywhere without him," he said.

The door opened, and Hanna raised a sonic pistol.

"Wait!" Kaya shouted. "Don't shoot!"

An old woman stood in the doorway. Elida.

The pistol aimed at her chest clearly didn't bother the storyteller. She hardly even noticed. Her eyes darted back and forth between Hanna and Lewis and the fallen professor. "I knew it!" Elida exclaimed. "They are real." She pointed to Kaya. "You're the girl from the theater. What are you doing here? Who are they?"

"Long story," Kaya replied.

"I'm accustomed to long stories," Elida said.

"Yeah, well, you're not getting one now," Hanna added. She stepped around Elida, leaned through the opening, then jerked back and closed the door behind the storyteller. "A half dozen more of them are rushing back into that control room. Our friends in the hall will wake up soon, too. Or someone will find them. Either way, we don't have long. This woman is a friend of yours?" Kaya nodded. Hanna eyed Elida for a moment, then held up the pistol. "Ever used one of these?"

"Once or twice," the storyteller said, "in my youth."

Hanna tossed her the sonic weapon. She caught it with one hand. Once or twice? She held it like it was an extension of her arm, Kaya thought.

"Okay," Hanna continued, "here's the deal: Anyone tries to come through that door, you knock them out. Understood?"

"Understood."

Maybe this wasn't the first time Elida had held a pistol, but she was old, frail. She'd just been in prison! "We can't just leave her—"

"I'll be perfectly fine," Elida said, interrupting her. "Besides," she added, nodding to the professor, "it seems you have more important matters to attend to."

Kaya moved back to Lewis's side. He was whispering to his father. "Come on, Dad. You can't give up. Not now. You finally did it! You proved everyone wrong. We have to get you back home. We'll get you better, and you'll be able to tell everyone . . ."

The words stopped coming out, and he leaned over the side of the cruiser, placed his head against his father's cold, wet chest, and started crying. A huge drop of water fell from the ceiling and splattered on the boy's back. He didn't react. Kaya watched as Lewis's dad pulled his hand away.

Wait.

He moved.

The professor moved.

Hanna grabbed Kaya's shoulder. They stared at the professor as he brought his hand up to his face and wiped his eyes. Lewis backed away, startled, too nervous to hope. The professor waved for his son to come closer. When he finally spoke, his words were low and weak, but Kaya could hear him clearly enough. "I'm proud of you, son, and I love you. But you can't stay here with me. Promise me that you'll let them help you get home. You and Hanna . . . you both need to get home. Promise me, son."

"I . . ."

"Please, Lewis.

He hesitated. "I promise."

The professor closed his eyes and smiled. Then he pulled off his wristpad, placed it in his son's hand, and closed his fist around it. "Take this with you. My Atlantis journals— everything is in here. All the proof anyone will ever need."

"But Dad—"

"No, let me finish," he continued, speaking with his eyes closed, as if he was devoting every bit of energy in his body to forcing out his whispered words. "I heard what you said earlier about finally finding this place. But it wasn't just me who found Atlantis, son. We discovered her together. The three of us." He reached up and held his hand to the side of his son's face. "Meriwether Lewis Gates, you truly are a great explorer."

18

SUDDENLY POWERLESS

THE LIGHTS of the cruiser faded into the dark tunnel as Naxos sped away. Lewis's dad was gone, rushed off to some mystery doctor somewhere in Atlantis. Would he ever see him again? Would his dad even survive? Lewis shook his head. He had to stop thinking that way. He promised his dad he'd get home. He promised him he'd survive. That's what he was going to do.

The wristpad was warm against his skin.

Hanna tightened the straps of her backpack.

Kaya finally pulled her hand off the tablet Naxos had given her and hurried them away from the entrance to the prison. She looked back at the old woman. "You'll be okay?" she asked.

"I've swum through far rougher waters in my life, child," the woman answered. "Hurry, now. I can hear them in the halls."

They raced only a short way down the tunnel before Kaya crouched over a metal grate set into the stone floor, gripped it with both hands, and pulled it open. "Let's go," she said. "Quickly."

Water was rushing below them.

"More sewers, huh?" Hanna asked.

"This is the safest and fastest way."

Hanna dropped through first.

"You're not going to get us lost again?" Lewis asked.

"No," Kaya said, "I'm going to get you home."

She climbed down, and Lewis lowered himself through after her, hung from the opening with both hands, then dropped to the floor. But what about the grate? If the Erasers got past the old woman, they'd see it and know where they had gone. And the old woman would never be able to move the thing. He started to climb back up the ladder when the grate was thrown over the opening. The old woman peered through the holes. "Well, are you going?"

Okay. Lewis made a mental note never to arm wrestle her. Or anyone in Atlantis, really.

The cold, ankle-deep water smelled like a pond. He splashed ahead.

Kaya pressed her hand to her tablet and marched on. They were moving at a near run. She asked about what had happened to them since the Erasers had grabbed them from her house. Hanna encouraged Lewis to tell the story. She was probably doing it to get his mind off his dad, he realized. But he didn't complain. Talking helped, and Kaya listened quietly. The only time she asked a question was when he talked about the man who had interrogated them. She wanted to know exactly what he looked like, and she seemed relieved when Lewis described him.

Once Lewis finished recounting their adventures, Kaya told them all about her meeting with Naxos, her grandmother, and her friend Rian. When Hanna asked about her dad, though, she changed the subject. Neither she nor Lewis pressed.

The prison, Kaya explained as they walked, was near the Erasers' headquarters, a series of offices, labs, and a factory all at the edge of the Atlantis, where the hidden world met the deep sea. At the factory, she said, they'd steal a warship and speed to the surface.

Hanna stopped. "That's the plan?" she asked.

"That's the plan," Kaya said.

"What about guards? Erasers?"

They started moving again, increasing their pace.

"Hopefully, they'll all be rushing to the prison," Kaya said. Or chasing his dad, Lewis thought. "Plus, it's the middle of the night, so most of them won't be here—"

"It's the middle of the night?" Lewis asked.

"Yes," Kaya replied. "The workday doesn't start for another few hours. We'll go inside, switch off the sentry system so they can't track us, and jump into a warship. By the time the engineers get to the factory, we'll be free and clear on the surface. Naxos even gave me the tones to control the vehicles."

Hanna stopped again. "How does he know so much about these warships?"

"Well, he kind of designed them."

If Naxos had designed the ships, that meant—

"He's one of the Erasers?" Hanna asked.

That information would have been super valuable to Lewis a few minutes earlier. "We just trusted him with my dad's life!"

"Kaya, you should have told us."

Kaya stopped and stared back at them. Seconds passed in silence. "You're right," she said at last. "I'm sorry. But he's trying to help us. I swear."

Maybe Lewis was putting too much faith in someone he'd just met. Someone from a completely different world. But he did trust her. "Then let's go," Lewis said. "Let's get home."

After winding through the darkness, stopping often so Kaya could check the map on her tablet—a super weird map that she read with her fingers, not her eyes, which Lewis still couldn't get used to—they came to a narrow, rusted ladder leading up into a hole in the rock overhead. They climbed into a dark, deserted hallway. Kaya felt the pad, then whistled. Blue-green light shined from the ceiling. What was this place? The headquarters of the Erasers reminded Lewis more of an alien spaceship than the caves and tunnels that shaped the rest of Atlantis. The walls were metal, but curved, and without the blinking lights and screens you'd see in a movie spacecraft. Okay, so it wasn't really space-like at all.

Kaya held her hand to her tablet and then pointed. "Just ahead. It shouldn't be far."

Her voice was quieter than usual. Nervous, almost.

Lewis didn't like this change. His heart was beating faster. He moved closer to Hanna. She glanced over at him, eyes scrunched, as if she was expecting him to say something. But he just wanted to be next to her. She switched the pistol to her other side and took his hand.

At a black glass door, Kaya stopped. She knelt, and Lewis thought he heard her whispering something about Naxos. Then the tablet played a six-note tune. A bolt slid back into the wall, and the door sprang open. They stepped through into a large room marked by a tall window that had to be ten or twenty long steps wide. The lights inside brightened automatically. On the other side of the glass stretched the darkness of the deep ocean.

Hanna gasped. "Whoa."

Lewis hurried over and pressed his palm to the window.

The lights in the room were a magnet for sea life, and soon the water was crowded with creatures. A long, wormlike fish floated into view. Tendrils hung from its body like tassels, and it glowed pink. Lewis could see its insides—its spine and organs. He bumped his forehead on the glass as he leaned forward for a closer look. "Whoops."

Hanna elbowed him and pointed to his wrist. Right. He might as well continue his father's work. He aimed the wristpad and recorded the scene.

"Follow me," Kaya said. She led them down a stairwell.

At the base of the stairs, they stopped in front of what looked like a train car, only way, way more awesome. The vehicle was identically curved at the front and back, like a giant glass vitamin. Hanna was studying the track below. "Magnetic levitation?" she asked.

Kaya shrugged. "I think so."

Once they were on the train, Kaya whistled six brief notes. Immediately, the doors shut and the train began moving. Lewis breathed out. Their plan was working.

He couldn't believe their plan was actually working.

Hanna stood and held one of the railings. "I can't sit," she said. "These Erasers need to be better about security. The same tune? That's like using the same password for every device."

Didn't everyone use the same password? His started with the word *chicken* and ended with one that rhymed with *nut*. He laughed quietly as he thought of it.

Hanna was switching the sonic pistol from her right hand to her left. "Kaya, can you make this fish swim any faster?"

The train quickly accelerated from a slow creep to a mad sprint through the tunnel. Lewis stared down at the wristpad. He couldn't help thinking of his father. Where was he? Had Naxos gotten him to the doctor yet? Was he even still alive? He gritted his teeth. If he could have crumpled up that thought like a piece of paper and tossed it down the aisle, he would have. But his brain wasn't made of paper, and it would probably hurt to reach inside his mind and—

Kaya stretched across the aisle and kicked him gently in the shin, then pointed up toward the ceiling. He tilted back his head. The roof of the shuttle was all windows. Glass stretched between the steel ribs of the tunnel, too, so they could see right up into the sea. The lights along the track shined out into the water, attracting all kinds of strange and wondrous creatures. They were brightly colored, transparent, slow-moving, like beautiful seaweed come to life, and as fluid as the water itself. He aimed the wristpad, recording it all, and watched the scene through his dad's eyes. Now, despite everything, he couldn't help smiling.

The shuttle slowed, and they lurched forward, holding tight to the rails and handles to keep from falling. Then the train stopped and dropped ever so slightly. The lighting inside the miniature station brightened. They hurried out, the doors closed behind them, and the train immediately took off toward its starting place.

Hanna scanned the room as she led the way inside.

Odd uniforms were hanging on the wall. No, not uniforms. They looked more like space suits. Kaya eyed them, and through a glass door, Lewis saw a small room with a dark pool.

"That's probably a way out to the ocean," Kaya explained. "We call them darkwater pools. Those dive suits look super advanced, too. They're built to hold up against the pressure of the deep, and they have really cool propulsion systems on the back. You can swim as fast as—"

"Believe me, I'm fascinated, and normally I'd be the last person to stop you from talking about tech," Hanna said, "but are we getting out of here or what?"

"Yes, sorry," Kaya answered.

She led them forward into the most spectacular room Lewis had ever seen. The factory was beneath a gigantic dome, the ceiling hundreds of feet above them. All the surfaces—the walls, the floors, the great dome that arched overhead—were made of glass, and the dark ocean surrounded them.

Almost everything here was built from glass, so they could see into the depths of the factory, built into some kind of giant trench on in the bottom of the ocean. A ramp in the center of the floor spiraled down as far as Lewis could see. The space below was divided into at least ten or twenty levels, and on each level there were hundreds of shining, silvery warships. They looked like teardrops. They were both beautiful and frightening.

"He was telling the truth," Kaya said.

"Who?"

"Naxos," she said. "Those are his ships. They're exactly as he described them."

"There are hundreds of them," Lewis said.

Hanna corrected him. "Thousands."

"Which means they probably won't even notice if we borrow one," Lewis noted.

"We're going home," Hanna whispered, almost to herself. "Kaya, you're going to be amazed! We'll show you everything. Mountains, valleys, cities—"

"And cows and chickens and goats, and chocolate, too," Lewis added. "You're really going to like chocolate."

The girl from Atlantis closed her eyes, as if she were trying to picture the mountains and valleys—and maybe even the chocolate. Hanna bit one corner of her lower lip. They were here. They'd made it. The ships were all around them, and the factory was empty. They hadn't seen or heard a single person.

They really were going home.

Overwhelmed, Lewis went to hug Kaya.

She pushed him away. Did he smell that bad? No. She was looking over his shoulder.

"What was that?" she asked.

Hanna reached into her backpack for a deadly trumpet. "The train. Someone's coming."

"I thought you said they wouldn't get to work until later," Lewis said.

"We did kind of break out of their prison," Hanna noted.

The shuttle doors opened.

Half a dozen Atlanteans sprinted toward them across the huge space.

Hanna practically threw Lewis behind a workstation, then crouched in front of him, holding out her weapons. "Kaya, come on! Get behind me!"

The girl from Atlantis didn't move.

Lewis recognized one of the Erasers immediately. "Weed Chin."

The man with the seaweed-colored beard growled in their direction. Mrs. Finkleman was beside him. Two other women, both dressed like Kaya in warlike yoga clothes, aimed weapons the size and shape of trombones, only without the slidey things.

The creepy old Demos guy was there, too, and another man. One Lewis didn't recognize.

This stranger pushed to the front of the group.

"Kaya? What in the world are you doing here?"

He knew her? How did he know her?

Kaya walked forward slowly and raised her hand in greeting. "Hi, Dad."

19
THE SECRET OF ATLANTIS

HER DAD'S hair was blond and long. More wizard than surfer, though. His pale, unwrinkled skin made it hard for Lewis to guess his age. Maybe a little older than Lewis's dad? His chin stuck out farther than normal, and his nose turned sharply down at its midpoint, as if someone had flattened it with a spatula. A really heavy spatula. There was something unusual about his eyes, too. They were an icy blue, almost arctic. The small gap between his front teeth probably made it really easy to floss.

Under the great factory dome, Kaya's dad swung around to face Demos. "Why didn't you tell me my daughter was involved?"

"You would have acted emotionally, not rationally," Demos answered. He motioned to the warships below them. "You have very important work to finish here. We couldn't afford to have you distracted by problems at home, so we intercepted all communications between you and your daughter, and your mother-in-law, too."

"You what?"

"This was merely an invasion of your privacy," Demos said. "We have much bigger invasions to worry about."

"Wait a second," Hanna said. "That's your dad, Kaya? I thought you said he was going to help us."

"Apparently I was wrong," Kaya said.

"Kaya, please—"

"No, let me talk," she continued. "I don't understand. I thought you were an engineer."

"I am an engineer," her father replied.

"One of the finest in Atlantis," Demos added. He held his arms out and up. "This factory was his design. Thanks to your father, and your weak-willed friend Naxos, we were able to build the most advanced fleet this planet has ever seen."

Kaya's dad was barely listening. He was staring at her. "I never lied to you."

"You didn't tell me you work for the Erasers!"

Still hiding behind Hanna, Lewis cut in, "That's kind of like lying."

"Definitely," Hanna added.

Weed Chin and Mrs. Finkleman pointed their weapons at Lewis and Hanna. "Stand up," Finkleman ordered.

Hanna refused. She held out her two sonic blasters like some kind of futuristic outlaw.

Then Weed Chin turned his weapon toward Kaya.

Reluctantly, Hanna placed her blasters on the floor.

Slowly, carefully, she and Lewis moved next to Kaya.

Demos pointed at Lewis's wristpad. "I'm glad you brought that with you, boy. We made a mistake in not searching your father closely enough when he joined us." He held out his hand. "Give it to me. Now."

"No," Kaya insisted. Lewis jumped a little; her voice had more power than usual. "Don't give him anything, Lewis." She shook her head and stared back at her dad. "How could you?"

"Kaya, please," her dad said. "I'll explain everything in time. I assure you, it will all make sense."

"How is this going to make sense? You're an Eraser! You told me the Sun People were a myth, but you knew they were real all along. Why?"

"To protect you, Kaya! My work with the High Council is critical to the survival of Atlantis. Please, just leave these creatures to the care of my associates."

"Creatures? They're not creatures! They're people!"

"Kaya," her dad replied, waving for her to come closer. "These Sun People . . . they're not who you think they are."

"Neither are you."

"This will make sense if you let me explain."

Hanna interfered. "Then explain."

Kaya's dad glanced at his colleagues. "Not here."

"What's there to explain, anyway?" Hanna asked. "You people locked us in prison, and we didn't even do anything. We just want to go home."

"We can't let you go home," Demos said. "You have seen far too much. But I will gladly return you both to your cell."

Kaya's dad lowered his voice. "I promise we won't hurt them if they cooperate, Kaya."

"What about my father?" Lewis asked.

"We'll find him, too," Demos said.

That meant they hadn't found him yet.

That meant he could still be alive.

"And you won't hurt him?" Hanna asked.

"No," Demos answered. "He is far too valuable. Heron, please, order your daughter to step away from these sunstruck invaders."

Wait. What? Lewis couldn't just let this go. "Your name's Heron?" he asked.

"Yes," Kaya's father replied. "Why?"

"I mean, you're named after a bird, and you live underwater. It's weird."

"It is," Hanna added.

Kaya's dad shook his head. "I'm named after a what?"

"Enough!" Demos shouted. "Heron, order your daughter to come here now!"

"You're not ordering her to do anything," Hanna snapped back.

Kaya's voice was shaky when she replied. "Please, Dad, just let them go home."

Her dad's face softened again. The way he looked at her—his expression was filled with love. Tenderness. Even Mrs. Finkleman appeared moved in some way, or maybe confused by this whole exchange between father and daughter. But Demos? Weed Chin and the others? Not so much. They were clearly ready and willing to toss Lewis and Hanna straight back into that underwater prison.

Heron's shoulders sagged, as if the strength were leaking out of him. "You don't understand, Kaya . . ."

"You keep saying that, but I do understand! Hanna and

Lewis and the professor shouldn't be locked in a cell. They should be celebrated! We should be telling all of Atlantis their story. If people knew the truth—"

"The truth?" Her father practically smacked her words back at her. A change came over him. The gentleness was gone. "The truth is that your two friends come from a world more violent than you could ever imagine. Their wars against each other have resulted in the deaths of millions of their own people."

"More," Weed Chin added.

"That doesn't mean we should lock the first ones we meet in a cell!"

"They've hurt us, too, Kaya," Heron said, his voice gentler now. "You and me."

"I know."

"You know what?" Hanna asked.

Kaya took a long, deep breath before explaining. "I know that my mother was killed on a peaceful mission to the surface when her ship was destroyed by the People of the Sun."

Her dad was stunned.

Demos was silent.

Lewis was shocked, too. Why hadn't she mentioned this? Had she known the whole time? He couldn't believe it was true. There had to be some kind of mistake.

"The submarine off New York," Hanna said. She elbowed Lewis. "Your dad's theory—he was right!"

Sure, maybe, but this wasn't the time to celebrate.

Not if Kaya had lost her own mother in the incident.

Heron could barely utter a reply. "How did you—"

"Grandmother," Kaya explained. "She told me everything."

"What's passed has passed," Demos declared. "Kaya, we don't do our work out of hatred or anger toward the People of the Sun. We do so out of love for our own people. This is why the High Council exists. For our survival. For the survival of Atlantis." He held out his hand, palm up, and stared at Lewis. "The wristpad. Give it to me now."

"Wait," Kaya said. She lowered her face into her hands, then dropped them to her sides with her palms facing the floor. She exhaled. "Let me talk to you, Dad, please. Just give me a moment? That's all."

"They're not going anywhere," Finkleman added. "Might as well."

Demos glared at her for speaking out of turn, but then he nodded, giving his approval, and Kaya stepped aside with her father. Lewis watched them closely. How was she going to help them now, exactly? Her father didn't seem like the sort to change his mind. Plus he wasn't even the one in charge. Lewis glanced over at Demos. The aged Atlantean was picking his nose with his pinkie finger. That didn't mean he wasn't powerful, though. It just meant he didn't have a tissue.

Finkleman was squinting in their direction, studying them again. "How old are you?" she asked.

Demos stopped his surgery. "Quiet," he snapped. "Say another word to these infiltrators and you can join them in their cell."

Kaya's voice rose, pulling the Erasers' attention away.

"We need to do something," Hanna whispered.

Sure, but what? Miles of water stood between them and

the surface.

Lewis wondered if they could call for help somehow. But he didn't even know if this was possible, and for that he blamed his classmate Ashley. They'd learned about sound and radios in science class earlier that year, but Mr. Brush had sat him right behind Ashley, and he'd wasted the whole unit trying not to look at her long curly hair. If only he had listened!

Now Demos watched him through narrowed eyes.

Lewis stared up at the huge dome. He thought of the probes that supposedly scoured the oceans, searching for this place.

Atlantis was safe because it was hidden.

The last thing the Erasers wanted was someone broadcasting their position to the surface. That would terrify them.

A few steps away, Weed Chin was staring at his wristpad. Demos was studying it, too.

The tech was a mystery to the Atlanteans.

Almost magical.

"I've got an idea," he muttered.

"Does it involve dancing?" Hanna asked.

"No," Lewis replied. "Will you back me up?"

"Sure?"

"Shut your mouths!" Weed Chin barked.

"Just say smart stuff, okay?" he added.

Hanna looked at him like he'd grown a third nostril. On his forehead. "Huh?"

Weed Chin and another Eraser started toward them. Lewis held up his hands. "I'm sorry. No more. We'll be quiet now. I promise."

"Then stop talking," Demos replied.

"I will."

"Now," Weed Chin growled.

"Ri—"

Lewis stopped short and pretended to zip his lips shut. Now the Atlanteans were the ones looking at him like he had a third nostril. Did they not have zippers down here? Nearby, Kaya's voice rose again. She and her father were arguing, and Hanna kept looking at Lewis, as if she were trying to read his mind, or find some clue to his plan. But he was thinking. Rehearsing, really.

The argument between Kaya and her father faded; she was staring at the floor now, slouching, as he did all the talking.

"Heron," Demos said, "we're tired of waiting."

Lewis was tired of waiting, too. He nodded to Hanna. She shrugged, confused.

Then he held his forearm out in front of his chest and hung his right index finger inches from the screen of the wristpad. He breathed in. He needed to sound powerful. Convincing. Heroic. He stared down Demos. "Tell them—" His voice cracked. He started over. "Tell them to lower their weapons."

Demos squinted, eyeing the wristpad. "Why would I do that?"

Lewis was shaking slightly. "Because all I have to do is touch my finger to this screen," he said, "and this wristpad will send a rescue signal out into the ocean—one that gives our exact location."

He paused, waiting. Kaya and her father had turned to listen.

Everyone was silent. Heron whispered something to Demos.

The old man laughed. "The dome is soundproof, you imbecile."

Okay. That was bad.

Where was Hanna with the smart stuff? He tried to kick her foot, but she was a little too far away. "Do you want to explain it to him, Hanna?"

She glared confidently at Heron. "You claim to be an engineer—"

"I am an engineer."

For a second, Lewis felt bad. This was Kaya's dad they were messing with.

Then again, Kaya's dad was trying to get them thrown back in prison.

His brain hurt.

"Well, that wristpad won't simply transmit our location," Hanna continued. "Once Lewis presses that screen, all of the data on the professor's wristpad—all the video and audio recordings and images he captured in these last few days, including our current location—all of it will be shared with the surface. Everyone under the sun will be able to see what we've seen and hear what we've heard. They'll know where we are and how to find you."

"That's impossible," Heron replied. "The dome will block the sound."

"But this technology doesn't use sound," Hanna replied. She breathed out heavily. "I'm sorry," she said sarcastically, "I keep forgetting how little you know about radiation. That wristpad pumps out powerful low-frequency radio waves. My mother invented this device, actually. It's pretty amazing. She's not always the best mother, since she's so busy all the time, but now that I've been away from her, from them—"Lewis edged closer and kicked her. She was getting sentimental now, of all times? He pointed to the screen. She shook her head. "Right. So, anyway, it doesn't use sound, and you're correct—if it did, we'd be in trouble. But at the moment, you're the ones who are in danger. Once Lewis here presses that touch screen, those radio waves will instantly propagate through the sea."

Propa-what? Lewis didn't understand half of what she'd just said.

Which was absolutely perfect.

He almost wanted to applaud. There had been a quick and unexpected crack in Hanna's impenetrable emotional armor, but now she was herself again. Brilliant and logical.

"Once I touch this screen," Lewis finished, "the secret of Atlantis will be out."

The Erasers were silent.

Heron's eyes were locked on the wristpad.

Demos was squinting at Lewis.

"You're lying," Kaya's father replied.

The rest of the Erasers—all but Mrs. Finkleman—raised their deadly trumpets and frightening trombones.

Hanna wasn't finished. Now that she'd started spinning and weaving this beautiful, complex scientific lie, she couldn't stop. "Maybe I should simplify it slightly, since you probably wouldn't understand all the technical details. Your work with gravity and sound is truly impressive, but electronics?" She winced. "Not so sharp, guys. You Atlanteans really have some catching up to do on that end."

Offended, Heron replied, "Our technology is far more advanced than—"

"I figured out your gravity drives," Hanna said with a shrug. "Took me . . . what? Fifteen minutes?"

"Less," Lewis said.

"She fixed up a busted blaster, too," Kaya added. "I'd believe them, Dad."

"I can explain more if that would make it easier for you," Hanna said. "The signals will first be picked up by communication drones near the surface, then relayed wirelessly through the air. Once that happens, the information will travel at the speed of light. Three hundred million meters per second, in case you didn't know. I can see already that this is too complex for you. I'm sorry—I'm really trying to keep it simple. Basically, though, I estimate that it will take three or four seconds before the most powerful nations on the surface know the location of Atlantis." She nodded to Lewis. She was kind of taking over his plan now. He hoped that if it did work, she'd remember that this was all his idea. It's not like he was going to interrupt her, though. There was an old saying about a rolling stone—you weren't supposed to lie down in front of it. Or maybe that wasn't the lesson. Anyway, he lowered his finger so that it almost touched the screen. "Of course, if you don't believe me," Hanna continued, "Lewis is happy to demonstrate."

His heart was pounding like a kick drum.

He was struggling to keep his finger from shaking.

Weed Chin was insisting that Hanna and Lewis were lying.

Good old Mrs. Finkleman wasn't so sure. She started pleading with Demos to believe them. "There's too much to lose!" she said. "Besides, they're just children."

"That's enough from you," Demos snapped.

Heron's face was contorted, as if he was thinking through every step.

Hanna started counting down. "Ten . . . nine . . . eight . . ."

Don't get to seven, Lewis thought.

"Seven . . . six . . . five . . ."

Stop at four. Four would be fine.

Please, please, please stop her at four.

But Hanna kept counting, and the Atlanteans waited.

Normally, Lewis didn't pray all that much. His dad wasn't very religious, and his mom and Roberts only dragged them to church on holidays. But now Lewis began to pray. Not to any particular god or goddess or ancient spirit. He was begging all of them. The Big Guy, with the beard and the robes and the throne on the clouds, the Greek and Roman gods, the cool Hindu ones, including that really smart elephant—even the Aztec spirit with the hard-to-say name, the one that sort of rhymed with pretzel. He pleaded with any and all mystical beings for help.

Meanwhile, Hanna was depending on herself, and the fears of the Atlanteans.

She was down to three.

Two.

"Well then, world," she said, nodding to Lewis, as if giving him a final order, "let us introduce you to the secrets of Atlantis—"

Heron placed his hand on Demos's shoulder. He whispered something in his ear.

"Wait," Demos ordered, his voice firm but calm.

Wait? This was good. This meant . . . their trick was working?

Yes. Demos was holding up both hands now, pleading with Lewis not to touch that screen. The pretzel god had listened. Or the elephant, or one of the Greeks.

Weed Chin was outraged. "They're lying!"

"One tap," Hanna said.

"That's right," Lewis added. "All it takes is one touch."

"What do you want?" Demos asked.

"Let them go," Kaya insisted. "Allow them to reach the surface and return home safely."

"Right," Lewis added. "What she said."

"Is that all you want?" her dad asked.

Lewis also wanted one of those Atlantean shirts that dried instantly. Maybe a gravity suit. And an extra bottle or two of the hot sauce. Or a case, even. But these requests were nothing compared to his one main wish. "And promise you'll leave my father alone."

"And that's all," Hanna said.

Demos stared up through the vast glass dome, then peered down at the thousands of sleek warships. The Erasers watched him, awaiting his decision.

After a long, deep breath, he said, "You may leave Atlantis. I'll program a ship to take you home. On one condition."

"Yes?" Hanna replied.

Demos pointed to Lewis. "That you give us your wristpad."

He held out his hand.

All of them were watching Lewis.

Were they seriously expecting him to give it up? He shrugged. "No way."

"We can't allow you to leave with that kind of evidence," Heron explained.

"Still no."

Hanna stepped forward. "And if we were to give it to you—"

"No, Hanna," Lewis said, his voice firm. "I'm not giving it to them."

She ignored him. "If we were to give it to you, what would prevent you from imprisoning us anyway?"

"His daughter," Kaya answered. She glared at her father. "If you lie to them, you lose me. I'll never speak to you again."

"She looks like she means it," Weed Chin added.

One of the other Erasers elbowed him.

"You have my word, Kaya," Heron replied.

His word? What good was that? Lewis wasn't giving up his dad's wristpad. This wasn't just some gadget. Of all people, Hanna should have known what it meant to him. To his father. To all three of them, really. She should've understood. So why was she offering up his most prized possession? This wasn't the kind of deal he'd imagined.

He should've been more specific with those gods.

He looked down at the wristpad.

Sure, he could give it to the Erasers, and then the two of them could return to the surface and tell their story and swear it was all true. But no one would believe them. Not without proof. Forget what people would say about him. He'd never hear the end of it at school, but he could deal with that. The worst part was that the world would continue thinking his dad was some kind of crackpot, and he'd never be able to convince anyone to try to rescue his father. His dad would be trapped in Atlantis forever. How could he give the wristpad away? If the files on the device were released, his dad would be part of history—one of the great explorers of their century. Of any century! Everyone would learn about him in school, not make fun of him.

The Atlantis journals would change everything.

And yet Lewis could never save his father's reputation if he spent the rest of his life locked inside a cell beneath miles of ocean. He'd never get home again. He'd end up bald and covered with warts.

Giving up the wristpad was their way home.

Slowly, he slipped the device over his hand. A thin layer of grime coated the underside, covering something that had been etched into the metal. He scratched it off with his thumbnail and revealed three letters: MLG. His own initials, engraved into his father's precious wristpad. His dad really did care about him. Of course he did. In a way, Lewis had been with him the whole time. Lewis squeezed the device in his hands as if he were giving his father one final hug. Then he handed the wristpad, and the Atlantis journals, to the Erasers.

20

BURIED IN THE MUCK

KAYA sat on the glass floor with her back against a railing. The Sun People stood apart, watching her father and the other Erasers. She still couldn't believe her father was really one of them. Her amazing, forgiving, loving father. The man who made her breakfast and helped her with her schoolwork and somehow prevented himself from yelling back at her when she shouted at him just because she needed to shout at someone. How could he be an Eraser? How could he agree with that old creep who wanted to throw her friends back in jail?

Her dad was standing at some kind of control station. Next to him, the ramp spiraled down into the huge factory. Demos stood beside him.

A series of high-pitched tones rang out.

Far below them, one of the ships backed out of its dock. Kaya watched through the glass floor as it floated up the ramp. There must have been thousands of ships down below. What if every one of them were to float up and out of this factory? She imagined them packed with soldiers. Thousands of warships and thousands of warfighters rising up out of this beautiful factory for their long journey to the surface.

This was the vision of the High Council, according to Naxos.

A vision that would lead only to destruction of the world above.

And maybe their world down here, as well.

She shuddered.

"Notice that no driver is necessary," her dad boasted. "That was my contribution. Impressive, isn't it?"

He was proud of himself? He should've been ashamed.

"Good for you," Hanna said. "We figured out driverless vehicles decades ago."

Demos had stopped paying attention to her father. He was studying the Sun People, and he wore the wristpad for all to see, as if he were taunting Lewis. He whistled at the device, hoping to switch it on. "How does it work?"

"You have to breathe on it," Lewis said.

"You need a password, too," Hanna added. "What is it, Lewis?"

"Cantaloupe," he replied.

"Don't say it too loud, though," Hanna noted.

Demos lifted the wristpad to his chin, breathed on the device, and whispered, "Cantaloupe." Nothing happened. He tried again. "Cantaloupe."

The People of the Sun smiled. Oh. This was a joke. She nearly laughed as the old man whispered the word over and over. Finally, Demos caught on; he glared at them.

"Just tap the surface," Hanna said with a shrug.

"That's enough," Kaya's dad said, motioning to her friends. "Follow me."

All around the base of the huge glass dome were darkwater docks. Transfer chambers, her father had called them. As Kaya understood it, a vehicle would move into one of these spaces, and its riders would secure themselves inside. Then a door would drop into place, seal the chamber off from the rest of the huge room, and allow it to fill with water. This wasn't an easy engineering job. The water in the chamber had to match the pressure of the deep sea, her father said. Kaya caught herself marveling at all this incredible tech, and beginning to feel a hint of pride that her father was involved.

No. Never mind the beautiful engineering. If these ships had been built to explore the seas, and the skies above, she'd be happy to marvel at them. But these were war machines. And these Atlanteans were called Erasers for a reason.

The Sun People were looking at her. She didn't move. She lacked the energy. Yet she forced herself to smile at them. Soon they'd be gone, and she'd never see them again. At least they'd be safe, though. At least they'd get home.

Maybe they could even warn their people.

Maybe there was some way to stop the war the Erasers were planning.

The shining warship drifted up the ramp and into the nearest darkwater dock. The front was shaped like the head of a humpback whale, but with a large glass panel stretching across the bow and lights in place of the huge beast's eyes. The body widened toward the middle, then shrank like the tail of a fish, tapering to a narrow point. The shell was made mostly of

Atlantean glass; the whole thing shimmered and shined like some kind of beautiful crystalline egg.

Hanna walked around the ship, inspecting it. Only the base of the hull was metal, and she bent down to stare at something on the underside of the ship. Kaya finally walked over, watched as Hanna studied a rectangular glass panel in the otherwise metallic base. "What's that?" she asked.

"An escape hatch," her dad explained. "The passengers will wear dive suits in case of emergency. If there's damage to the ship, they can exit safely into the water."

"Kind of like soldiers parachuting out of a helicopter," Lewis said.

"Yeah," Hanna replied, standing upright again, "but at the bottom of the ocean."

"They can also go through these hatches and come back in if they need to inspect the outside of the ship or merely explore the surrounding water," Kaya's dad said.

"Do we get suits?" Lewis asked.

"No," Demos snapped.

"This isn't a tour," Weed Chin snarled. "Inside. Now."

Kaya winced. Why did they have to be so rude? What was wrong with them?

She wanted to say goodbye privately, but the green-chinned Eraser rushed over and stood between them before she could get close. "Onto the ship," he ordered.

"The ship will take you safely to the surface," Demos added.

Kaya looked to her father. "Can I at least say goodbye to them?"

"You just did," Demos answered. "Stop acting like a child."

Her father spun to face the old man. "Sir, that's my daughter."

"Your daughter has caused us a great deal of trouble, Heron. By helping these invaders, she endangered the very existence of Atlantis. I believe we have been lenient. Need I remind you that others on the High Council might not be so forgiving?"

Kaya started to reply, but her dad cut her off. "Of course, sir," her father answered. "You're absolutely right."

Did he actually agree with Demos?

Had she really threatened the safety of Atlantis?

"But, Dad, I—"

"Enough, Kaya," he said. Then he pointed to the sleek, gleaming warship and ordered the Sun People inside. "Leave us before we change our minds."

The same Eraser tried to intervene again; the woman with the short blond hair. "Demos, sir, I don't think—"

"I warned you already," the old man replied. "I will not do it again."

The woman said nothing more.

"Kaya," Hanna began, "I'm sorry—"

"No, I'm sorry," she answered.

"Thank you," Hanna added, "for everything—"

"Go," Kaya's father said. "Now."

Poor Lewis was still looking at the wristpad. Hanna was already a step into the warship, and she turned back and grabbed his sleeve at the shoulder, pulling him inside. He moved, wrestling free of her grip, but he didn't beg for the device. His jaw was tight, his face stern. If anything, Kaya thought he looked determined, as if he'd come to some kind of decision.

The door to the warship closed.

A glass pane dropped down from above, sealing off the darkwater dock from the factory floor. Water flooded the chamber, rising up around the ship. Her friends were safe now. Their path to freedom would open soon. Their path home. This was what they wanted. What she wanted. Yet Kaya couldn't watch. She hurried back toward the train to wait for her father there. And then what? Back home? Back to her supposedly normal life?

No. That was impossible.

Nothing would ever be the same.

Kaya stopped outside the entrance to the tunnel.

Her breathing was quick and shallow.

Her father crossed the factory floor.

He stood at her side as the train waited with open doors. "Let's go, Kaya. Let's get you home."

She turned to catch one last glimpse of her friends.

The warship had already disappeared into the darkness of the deep.

Demos stared up and out through the dome with the other Erasers at his side.

As she followed her dad to the train, and thought of the warship soaring up out of the sea toward the sun, it struck her—the glaring flaw in this plan. The Erasers weren't merely trying to keep the secret of the surface world from the people of Atlantis. They were working to make sure that as few of the Sun People as possible knew Atlantis existed.

So why had they given her friends a warship?

The technology of the two civilizations was nothing alike, according to Hanna. The People of the Sun didn't even have basic gravity drives. And yet her friends were traveling in an Atlantean warship. The other Sun People would know immediately that this vehicle was from another world.

Forget the wristpad, the journals.

The warship itself was proof that Atlantis existed.

Suddenly, Kaya understood the truth.

The Erasers had never meant for that ship to reach the surface.

Her friends would never get home alive.

She stopped.

Her father was waiting in the doorway of the train. "What is it, Kaya?" he asked.

Did he know? Was this part of his plan?

"N-nothing," she lied.

The tunnel back to the ridge stretched out in front of the train. The deepwater suits still hung on the wall nearby, outside the room with the pool. The suits looked far more advanced than the one she'd left back in Edgeland. Probably faster, too.

The beginnings of a plan were forming in her mind. But it wouldn't work with him here.

She faked a smile and walked toward her dad. He stepped inside the train, turned, and sat. He started to pat the seat next to him, then pulled back his hand, unsure of himself. But Kaya had no intention of sitting there. Or anywhere else on the train. She placed one foot inside, whistled the six-note tune to set it in motion, and leaped back as the door closed.

The shuttle sped away as her father banged desperately on the glass.

The train was fast, and would return in a few minutes.

Kaya checked the suits quickly, then hurried back to the main floor. The Erasers would've heard the train leave—they'd assume she and her dad were gone. She stopped a safe distance away, careful not to be seen. Below her, several more warships were rising up the ramp. Demos was directing the others. The group was huddled on the opposite side of the factory, listening to his orders, but sound carried well in the space, and she heard him clearly enough.

"You are to track and destroy that vehicle," he said. "It will be disappointing to lose one of our ships, but I want every scrap of them buried in the muck and detritus of the seafloor."

≋≋ 21 ≋≋
NEVER OUT OF RANGE

LEWIS rubbed his forearm where the wristpad should have been and stared out through the glass. There wasn't much to see. The water all around them was dark and lifeless. Hanna was obviously worried about him; she kept asking if he was okay.

"I'm fine," he said.

And he would be fine. He'd decided something back at the factory, as he'd stood inside the ship, looking out at the Erasers, and Kaya, and the fantastic dome, and Atlantis hidden in the distant ridge. He was not going to let his father's work or his discovery go unrecognized, with or without the wristpad. People could laugh and mock him and call him crazy for the rest of his life. He didn't care. He was going to tell his father's story—their story. Hanna's, too. He'd shout it, sing it, even dance it if he had to. He'd tell it to anyone and everyone who would listen.

The truth about Atlantis would live.

His father would survive, too. Naxos would take care of him and get him to the healer. Hopefully, Kaya would talk some sense into her dad, and he'd help. The Atlanteans weren't all war-crazy like Demos. Mrs. Finkleman seemed to have a little sympathy for them. But if needed, Lewis would return to Atlantis and rescue his father himself. Whether it took him a month, a year, or even a decade, he'd find his way back.

And next time he'd be ready.

He'd bring more snacks, too. Maybe a pair of swim fins.

But this was all ahead of him—or them—in the future. What mattered now was that they were going home. Lewis tried to steer his thoughts in that direction. He pictured his house, his room, his stepfather and little brother, and most of all, his mother. When he closed his eyes, he could almost hear her voice.

"You with me?" Hanna asked. She was gritting her teeth. Her eyes were darting back and forth, staring out into the water.

He exhaled. "I'm here."

"That was a pretty good bluff, you know," Hanna said. "The whole wristpad thing."

He kind of wished his dad had seen him in action. "Thanks," he said. "It wouldn't have worked without you."

"The 'smart stuff,' you mean?"

"Was that all true?"

"Mostly," she said with a shrug. "Radio waves don't actually travel well at all through the water, though, so that was kind of a gamble."

"Kind of?"

"I had to think of something, and they didn't seem too knowledgeable about the electromagnetic spectrum," she explained. She stopped staring out the window and studied the dashboard of the strange ship. "I don't want to freak you out or anything, Lewis, but we're not quite golden yet."

"What? Why not?"

She sat in one of the two chairs at the dashboard. A small touch pad extended out from each armrest. She placed her hand on one of them and slid it forward. The ship turned gently to the right. Hanna laid her hands down on both pads, then slid them forward at the same time. The warship accelerated. "Nice," she said.

"What are you doing?" he asked. "Demos said it's programmed to take us to the surface."

"Right," she said. "That's the problem."

"Why is that a problem?"

"Do you really think they just gave us one of their most advanced warships? There's nothing like this on the surface, Lewis. This ship is proof that Atlantis is real. We could reverse-engineer this thing and basically steal one of their best inventions. You don't give your best toys to your enemies, Lewis. No way they're really letting us go."

Okay. This was bad. He jumped into the other seat. "What now?"

"Well, I figure if I can learn how to steer her—"

A dull thunk sounded below them, as if something had struck the underside of the hull.

"Whoa," Lewis said. "What was that?"

They looked out through the glass. The one area they couldn't see was the bottom of the ship—that was made of metal. "I don't know. We couldn't have hit anything. Or at least

I don't think so." She held her hands out over the ship's wide instrument panel. The surface was crowded with knobs and dials, switches and tablets. "I was looking for cameras. I keep forgetting—no screens. No cameras, either."

"I'm not sure we hit something," Lewis said. "It felt more like something hit us."

"But what?"

He heard more movement below them.

"Whatever it is, it's still there," Hanna said.

He pointed to the pads on Hanna's armrests. "Maybe if you turn or roll the ship, we can shake off whatever's on there."

Another gentler thud sounded from below them.

Then another.

"Try turning," Lewis said.

Hanna pulled her right hand back on one pad while pushing her left hand forward on the other one. At the same time, she pressed down with the heels of her hands, and the pads tilted back. Immediately the ship veered up and to the right, changing its course, but the noise on the bottom of the hull only grew louder. Now it sounded different, though. Almost like . . . knocking?

A speaker on the control panel began crackling with static.

"What's happening?" Lewis asked.

"Maybe they're trying to contact us."

The static began to clear, and they heard what sounded like a voice. Lewis reached over to a knob below the speaker—the volume, he hoped. He turned it up.

"Let me in!"

Lewis looked over at Hanna. "That sounds like Kaya."

There was no obvious microphone on the control panel. So Hanna just spoke, hoping there was a hidden one somewhere on the dashboard, and that their friend would hear them. "Kaya, is that you?"

"Yes, and I need you to stop turning the ship! I'm trying to get inside."

"Where are you?" Hanna asked. "And what are you doing?"

"I'm latched on to the hull, and I need one of you to open the escape hatch—no, wait. Something's coming from behind us. Can you hear me?"

Lewis started to answer, then flicked both his hands at Hanna, signaling for her to go ahead. "We can hear you!" Hanna said. "What's wrong? What's going on?"

And why was she holding on to the outside of their ship?

"I need you to turn again when I tell you turn."

"Which way?" Hanna asked.

"Any way," she said, "but do it quickly. When I say."

"What's going on out there?" Lewis asked. "What's happening?"

"Ready?" Kaya asked.

Lewis and Hanna hurriedly buckled into their seats.

"Ready!"

"Wait . . . wait . . ."

Hanna held her hands over the pads. Lewis was frozen, gripping the armrests of his seat.

Kaya's command blasted through the speaker. "NOW!"

The warship swung down and to the left, as if Hanna were planning to steer it straight into the seafloor. Holding on tight, Lewis stared out through the side of the ship and watched as something streaked past them, leaving a trail of bubbles that looked like the smoky tail of a rocket. "Was that a torpedo?" Hanna asked.

Whatever it was exploded, sending waves pulsing through the water in all directions.

Their warship flipped upside down and then turned over onto its side.

If Lewis and Hanna hadn't buckled themselves in, they would've smashed into the windshield or been thrown around the rolling, tumbling ship like a pair of sneakers in a dryer. The aftershocks passed. Hanna moved her hands along the pads and righted the ship.

"See? They were lying to us," Hanna said. "The whole time."

A strange fish drifted into view outside Hanna's side of the ship.

Lewis squinted, then pointed. No, that wasn't a fish.

Kaya was swimming beside them, protected inside one of those underwater space suits Lewis had seen at the factory, with some kind of jet pack on her back. She was pointing to the underside of the ship.

"She's trying to tell us something," Lewis guessed. "Her radio must not be working."

"The hatch," Hanna said. "She said something about the escape hatch—her dad said you can use it to get inside. It could be like the transfer chamber in the factory. Get it open, Lewis."

Lewis unbuckled himself. All he saw behind him were long benches on either side of the ship with storage racks above them. And a small bathroom at the back—he'd already made a quick visit, and had propped open the door afterward to air it out. "Nothing," he said.

"What about down below?" Hanna guessed.

"There is no—"

He stopped, spotting a panel in the floor. The frame was wider than his shoulders but shorter than he was tall—about the size of someone from Atlantis.

"What do you see?" Hanna asked.

"Give me a second."

"I don't know if we have a second."

A circle with a handprint in the center was etched into the metal. He placed his hand over the etching, pressed down, and turned the circle clockwise. The panel sprang up and slid to the side, revealing a thick window looking into a tub full of water with a girl in a space suit squeezed inside. "Kaya!"

"You've got her?"

Not yet. She was mouthing words, trying to tell him something, but he didn't understand.

He watched her lips. Butt?

No.

Button.

Of course. She was telling him to search for a button, and he found one set into the frame. He pressed it with his thumb, and the glass immediately slid away. The chamber was closed below her, not open to the ocean, and Kaya quickly sat up and pulled herself out. Ice-cold water splashed across the floor and onto his lap. Lewis sealed the hatch shut again.

"Are you okay?" he asked.

Kaya popped open her face mask, already rushing to

Hanna's side. She pulled off her helmet and tossed it on the floor.

"They're attacking us," Hanna said.

"Move over," Kaya replied.

The girl from Atlantis tore off her dive gloves and leaned over the controls. Her hands frantically turned dials and flipped switches before she set them down on the steering pads. An alarm sounded. She turned and looked out the back of the ship. "Strap in, Lewis," she warned. "There's another one coming!"

The warship nosedived, then swung back up.

The explosion shook the ship before Lewis could strap himself down. The whole vehicle pulsed as he flew backward, somersaulting across the deck and into the tiny bathroom. He threw back his hands at the last second to protect his head from slamming into the toilet bowl.

His ribs felt busted. The bones in his hands felt like they'd splintered. It hurt to breathe. He crawled back to a bench seat just behind the pilot's chair and buckled himself in. His pants were soaked, his bare feet frigid.

The ship accelerated, shooting through the water like a bullet. Kaya explained what had happened. She doubted her father would help her, and she'd heard the old man's orders. So she had sent her dad back to headquarters in the shuttle, stolen one of the dive suits, and chased after them.

"You risked your life for us," Hanna noted. "Thank you."

"Yeah, thanks," Lewis added. And he did appreciate it. Definitely. He just wasn't exactly sure how it solved their problem. Now all three of them might get blasted out of the water.

"What do we do now?"

"I have a way to guarantee your safety," she said.

"We need to get out of range of those torpedoes," Hanna said.

"As long as we're in the water, we're never out of range."

"So then what's your plan?"

She pointed ahead of them.

The dull light of the dome appeared in the darkness ahead.

The factory looked like a gigantic jellyfish sitting on the ocean floor. And they were driving toward it. Lewis felt faint. His head spun. Had they been tricked again? Had Kaya turned to her father's side? "I don't understand," he said. "Wh-what are we . . ."

Hanna nearly screamed. "Why in the world are we going back to Atlantis?"

"Because they won't kill one of their own," Kaya said.

Four ships circled ahead of them, near the factory, then swung around to point in their direction.

Something rose out of the base of the dome. "Another torpedo!" Lewis shouted.

Kaya calmly pulled back on the pads. Their warship slowed until it was hovering in place, suspended in the water. "It's not a torpedo," she said. "It's a ship."

The five ships roared out from around the dome like wasps bursting out of a shaken hive. Now it was five against one. This was her plan?

"What are you doing?" Hanna asked. "You're putting us right in their line of fire!"

Kaya stared straight ahead. "I'm trying to talk. They'll think we're surrendering."

The ships hovered in a starlike pattern.

"You sure about that?" Lewis asked.

Kaya reached over to a small pad attached to the control panel between her and Hanna. Her right index finger moved across the surface as if she were doodling. Low-level static bristled out of the speaker. Then a voice came through: "Give up control of the ship, and we will consider returning you to your cell."

"I live in Ridge City, not in a cell," Kaya answered. "My friends do not live in a cell, either, and they never will."

Lewis heard muffled shouts through the speaker.

Then a familiar voice replied, "Kaya, please don't tell me you are on that ship."

"I am," she said.

The lights of all five warships brightened at once, flooding their cabin. Lewis shielded his eyes with his arm. Hanna ducked. But Kaya sat taller. She leaned forward and stared defiantly through the glass. "You lied," she said.

"You don't understand. I didn't know—"

Another voice came through the loudspeaker. "We have orders to fire, Heron. I don't care who's on that ship."

"That's Weed Chin!" Lewis shouted.

"What?" Hanna said. "Turn around, Kaya! This isn't working."

"You can't kill an Atlantean," Heron added, pleading with the others.

"Of course we can," Weed Chin replied. "Erasers, ignore the engineer and fire on my count. Three—"

Her father shouted, "Kaya, MOVE!"

Kaya placed her hands on the pads. "Hold on!" she yelled.

Their ship raced up over the warships and the huge dome.

The whole vehicle shook from repeated explosions.

The ocean was rocking madly.

Yet the sub hadn't sprung any leaks. They were still safe, still moving. Lewis turned to try and see the scene below them. The water was roiling. Huge clouds of muck and dust were exploding off the seafloor. "What's happening?" he asked. "What are they doing?"

Another torpedo smashed against the side of the dome.

Kaya steered them back around. The clouds began to clear; the current was sweeping them away. By the light of the dome, Lewis saw three vehicles lying around the base. Or what was left of them, anyway. The ships were shattered. Even the metal hulls were busted into pieces.

"What happened?" Lewis asked. "Was that you, Kaya?"

"I didn't fire," she said.

"Over there!" Hanna shouted. "There's another one coming over the top of the dome!"

Lewis spotted a second surviving warship closer to the seafloor. He pointed it out to Kaya. And then he noticed that neither ship was turning their way. The water had cleared; he was sure the Erasers could see them. "What are they doing?"

"They're not firing on us," Kaya said. "They're firing on each other."

A torpedo blasted out of the ship speeding over the top of the dome.

The warship near the seafloor swung hard to the right.

The undersea missile glanced off the side of the speeding ship and exploded in the muck.

Another thick cloud of seafloor debris bloomed to the size of the factory dome.

The first vehicle fired again.

And again.

Lewis couldn't see anything in the cloud. The other ship had to be destroyed.

Why were they still here? Why were they watching the battle? They should have been speeding away as fast as possible. Lewis started to speak up when Hanna jumped in. "Kaya," she began, "drive us out of here now!"

The girl from Atlantis was silent. "No," she said. "Not yet."

The ship that had fired the three torpedoes was turning their way.

She turned a dial on the dashboard. "Dad, is that you?" she asked.

"No, your traitor father is gone."

Lewis recognized the voice of Weed Chin immediately. He was about to shout back at the kelp-bearded Eraser, but someone else replied first.

"No, I'm not gone," Heron replied. "I'm right behind you."

All three of them were watching the scene, so Lewis didn't really need to point, but he did anyway. The last warship, the one they thought had been destroyed, had sped up out of the cloud of muck. Now, far below them, it hovered behind Weed Chin and launched its own torpedo. The Eraser turned his ship, but not soon enough.

The explosion spun the vessel.

A cloud of bubbles and debris erupted.

Another torpedo launched from the underside of Weed Chin's hull.

No, not a torpedo—something smaller.

"He's escaping," Hanna said. "He must be wearing one of those suits."

Kaya wasn't paying attention to the escaping Eraser.

She was watching the factory.

A jagged crack had begun to spread out from where a torpedo had smashed into the glass.

The crack branched and widened, faster and faster.

Soon it had spread all around the dome.

And then, in a rush, the entire factory collapsed in on itself.

The weight of four miles of seawater drove the glass, the inner walls, and the thousands of ships below into the depths of what had been the factory's lower floors. The force of the implosion roared back up and out through the water. Waves rocked their ship; Lewis gripped his seat as they were flipped over at least three times.

When the water finally calmed and Kaya had righted the vessel, he could only manage one word: "Wow."

Kaya's dad's voice sounded through the speaker again. "Go," he said. "Go quickly."

"But Dad . . . what are you going to do?"

"Please, go," he said. "I'll take care of myself. Get your friends to safety, and tell the boy I'll do my best to protect his father. Now hurry, Kaya. You don't have much time. And you Sun People . . ."

Hanna leaned forward and spoke into the control panel. "Yes?"

"Take care of my daughter."

Kaya didn't reply, and she didn't look back. Lewis watched tears pool in her eyes as she pressed forward on the pads, pushing the warship away from the ruined factory as fast as it would go. Not one of them spoke. Lewis couldn't imagine what Kaya was thinking. But he counted each passing second, each minute that they powered through the darkness and a torpedo did not scream toward their stern.

Then Kaya exhaled dramatically.

This was their signal.

Hanna let out a whoop.

"We're safe?" Lewis asked.

"I think so. Kaya?"

"Safer," she replied.

The girl from Atlantis wasn't really with them. Not entirely. He wondered where she'd gone in her mind. Home? Or to some other time, before she knew the truth about her father? The thought of his own dad, inside that ridge somewhere, lost in Atlantis—

"Music!" Hanna announced. She was out of her seat, clenching and unclenching her fists, walking in circles.

"What?" Kaya asked.

"This thing has speakers, right? We need music."

"We're probably out of range of the soundscape," Kaya said. "I don't think we'll be able to pick up any of our stations."

"Not your music," Hanna said. "Our music." She slipped the electronic ring off her finger. The little device had a speaker, but not a strong one. She turned it up as loud as possible. Lewis could barely hear a note.

"Let me try," Kaya suggested, and she placed the ring over what Lewis guessed was a small microphone on the dashboard. Hanna tapped the metal, switching songs, as Kaya turned up the volume. Lewis didn't love the tunes, but he didn't care. Anything to get his mind off his father, her father, the idea that they would never be out of range of the torpedoes as long as they were in the water. Kaya wasn't into the music choices either, though, so Hanna kept switching songs.

Then Lewis heard a familiar voice. This wasn't a song, though.

"Stop," he said. "Go back."

Hanna scrolled back to the previous file; now she recognized the voice, too. "I totally forgot about this . . ."

Lewis was pointing at the dashboard, jabbing his finger. Was it really him? "What is this?" he asked.

"That's your father speaking, isn't it?" Kaya asked.

"He borrowed my ring to make a recording when his wristpad was full," Hanna said. "When we were sneaking him through Edgeland."

"Wait," Lewis said. "Quiet."

They were listening to one of the many voice memos his father had made since they'd left on their journey—the only one that hadn't been handed over to the Erasers. A piece of his Atlantis journals. Now it felt like his dad was right there with them. He'd made the recording when he was hidden inside the tank and they were wheeling him through Edgeland like some giant illegal fish. Lewis couldn't help smiling as he heard that low, growling voice. Sure, they'd told him to stay hidden under the tarp. But his father hadn't been able to resist peeking out.

"I'm in some kind of tank used for storing rare fish," his father said. "I'm too large to be seen on the street. Note to self: Eleven cookies per day might be too many. Ha, ha. No, it's the height. They're all small here. And the streets . . . do they even call them streets? Don't know. Will find out. They told me to remain hidden, but there's too much to see. A slight opening between the tarp and the top of the tank, just enough for me to peek out. Shops line the streets, walkways, whatever you call them. Strange fish in the windows . . ." There was a pause as he stopped to study his surroundings. Lewis heard his own voice in the background of the recording. Hanna's, too. She reached over and squeezed his shoulder as his father started talking again. "And the gadgets in the stores! The devices here are like none I've ever seen. No screens. All audio and touch. Oh, and the crowds, the crowds, the crowds! Never would've thought there'd be so many people down here. Life is everywhere. In all forms. Vibrant, stinking, sweaty life.

"So, to all of you out there who never believed, all of you doubters and skeptics and closed-minded cranks who thought it was impossible, absurd, ridiculous . . . to all of you, I have one thing to say. Something I can now say with absolute and complete certainty and real, verifiable proof.

"Atlantis is real!"

22

THE LONG DREAM

THE SHIP burst up out of the water like a great fish.

Kaya's friends cheered as they soared into the sky.

The gravity drive turned on automatically, and they coasted above a glassy sea.

The surface—Kaya had sped straight through the roof of her ocean world and made it to the surface. The sky was endless. Infinite. Her whole life, she'd lived in a world with walls. But this place went on forever, and the light and colors were like nothing she could have ever imagined. She was too stunned to speak. The horizon began to glow orange and red. Then a kind of fire appeared over the water, far in the distance. The fire grew into a burning ball of flame that rose higher and higher in the sky, and soon everything all around them was blue. The sky was a bright, painful blue, the ocean below a deep, dark blue. And the fireball cast its powerful light over everything.

Her eyes ached. She had to squint. "What is that?" she asked, pointing into the distance.

"The sun," Hanna replied.

Of course! The sun. She'd made it to the surface, into the light of the sun, and it was all so much stranger than she could have imagined.

"Don't look straight at it," Lewis warned. "It's bad for your eyes."

"We might need to get you some sunglasses," Hanna said.

"Cool ones," Lewis added.

"Right," Hanna replied. "I'll pick them."

Kaya placed her hands on the pads and steered the ship higher so she could see more of the water. The color of the sea changed to an even darker blue in the distance. But the sky—the sky was this bright, radiant blue in all directions, as far as she could see. And there was just so much space! The aquafarms and cities were the largest open areas in Atlantis, and you could still stand at one end and see the far side if the light was bright enough. But the sunstruck surface of the planet and the great dome of the sky all around her stretched on and on and on—forever.

"Do you know where we're going?" Lewis asked.

Kaya certainly did not.

"West," Hanna answered. "Keep the sun behind us, and we should reach the coast before long."

Lewis rubbed his wrist where the watch had been. "My compass would be helpful right about now."

"Hey," Hanna reminded him, "it was worth the trade. We're here, aren't we?"

He nodded, then turned quiet. Thinking of his father, Kaya guessed.

After playing the clip of the professor's journal several times, they'd switched back to Hanna's music, and Kaya listened, almost liking some of it, as they soared over the water, cruising west. Sea creatures appeared and swam below them, as if they were being welcomed—or welcomed back—to this upper world. A pod of hundreds of dolphins churned through the water ahead. She'd heard of these beautiful swimmers but had never seen one herself.

Kaya panicked when Hanna pointed to something flying high above them. They laughed, wondering why she was frightened, and explained that this thing was called a bird. What had they expected? There were no birds in Atlantis—no flying creatures at all, except for Atlanteans in cruisers and gravity suits. Kaya wondered, as she watched the bird, what else she was going to see and learn. What other strange mysteries lay ahead?

The ship flew over huge islands of garbage and plastic that stretched for miles. This was the pollution that had inspired the Erasers to attempt that fateful meeting with the surface, and later plan their attacks. Her friends looked ashamed as they coasted over this refuse, this clear sign that the People of the Sun really were poisoning the seas.

After they'd been cruising for several hours through the clear air, a metal bird appeared high above them. "What's that?" Kaya asked. This time she tried to seem casual, not quite so surprised.

"A jet," Lewis said. He turned to Hanna. "They're tracking us."

"Escorting us home, I hope," Hanna replied.

So the Sun People had airborne machines, too. Not quite as elegant as the ones in Atlantis, Kaya decided, and shockingly loud. But the thing was certainly fearsome and fast. Soon it was joined by another flying craft, one with some kind of spinning blade that held it aloft. This vehicle—Hanna explained that it was called a helicopter—flew closer to them. There were several people inside, and a man studied them through one of the windows. Lewis held up his hand, waving, and then raised his right thumb. The man smiled back, returned the thumb signal, and then patted the pilot on the shoulder. Kaya would have to remember the thumbs-up signal. Maybe this was the way Sun People said hello.

"How long have we even been gone?" Lewis asked.

Hanna laughed. "I don't know, but it feels like a year."

The machines were leading them now. Before long, more jets were flying above them, and more helicopters surrounded them, too. Kaya was thrilled. When a wide, blurry form appeared on the distant horizon, however, she was stunned speechless. For a while, she simply stared at the growing mass above the water. She almost didn't want to ask. Finally she summoned the courage. "Is that land?"

"That's home," Lewis answered.

Kaya laughed to herself. She was within sight of a world she'd only dreamed about. A world most of her people insisted didn't exist. And she would tour the surface, their towns and cities and mountains. She'd play their games—this soccer thing Lewis had started talking about. Chocolate sounded interesting, too. And she'd definitely have to see the animals. Well, except for the goats. She didn't want to see the goats. But then what? She couldn't stay here. Her dad was in trouble. He needed her, and she needed to understand why he had done what he had done. She needed to understand why he was an Eraser. She had to learn more about what had happened to her mother, too, and she hoped he would finally tell her everything. No matter who he worked for or what secrets he'd kept from Kaya, he was her father. She loved him. And he was going to need her help.

Yes, she'd see the Sun People's world, the marvelously dry and sunburnt surface, but she wouldn't stay long.

She had to return to Atlantis.

≋ EPILOGUE ≋

MICHAEL yawned and staggered down the hall. He'd been wearing his brother's T-shirt to bed at night; it reached his knees. He pulled the collar up over his nose and mouth. Even all these days later, all the nights sleeping in the shirt, it still smelled like Lewis.

When was his brother going to come home?

His dad changed the subject whenever Michael asked. And his mother? She always hurried out of the room without even saying a word. He dug some crust out of the corners of his eyes and wiped it on the wall. "Mom?" he called out.

The kitchen was empty.

The living room, too.

He glanced outside. Clear skies.

"Mom?" he called out again, louder. "Dad?"

He rubbed his eyes. He'd had a terrible sleep. Nightmares, maybe. With pumpkins. Or maybe animals? He couldn't remember and didn't really want to. Some kind of alarm had gone off in the middle of the night, too. But not his dad's alarm. This one was loud enough to shake the house. It had been dark at the time, though, so he'd fallen back asleep and dreamed of lions. Yes, that was it! He had dreamed that endless grasslands stretched out in front of their house instead of trees and that lions were stalking him.

He slipped on one shoe, just like his brother. Several of his friends were doing it now, too. Lewis was right; the trend was definitely catching on.

When Michael pushed open the front door and stepped onto the porch, the old familiar yard was there. No savannah. No lions.

But no parents, either.

He called out again. "Mom?"

He walked to the end of the porch and saw her standing in the yard. A small crowd was gathered around their property. Their neighbors and a few other parents and kids. Some of Lewis's friends were there—Jet was wearing only one sneaker. And Michael's mom was staring over the treetops at the clear sky, holding her ear, listening to someone on the phone. Then she dropped her hand.

He called her name again, but she didn't hear him.

Michael could barely hear himself.

Dozens of hovercars and a few helicopters were flying low over the trees, heading in their direction. The flock surrounded a weird glass vehicle with a metal bottom. It was shaped almost like a teardrop or some kind of whale, and it had no wings. No fans that he could see, either. He wasn't sure whether to run back to the house and roll under his bed or race to his mother's side. She turned and saw him; Michael hurried to her. She knelt next to him and held him tight. "It's okay," she said. "Don't worry. It's okay."

Only then did he notice that she was smiling.

For the first time in a week, his mother was smiling.

The glass ship turned sideways and drifted silently down to the grass. No wings. No fans. No noise. Was it magic? Michael kept glancing at his mother. She was biting her lip. A door in the side of the ship opened, and his older brother stepped out into their yard. He paused for a second, as if he were breathing the air for the very first time. Then Lewis ran toward them barefoot across the wide grass lawn.

Members of the Board,

Recent developments indicate that Gates has discovered the location of Atlantis. Our estimates were off, and their technology is even more advanced than we anticipated.

Needless to say, this changes our plans. I suggest convening an emergency meeting to discuss next steps. We must act now or risk losing everything.

Sincerely,

R.B.

MAP OF NORTHERN ATLANTIS

EVENOR

CLEITO

EAST TO
THE RIFT &
COLLAPSED
EASTERN
CITIES

RIDGE CITY

PELLA

ACHERON

KEY #2

 Collapsed City

 Vacuum Tunnel

Waterway / Tunnel

 Aquafarm

THE SCIENCE OF THE ACCIDENTAL INVASION

The earliest mention of Atlantis dates back to an old Greek thinker named Plato. Smart dude, great robe, weird dating habits. Anyway, Plato told a story about a highly advanced, ancient civilization, an island nation that later sank into the sea. For one reason or another, people never really gave up on the idea. Some explorers are still on the hunt for evidence of this vanished world.

The way I see it, if Atlantis did exist, and its people found a way to survive under the sea, it wouldn't involve living as fish folk. I've been trying to be a fish since I was eight years old. It's really hard. So I imagined a different kind of Atlantis, one in which the people sealed themselves off from the sky as their land sank, and gradually built up a world below the seafloor. That led to a few questions.

How Would They See?

That big orange-yellow thing up in the sky is pretty important. Sure, we have electric lights inside and outside our homes and buildings, but without the sun, our world would be a pretty dark place. So how would the Atlanteans make their way around? I thought about having them use echolocation, kind of like bats, but then Lewis and Hanna would've been bumping their way through their story. Instead, the

Atlanteans develop technology based on bioluminescence, in which life-forms generate their own light. One source of inspiration was these weird little glowworms that hang out in caves in New Zealand, casting an eerie blue light. Look them up. The photos are wild.

What Would They Breathe?

Up here on the surface, we get to breathe this stuff called oxygen. The Atlantis in this story is filled with aquafarms and greenery because the people down there would need a source of oxygen, too. Granted, algae and other sea plants need sunlight to crank out oxygen, and that wouldn't work in Atlantis. So, instead of sunlight, the artificial and bioluminescent lights in the caves provide the necessary energy to make enough breathable air. Think of them like the grow lamps people use in indoor farms or even on the space station . . . only Atlantean. Plants prefer blue light anyway.

What Would They Eat?

There would be no hamburgers in Atlantis. I'm sorry. It just wouldn't work. First you'd have to get all the cows in SCUBA gear . . . no, it just isn't reasonable. The Atlanteans would survive on a diet of sea vegetables and fish of various kinds.

How Would Their Technology Be Different?

Humans are a pretty smart bunch. All of us; not just the famous or powerful folk. Now imagine you trap a whole bunch of us down in an enclosed world like Atlantis, and give us a few thousand years to think and invent and tinker, without connecting or sharing our ideas with anyone up here on the surface. Don't you think these people would come up with some neat inventions? I do. And since they wouldn't have sunlight to study, or stars to gaze at, they'd probably focus their efforts in other areas. Sound, for example. Or even gravity! Our scientists up here on the surface don't really, truly understand gravity, or how it works. But maybe if we'd spent the last few hundred years focused on that, instead of working on fine-tuning lasers and splitting atoms, we might all be drifting around like Kaya.

Would They Be Mermaids?

Now, I love mermaids. Totally. Always wanted to meet one. But it just wouldn't make sense for Atlanteans to be swimming around in the open ocean. The pressure that deep is crushing. The water is frigid. And you'd need gills! Evolution has done some amazing stuff on this planet. But as the professor notes in the story, a few thousand years wouldn't be enough time for evolution to give Atlanteans the ability to breathe underwater.

Would They Be Angry?

Yes, yes, and yes. Given what we're doing to the seas and the skies, Atlantis would be livid. That's our next topic.

Why Atlantis Would Be Furious

If a highly advanced civilization really lived down on the ocean floor, they really would not like us very much. Sun People like you and me are filling the ocean with plastic. The greenhouse gases our cars and factories are pumping into the air are also sinking into the ocean, harming all types of sea creatures. Warming temperatures and melting ice could even change the way currents move around the world. I asked the marine scientist Chris Reddy if he thought any of these changes would impact Atlantis. He said that scientists who study the oceans compare the movement of water to a giant conveyor belt. If our glaciers keep melting, and more freshwater flows into the ocean, then that conveyor belt will stop moving. "If the conveyor belt were to stop, Atlantis would be in trouble," Reddy told me.

But I have to think the Atlanteans would be really angry about all that plastic. The researcher Jenna Jambeck and her colleagues found that roughly eight million metric tons of plastic entered the world's oceans from 192 different countries in the year 2010 alone. That's the weight of about four million SUVs!

So where does it go? One group of researchers estimated that more than five trillion pieces of plastic are floating on the sea surface. Some of it drifts below the surface or washes up on shore. And some sinks all the way down to the bottom. Scientists have even found plastic in the Mariana Trench, miles below the surface.

This isn't just about the bottles and caps and straws you'll find during the average beach cleanup, either. Scientists are also focusing on microplastics—tiny threads or fragments that wash right off our clothing. Say you live in the Midwest somewhere, and you wash your favorite fleece jacket. The water that rinses it clean also pulls off tiny bits of plastic in the fibers. Next the water probably flows to a treatment plant, where it's cleaned up a little, then pumped into a river system. Treatment plants don't filter out the microfibers, though, so the plastic bits rush out right with the treated water, into larger rivers and, eventually, the sea.

When scientist Ian Kane and his colleagues removed a sample of stuff from the seafloor off the coast of Italy, they discovered

1.9 million little pieces of plastic in a tiny area just one meter—
or about three feet—on a side. "Microfibers are the dominant
plastic on the seafloor," Kane told me.

So what's the big deal? The marine scientist Chris
Reddy said it is helpful to think of the ocean like a factory. Normally, in a factory, you add stuff in, like cotton fibers, and then
you get stuff out, like nice new T-shirts that don't smell like
armpits. (Reddy didn't talk about armpits; that's me.) Well, now
we're putting the wrong stuff in the oceans, so we should expect
to get the wrong stuff out. Toxins and chemicals can latch on to
these tiny plastics. Little creatures gobble them up. Then bigger
creatures munch on them, and the little bits of plastic and chemicals move from one life-form to the next . . . all the way, in some
cases, to the fish on our plate. Scientists don't really know what
they do, or how much harm they inflict. But it's not likely that all
this plastic is healthy, either for us or the ocean's many creatures
and critters.

So what can we do? What can you do? Well, first of all, don't
leave it to the adults. I asked a few scientists and ocean activists
what they thought, and the filmmaker and photographer Shawn
Heinrichs, one of the leaders of the ocean conservation group
SeaLegacy, started off with one very clear point. "Don't wait for
your parents to make a difference," he suggested. "If you wait for
someone else to fix it, then it's not going to happen. You have the
power to communicate, and people are starting to listen to your
voice. There's nothing stopping you from putting down TikTok
or Instagram, becoming informed, and turning yourself into an
ocean ambassador."

"Individual efforts matter," added Rachael Miller, the
cofounder of Rozalia Project for a Clean Ocean. "Lots of little
efforts can have a positive impact." That could mean organizing

a beach cleanup, or changing your own behavior to reduce the amount of plastic that you contribute to the ocean. Going for ice cream? Bring your own spoon. Thirsty? Carry your own water bottle. Try not to use single-use plastic items or things that can't be recycled. Try to wear clothes made from natural materials. And if your clothes do have artificial fibers, don't wash them too often—unless the smell is so bad that people start fainting as you walk past.

You really can make a difference. Honestly. "Those individual choices that don't feel like they make a difference really do," Jenna Jambeck told me. "Kids have more power than they realize. Kids motivate companies and governments to change because when kids communicate, it has more power." Where I live, local kids got together and banned the use of plastic straws and small plastic water bottles. The adults listened! Check out organizations like the Ocean Heroes Bootcamp, which helps kids start campaigns to fight ocean plastic pollution, or Bye Bye Plastic Bags, the worldwide group started by two young girls in Indonesia. Maybe you'll be inspired to start a group of your own. Whether Atlantis is real or not, our oceans are worth protecting.

ACKNOWLEDGMENTS

Nika, Clare, Eleanor, Dylan, and Bobby. Wait, who's Bobby? Ha. Just made him up. But the first four . . . really, thank you. Life is fun with you, in and out of the water. Mom and Dad, who are still good at the mom and dad thing. My early readers, including C&E and Georgia and Lucy. The Gales, Thayers, Albrights, and Walkers for hosting a wandering, school-visiting jester. Aquin-Aqua. Carl and Marvin. Editor extraordinaire Howard Reeves ("Make it funnier") and Andrew Smith for guidance, faith, and action figures. Russ Busse for fantastic editorial insight and sharp comments. The rest of the amazing crew at Abrams, including, in no particular order, Jody Mosley, Jessica Gotz, Brenda E. Angelilli, Megan Carlson, Bobby, Hallie Patterson, Jenny Choy, Patricia McNamara, Sara Sproull, Kim Lauber. Janet Zade. Bill Nye, for sneaking me into Abrams in the first place. My fantastic agent, Jennifer Carlson. And of course Nika, again, for everything.

EVEN AN ACCIDENTAL INVASION HAS DIRE CONSEQUENCES . . .

Read on for a sneak peek of

ATLANTIS:
THE BRINK OF WAR

From: Porter Winfield

Director, National Security Agency

To: President Laura Moffat

The White House

Madame President,

I am pleased to report that we successfully interviewed the two young people who recently returned from Atlantis. You will receive a more detailed description of their journey in the coming days, but we have reason to believe their account is truthful. The vehicle that carried them is unlike any technology we've seen and the girl with them is strangely alien in her features. We believe that she is an Atlantean, but she has thus far refused to speak with us. Also, the agency received your note communicating your distaste for long, unbroken paragraphs, so here is a brief, bulleted summary of what we know:

- Three individuals—including former professor Richard Gates; his son, Meriweather Lewis Gates, twelve; and Hanna Barkley, sixteen, daughter of Eyetide founder Miriam Barkley and investor John Barkley—survived the most recent tsunami in a custom-made submarine.
- The crew of three entered Atlantis on July 9.
- The boy, who goes by Lewis, assured us repeatedly that no cannibals were present. We are not sure why he was

expecting cannibals, but he asked that we include this in any reports.

- Upon their arrival in Atlantis, they met the Atlantean girl, Kaya, and were mistaken for invaders. With Kaya, they spent several days attempting to evade capture as they traveled through the subsea world.

- Atlantis is much larger than we anticipated. It consists of perhaps 100 million people and many major cities.

- The technology of the Atlanteans is far more advanced than we realized. They use sound-based, nonlethal weapons and have learned how to control gravity.

- We can confirm that Atlantis is responsible for the devastating tsunamis that have plagued the world's coasts for years.

- The hot sauce in Atlantis is fantastic. I would not have included this point, but Lewis repeated it on numerous occasions. Our codebreakers are working to determine if there is some kind of hidden message in this statement, but it may be that he just really liked the hot sauce. Given your fondness for this condiment, we will try to get you some.

- The three travelers were eventually caught and imprisoned in Atlantis. They managed to escape, but Professor Gates risked his life in the process, and has remained in Atlantis under the care of a local. We do not know if Gates is alive or dead.

- Hanna, Lewis, and Kaya then returned to the surface in a stolen Atlantean warship, destroying a factory in the process. The factory was designed for mass manufacture of the warship.
- The three young people returned on the morning of July 15, where they have remained in quarantine due to concerns about possible Atlantean viruses.
- Neither Hanna nor Lewis will reveal even the rough location of Atlantis; we suspect the Atlantean girl has requested this of them. We tried bribing the boy with sneakers from Ambassador Jordan; he accepted the gift but did not return the favor.

Again, we will provide you with a more detailed report in the coming days. As for Professor Gates, I strongly advise against any attempt to rescue him. This situation is far too delicate. Many questions remain about the intentions of the Atlanteans, the tsunamis, and their potential plans for war. Needless to say, we should prepare our Armed Forces for battle. We hope to have our remaining questions answered soon, and we strongly advise that this journey, and the existence of Atlantis, remain a secret.

Sincerely,

Porter

1
THE SURPRISE SPY

RIAN sprinted through the dark, narrow tunnels of the sewers beneath the city. The air was hot and thick. His feet splashed through small puddles scattered along the path, and the waterway beside him carried fish scraps, sea greens, and other trash out of the city toward giant recycling and filtering pools. He stopped and listened. All he heard was the steady rush of the water.

No one was following him.

He ran faster.

When Rian finally neared the basement of Capitol Tower, he was breathing heavily. His heartbeat had accelerated. Was he scared? Maybe. Nervous? Definitely. Rian was a scrawny fourteen-year-old kid with a talent for sneaking around Ridge City. He wasn't a spy.

Not until today, anyway.

He could stop now.

Go home.

That would be the smart choice. The safe one, too.

But would Kaya give up now? Not a chance.

When he came to the rusting steel door to the basement of Capitol Tower, Rian reached into his pocket and pulled out a small cylindrical device known as a lock whisperer. The gadget was capable of speeding through endless combinations and sequences of notes. Given enough time, it could find the string of tunes to open any door in Atlantis. He switched it on and listened. The sounds played so quickly, and so chaotically, that he had to cover his ears. Before too long, though, the heavy door slid open, and Rian stepped into the large, high-ceilinged basement.

The sewer water was slightly cleaner here, upstream, and it flowed out through small gaps below the walls. After a deep, steadying breath, he tightened his gloves and ankle straps. He checked his chestplate. Everything was powered up. Whistling quietly, he turned on his gravity drive—or Kaya's really, since he was borrowing her gear—and his feet rose off the ground.

He drifted to the ceiling; it felt like he was swimming through the air.

The air vents and trash chutes that snaked down from the building's upper floors all ended here. Each one was neatly labeled. The lights in the walls were faint, but bright enough so he could see the numbers.

A rattling, sliding sound was coming from one of the openings.

Rian peered up into the dark space, then jerked back.

A clump of trash plummeted down and splashed into the water below.

His instructions were to find chute 14B. With his back to the water, he moved along the ceiling like a spider, his hands and feet pressing lightly against the damp stone, until he found the narrow tunnel, pulled himself inside, and rose. His nose itched. His shoulders brushed the sides as he floated higher and higher. There was no way an adult would ever fit inside. And one of those giant Sun People? Impossible.

Sometimes it wasn't so bad to be small.

The antigravity suit carried him smoothly to the upper floors.

Metallic-tasting air rushed out as he passed vents to other rooms.

Twice he had to scrunch his nose to stifle a sneeze.

Above him, he heard angry, passionate voices bouncing off the tunnel walls.

He drifted toward the source and hovered in the dark and narrow passageway. A faint green light flooded into the chute. The same metallic air, too—it was cool against his face. The mouth of the vent was close to the room's ceiling, and a square screen covered the opening, so he wouldn't have been able to see the people inside if he'd tried. Yet he did recognize a few of the voices. He'd heard them on the soundscape.

These were the members of the High Council.

The leaders of Atlantis.

And Rian was spying on them. He swallowed quietly.

Follow the instructions, Rian told himself. Kaya's dad, Heron, had entrusted him with this mission. He'd asked him to record every word in secret, then hurry home and transmit the audio through a specific channel on the soundscape.

The whole arrangement was odd—Heron hadn't even asked him in person. Instead, he'd requested Rian's help through a recorded message.

Now Rian reached up and tapped his earpiece. He was late; they were deep into a debate about the Sun People. Several of the voices were gravelly and tired. One of the women sounded like she needed to cough, and the argument was growing like a wave as it neared the shallows.

"They are poisoning our oceans and our cities are collapsing at a frightening rate!" a woman with a deep voice proclaimed. "We have to find a new home on the surface."

"Our civilization has survived under the sea this long," countered another woman, whose voice was garbled, as if she had an oyster lingering in the back of her throat. "We can manage for a few more centuries."

"How can you be so sure?"

A man slapped his fist on the table as he spoke. "Why should we fight the Sun People? Let them fight each other, as they love to do, and Atlantis can rise in the ashes of their civilizations."

Rian had only learned about the existence of the Sun People a few days before. His whole life he'd been taught there was no life on the surface. There were people like Kaya who believed the government was lying to them, but they never had proof. Based on what he was hearing now, though, it sounded like the High Council had known about the Sun People all along.

They'd been lying to the rest of Atlantis.

The debate turned into a shouting match.

"Their machines are mining and ravaging the seafloor. It won't be long until the Sun People tunnel straight into one of our cities in search of their precious metals and oils. We must act now!"

"The surface was ours once. Let it be ours again!"

"The people of Atlantis deserve to know the truth."

"We should try to negotiate with the Sun People first."

"Negotiate?!" someone yelled. "The last time we tried that several of our brightest young minds were killed!"

"Including my son," added another voice.

The room turned suddenly quiet. Rian recognized the man's low, forceful growl. He'd heard that voice on the soundscape. His parents always made Rian listen to the news. But he couldn't remember the man's name. A chair was pushed back from the table, its stone legs grinding against the stone floor. The man continued. His voice was calm and assured.

"We sent that delegation on a peaceful mission and what did the Sun People do? They blasted a dozen innocent Atlanteans out of the water. So, while I appreciate your opinions, and would prefer to live in peace, we cannot ignore the facts. They poison our oceans, making it ever harder for us to grow and raise enough food for our people. They will not stop, either. Their hunger for metals and oil draws them to the depths. Some of you have said we can survive for centuries, but what if you're wrong? What if we only have a few years? Their submarines have been scouring the seafloor in search of our world and now they've found it. Their invasion was a success—they stole one of our warships, and I wouldn't be surprised if they are copying it right now, building a fleet of their own. Their next attack will be devastating if they have Atlantean technology." His voice had risen in intensity. The man paused, breathed. When he resumed, his tone turned solemn. "Yes, I lost my son to these heartless creatures from the surface, but I have not let that muddy my judgment on this issue. This is not about my son. This is about Atlantis. We need to stop the Sun People before they invade again. It pains me to say this, but a direct attack is our only choice, my friends. I move to vote."

Rian had to stop himself from interrupting. None of this sounded right. Invaders? He'd met the Sun People. They were kids! And they were completely harmless. Especially the boy, Lewis. If he were a fish, he'd be a minnow. The older one, Hanna—she was different. Smart. Powerful. Strong, too. But neither of them were soldiers. Not even close. Rian wanted to push through the grate and tell the High Council all that he knew. What he'd seen! Yet he'd been urged not to whisper a word.

One of the women spoke up again, her voice solemn and insistent. "First we must inform the public of the existence of the Sun People."

"No, we must vote now or—"

"Demos, must I remind you again that you are one of twelve equal elected members of the High Council? You are not our leader."

This time the man said nothing. Rian could practically sense him glaring.

"Agreed," the woman with the oyster voice said, "but I second Demos's motion to vote on war. The invaders he encountered are likely only the first wave."

The arguments started up again. Practically everyone was shouting at once. Finally, someone called for order, and the woman with the solemn tone spoke. "An attack on the surface is a very serious matter, but Demos has raised serious concerns. We will all need time to think. I suggest we reconvene at this same time, in four days, to vote for or against this war."

The other members of the High Council agreed. Chairs scraped against the floor as the meeting was called to an end. The conversation broke into pockets of murmurs and whispers. Rian waited until he heard the whoosh of doors opening, the shuffle of footsteps, and then a stretch of unbroken silence after the last of the High Council members exited the room. The green glow of the room's interior lights faded to darkness, and the cramped tunnel now felt strangely cold. Rian wanted to get home as fast as possible. Most of all, though, he wanted to talk to Kaya, to tell her what he'd learned, and find out what she knew. But he hadn't seen or heard from his friend since she hurried off to rescue the Sun People a week before.

He didn't even know if she was alive or dead.

Gregory Mone is the author of several bestselling works of fiction and nonfiction for both children and adults, including the Jack and the Geniuses series with Bill Nye. He is a contributing editor at *Popular Science* and an award-winning science writer. Greg makes school and library visits throughout the country. A graduate of Harvard College, he lives with his wife and three children on Martha's Vineyard.